SUBTERRANEAN:
Tales of Dark Fantasy 3

EDITED BY WILLIAM SCHAFER

Subterranean Press 2020

First Edition

ISBN
978-1-59606-966-4

Subterranean Press
PO Box 190106
Burton, MI 48519

subterraneanpress.com

Manufactured in the United States of America

Table of Contents

An Orderly Progression of Hearts | by Kat Howard | 9

Cherry Street Tango, Sweatbox Waltz
| by Caitlín R. Kiernan | 13

Estate Sale | by Bentley Little | 29

Twisted Hazel | by Stephen Gallagher | 37

Death Comes for the Rich Man | by Robert McCammon | 51

At the Threshold of Your Bedchamber
on the Fifth Night | by Sarah Gailey | 83

Final Course | by C. J. Tudor | 95

Lamagica | by Ian R. MacLeod | 125

Razor Pig | by Richard Kadrey | 161

Skin Magic | by P. Djèjí Clark | 197

For
Kim and Tony,
and Alexander and Avery,
family

An Orderly Progression of Hearts | *Kat Howard*

You are born with a heart of flesh. You are human, when you are born, and so this is the usual, expected thing. You grow, and your heart grows with you. Most times, you hardly know it is there—your blood moves through your body as it should, and it is only when your heart moves strangely, when it races in terror or jumps and flutters in your chest that you think of its presence.

And so you go about your life as anyone else would.

One day, this changes. Your heart changes. There is a hollowness where your heart should be that at the same time feels like pressure, like you might burst from the strength of it. Your heart, which you have never before had to consider like this, aches so strongly that you cannot eat or sleep for the pain. The hurt is so present, so all-consuming, that you begin to wish that you had no heart at all, or that if you must have one, that it was not this fragile and easily-wounded flesh.

You wish and you wish and your wish is more powerful than heart-break, your wish is stronger than flesh. Your heart changes.

You feel it change. It beats more slowly, and grows heavy in your chest.

You have never done magic before, never considered it real enough to try, but the transformation of your heart seems like a magic that is just, that is right. On the day your heart turns to stone, you feel nothing but quiet and calm, and you are glad for the unmoving weight of it, safe behind the cage of your bones.

You are happy like this for some time.

A HEART OF stone does not beat. It does not race or flutter. It does not hesitate from either joy or fear. You grow accustomed to the stillness, and then you grow to enjoy it. You remember before, when you had your heart of flesh, and how you could ignore its beating presence. This, you think, is better still, this heart that is unmoving and strong.

There is a clarity that comes with having a heart of stone. You see things in starkness, free of any haze of emotion. Your thoughts become knife-edged in their precision.

There is power in the transformation of a heart, and this power sits, proud and heart-shaped, inside you. You consider that this power came from the wish that you made, and you choose to focus it, to practice magic—enchantments and illusions. A heart of stone is useful in this practice. You see things more truly now, unaffected by the galloping caprices of a heart of flesh, and in seeing things truly, you learn how to deceive.

You find that it is still possible to feel love, even with a heart of stone. You had thought to leave that emotion and all its messiness behind when you left your bloody and messy first heart, but this is a steadier love, one as cool and soothing as the dusk, and so you allow it to remain.

But just because a heart is made of stone doesn't mean that it cannot break. The crack is a small one at first, so small you barely even notice it—your heart does not beat, and so surely such a small thing does not matter.

Everything matters when it comes to hearts.

A small crack is all it takes, and one day your stone heart shatters. You feel the grit and the hollowness of a heart that has turned to dust in your chest. It is empty, irritating.

And so you call on your magic, deliberately this time, and you press hard on the emptiness in your chest. You compress it into the smallest of spaces. You gather the dust and fragments of your shattered stone heart, and compress them as well.

Your heart shrinks, grows harder, changes. You dwell in the transformation, guiding it. You think of your magic, your illusions and enchantments, and you shape your heart in service of them. When you are finished, an emerald beats in your chest, the deep green heart of the deathless sorcerers. You like its smallness, its facets, but there is something about this heart that still feels wrong.

It is too close, too much a part of you. You must cast it out.

You take a knife, sharp enough to cut a shadow, and you slice through skin and between bone. You reach in to the core of yourself and you pull the emerald out, the dark green streaked with red so deep it looks black.

You feel so much better.

But still, as you see your heart, gleaming there in your hand—so small, so perfect—an uneasiness lingers. It could still be lost or broken. Hearts, it seems, have an inherent fragility to them. Why else would yours have been so faulty?

You decide you will hide your new heart—if it is apart from you, it will be safe. There will be no danger of it breaking. You find a robin's egg, pale and perfect blue, and you pierce its shell, pouring out the contents. You place your emerald heart inside and close it back up. You take the egg past borders and boundaries, over water and land, to a forest as thick as secrets. There is a tree in the center, and you leave your heart there, alone.

You return to your home, and you don't miss your heart at all. You practice your magic, your power stronger still. You are not tempted by the weakness of love.

Nothing changes except your dreams.

You dream of a forest, its air resinous and cold. You dream of the sky, as blue as eggshells and haunted by feathers and wings. You dream the slow thoughts of trees, their roots dark in the earth.

The empty space inside of you aches for a heart, and the ache grows larger, devouring.

Perhaps your heart was not such a frail and faulty thing after all, if it can hurt you from such a distance. You repeat the long journey back to the forest.

When you arrive there, you remove the egg from where you placed it in the tree and you hold it in your hand. There is a stony weight to it that is much heavier than you remember. You crack the shell, letting the two pieces of fragile blue sky fall to the earth. You bury your emerald heart in the ribcage of the tree's twisted roots.

You step into the tree. Enfolded by branches, you use your magic one last time. You wish and you wish and you become, beating, a heart of flesh.

Cherry Street Tango, Sweatbox Waltz | *Caitlín R. Kiernan*

1.

The hotel room is hot as blue blazes, and it smells hot, and it also smells simultaneously of dust and mildew, both dry and damp. The room is, in fact, almost *unbearably* hot, and I sit on this sofa, alone in my private darkness and I sweat and listen to the radio. Usually, there's only music, jazz from a hundred years ago, discord and jangle and a thousand arrhythmic anti-harmonies on piano and clarinet and baritone saxophone that seem composed to mock my disorientation. But then I am a paranoid woman. It comes with the job, the paranoia. That is, either you bring it with you to the job or you pick it up soon afterwards – or you don't live very long. And sometimes you don't live very long anyway. So, the radio plays and I sit here listening to the jazz, sweating in someone else's silk bathrobe, cradled in frayed upholstery, alone in the darkness behind the bandages that cover my flash-burned eyes. I might have been sitting here for hours. I lose track of time, in between sleeping and being awake. But finally the music stops, as it periodically does, and a man with a heavy Hungarian accent comes on in its place, and he wants to know if I'm feeling any better than I felt the last time we talked. I tell him sure, I feel like a million bucks, and he reminds me how snark and sarcasm isn't going to cut it. His time is precious. On the other hand, my time, like my life, is disposable, expendable, no kind of rare dish, me, and I should therefore behave accordingly. Which is to say I should behave.

"Last name first," he says. "First name last."

I have lost count of how many times I've given my name to the man on the radio. I lick my dry lips, wishing for anything wet besides my own inner sea leaking out of me. "Sakellarios," I reply. "Elenore."

"Are you in pain tonight, Ms. Sakellarios?" the man with the Hungarian accent wants to know.

"Nothing has changed since the last time we talked," I say.

The radio crackles with a burst of static, and I wonder if that's all I'm going to get from him until next time. Sometimes it's just that short. Other times I think he's gonna yammer on forever. Anyway, this time the static fades and he's still here with me. Sweat runs down my face and drips onto my hands where they lie folded together in my lap.

"It's a dream-kill-dream world in here," says the man on the radio.

"Yeah, but ain't it always," I reply.

"I'd like to hear about the dog again," he says. "The dog on the beach." He sounds as if he's reading off a script, just like every time before. He sounds like he's reading cue cards.

"I've already told you about the dog, what, a dozen times over?"

"Indulge me," he says calmly, flatly, indifferently.

"How about you tell me how much longer I'm gonna be here, wherever here is?"

"Why?" asks the man on the radio. "Have you got somewhere else to be? Please, tell me about the dog."

I dig my nails into my palms and try not to think about the heat or the stinking room or how badly my eyes ache. It seems like they ache worse whenever I'm talking to the man on the radio, but always I tell myself how that's probably just a product of the aforementioned paranoia.

"I was seven years old," I tell the man on the radio.

"Last time you were eight," he reminds me.

"Well, *this* time I was seven. I was seven years old, and the tide was out, and I was dragging for scrap in the muck. My father ran a junkyard up in Queens."

"Last time," says the man, "his shop was in the Bronx."

"Fine," I say, "it was in the Bronx."

"If you would, please finish this sentence, Ms. Sakellarios: There is another shore, you know –"

I want a cigarette so bad it hurts, almost as much as my eyes hurt. "– upon the other side," I reply.

"Tell me about the dog, please, Elenore."

"I was seven years old, and I found the dog in the mud at low tide. It was dying when I found it. The sea lice had been at it. They were bad that year."

"So, had you killed the dog it would have been an act of mercy," says the man with the Hungarian accent.

"If you want to think of it that way, fine."

"Why didn't you kill the dog?" he asks me. "It was suffering."

"It was dying anyway," I reply.

"If you would be so kind, please finish this sentence, Ms. Sakellarios: Then turn not pale, beloved snail –"

I swallow. My throat feels like a sandstorm. I cough and wipe sweat from my face onto the sleeve of the borrowed silk robe. It always seems hotter whenever I talk to the man on the radio, but that's also probably only my imagination.

"– then turn not pale, beloved snail," he says again.

"– but come and join the dance," I say, hardly louder than a whisper. I clear my throat and cough again.

"Are you in pain?" asks the man.

"My eyes ache," I tell him. "My eyes ache, and I'm thirsty, and I need a fucking cigarette."

"You didn't kill the dog that was being eaten alive by the sea lice, did you, Elenore," he wants to know.

"Up till then, I'd never killed anything in my life."

"That day at low tide, did you kill the dog, Ms. Sakellarios?"

"Yeah, sure. I picked up a rock and bashed its brains in."

"Please complete this sentence: They are waiting on the shingle –"

"– will you come and join the dance?"

"When you were seven years old, or eight, did you kill the dog or didn't you?"

"I don't remember," I lie. It always feels good to lie to the man on the radio.

"In Trenton, were you paid to botch the hit? Or did your failure follow from mere incompetence?"

I want to stand up and leave the room. I've memorized the path from the room with the sofa to the room with a bed and a toilet and a sink. It isn't a long walk, not even for a blind woman. But I've not yet had the nerve to walk out on the man who speaks to me through the radio, and if wishes were horses, beggars wouldn't go around hungry, just like they say in the funnies.

"I *did* my job in Chinatown," I say, sounding more angry than it is wise to sound. "Before the grenade went off, I did my fucking job. Don't you try and tell me otherwise. I know better."

"Did the dog have a name?"

"How the shit would I know?"

"Most dogs do," says the man.

"Not strays. Not dogs no one has ever bothered to name."

"Why didn't you kill the dog, Elenore? It must have been in agony."

And I'm sitting there, sweating and smelling dust and mildew and my own stink, my own filth, and I'm wondering whether the man on the radio *is* a man or whether he's only tick-tock or AI. I'm sitting there in the darkness wrapped around my face, just wanting him to go away and let the music play again. I'm sitting there trying to remember if there really was a dog.

"There were a lot of strays along the waterfront," I say. "I knew an old man who shot dogs for the constable, for the bounty money. Ten bucks a head. Twenty for a pregnant bitch."

"You haven't answered my question," notes the man, just as cool as a scoop of vanilla ice cream.

"My eyes hurt," I tell him.

"Rubbing doesn't help," he says, and then he asks me why I didn't take the shot in Trenton. He asks me why I froze.

"I took the shot," I reply. My hands have begun to tremble.

"It's a dream-kill-dream world in here," he says for the second time.

"Don't you know it, Mister," I reply. And then he's gone and the jazz returns. He's gone and I'm alone, and I lean back and try to think about anything at all but whether or not the dying, writhing dog is a real memory or something else. It's so hot that I can almost believe the world is ready to catch fire, and that would be a mercy, too.

2.

I'm on my second Scotch and soda, when Mercedes Bélanger strolls into the place. She's almost an hour late, but that's nothing much to make a fuss over. That is absolutely no sort of surprise, not to me and not to any other blackstrap who's ever had cause to deal with the Turk. His merry band of goons and gunsels are not known for their punctuality. But that's fine. I'm not in a hurry. I have just been sitting here getting very slightly drunk and watching the river burn. Out on the Delaware, a petro barge caught fire right after sunset, and the low-slung underbellies of the clouds glow like the roof of Hades. More likely than not, someone neglected to pay someone else this, that, or the other bribe, and so the barge was torched. Anyway, I am sitting there sipping my Scotch and thinking how if the fire keeps drifting downriver towards the ramshackle span of the Calhoun Street Bridge, it is gonna be a bitch getting back over to Levittown. Mercedes Bélanger, she spots me and comes weaving her way through the joint, just as slick as Cleopatra's asp, easy as the snake in Eden, between the tables and chairs and all the other gawkers watching the fire. Right at the last I let her know that I have seen her. Then I go back to watching the river. She sits down in the booth across from me and lights a cigarette, and she does not say one word about being late. A waiter flits over, and the Turk's woman orders tequila, and then the waiter flits away again.

"And, what's more, they don't even charge extra for the floorshow," she says, then blows a smoke ring that drifts lazily up towards the ceiling. Her accent sounds like South Philly, but fuck only knows. It could be a coverall. Everything about her might well be a cover, for all that I can tell, from her rust-colored hair to her shiny black shoes. Me, I have learned not to bother looking too close when dealing with the Turk. If he wants to play hide the Nazi with masking socks, that is more than his prerogative – just so long as I get paid my due. Just so long as he does not decide to cut corners by popping the folks who do his dirty work.

"You got the box?" I ask the woman sitting across from me.

"Well, ain't you all business," she smiles.

"Yeah, ain't I just."

"How long has it been burning?" she wants to know, and Mercedes Bélanger, she points at the window with her cigarette.

"Long enough that I am pretty sure no one is coming to put it out."

"The Turk, he don't do arson," she says, like maybe I have said he does.

"No, Ma'am," I say. "I am sure he has never in his life struck a match, save to light his fat cigars."

She sits back and she stares at me. Her eyes are lined in crimson smudge and filled up with flecks of gold and silver, and that right there is when I decide this one is exactly as she presents herself. Nobody would go to all the trouble and discomfort to mask and not hide those cheapskate implants.

She says, "I was told you don't know when it's best to keep your mouth shut. I see I was not misinformed."

"Do you have the box or don't you?" I ask the woman with artificial eyes.

"Is there a hurry-up on this evening that no one told me about?" she wants to know.

I finish my drink, then go back to staring at the river.

"If I had known it was a courting," I say, "I would have brought you flowers. Shit, I would have brought you a box of chocolate bonbons."

Mercedes Bélanger points at the fire again. "Use to was round here," she says, "folks wasn't so sloppy they let shit like that go down. Use to was, everyone knew his place, and if a ship's toll needed paying, it got paid, and if a fire was burning, someone in a yellow hat showed up to put it out. Yeah, Ms. Sakellarios, I got the box, but my instructions are that we talk until half past ten, and so we still got fifteen minutes left to go. Think you can make do with that?"

"If those are the rules."

She grins and says, "I hear you were soldier, use to was. I hear it you did a couple tours down in Nuevo Léon, right after the uprising."

"I never got anywhere near Nuevo Léon," I tell her. "I did my stint down on the Yucatán, mostly."

"Oh, I see," she says. "Is that where you acquired your fascination with fires? 'Cause what I heard is you were a sprayer for the infantry, one of the blowtorch brigade, but if that ain't so, you should set me straight."

I take a quick hinge at her, a glance at those stark metallic eyes, and I'm about to say something – I do not recall just what – when the waiter flits over with her tequila. I order another Scotch and water and the waiter goes away again.

"I was a breaker, a translator," I tell Mercedes Bélanger, instead of whatever it was I'd meant to tell her before the waiter interrupted. "I'm good with code."

She raises an eyebrow, plucked thin as a razor's edge and she wants to know, "Then why is it you're running meat wagon for the likes of Constantin and not decrypting for the highest bidder?"

"I am not that good," I reply.

She takes a sip of her tequila. "Yeah, well, what's it the spielers out on the strand all say? The clutch of life and the fist of love, right? Ain't that something from the Bible?"

I tell her how she's asking the wrong person. And frankly, this whole scene is beginning to wear on me, and I want to get the package and make my exit. Still, it isn't that I don't know what is and what is not in my best own sweet interest, and right here it *surely* is in my best interest to play along and trust that there's no way through this palaver but straight down the middle and that Mercedes Bélanger isn't up to something. I know her by reputation. She's the sort the Turk sends round when he is not taking chances. She is not the sort to offend with impatience. I need the work, and I do not need the black star next to my name. So, I let her talk, and I sit there counting off the minutes in my head and I listen. Every again and now, I try to contribute something, and I watch the barge burn.

"Well, it's been a pleasure," she finally says, "more or less." She finishes off her tequila and mashes out the butt of her cigarette, and then she reaches into her handbag and takes out a shiny little brass cube just about the same size as a lump of sugar. "I trust you know what to do with this," she smiles, "a smart cookie like yourself." She slides the box across the table, and I make it vanish into my jacket.

I say, "Please relay my respects to Mr. Constantin, and let him know I said how much I appreciate the job, same as ever."

And she tells me, "Just don't fuck it up, lady."

Right then, the barge collides with the span of the bridge, and the resulting explosion rattles the tall plate-glass windows of the joint. There's a chorus of appreciative oohs and ahs from most of the other gawkers, and when I go to turn my attention back to Ms. Mercedes Bélanger, to assure her I do not make a habit of fucking it up, she is nowhere to be seen.

3.

In the moldy, dry room – in the sweltering room that is so much like a fire on a river – I sit smoking and listening to the man on the radio, the man with the Hungarian accent. Someone else is here with me now. I think that it is a woman, but I cannot be sure. They do not speak. They have not let me touch them, and my eyes are still hidden behind the bandages, and if they were not I still probably could not see my whoever-come-lately companion. But they brought me the cigarettes and a lighter and a bottle of cold water, and they linger somewhere nearby. The spicy, pungent smoke from the Javanese kreteks tastes like cloves and cumin, nutmeg and tobacco. I have to be careful not to burn my fingers, but I'm managing. A magician, I am.

"It was raining," says the man on the radio.

"Yeah, that's what I said, isn't it? First, it *wasn't* raining, and there wasn't a cloud in the sky. And then it *was* raining, so hard I thought I might drown every time I drew a goddamn breath. I was running across the catwalk in the fucking rain, trying not to drown, or lose my footing, because it was a hundred feet down to the street. I was also trying to stay far enough ahead of the dogs – the dogs that no one bothered to tell me to worry about – that they wouldn't be taking a plug out of my ass."

"The wolves," says the man on the radio.

"Wolves, dogs, whatever."

"Earlier, you told me that they were wolves."

I take a long drag on my cigarette. I hold the smoke in so long that my ears start to buzz. I exhale and wish the man would stop talking and let the jazz come back.

"Either way, I was not warned to expect them. They weren't on the manifest, not dogs and not wolves, and, for that matter, also not rain. None of that shit was in the box."

"You were running on the rooftop," says the man on the radio.

"Not on the rooftop. On the catwalk dangling fifteen feet *above* the rooftop. The goddamn dogs were down there on the rooftop."

"Not wolves, dogs."

"I figure, no matter which they were, they get their teeth in you, it's gonna hurt just about the same."

"You said the sky was clear," the man on the radio tells me.

"And then it was raining. I said that, too."

"Elenore, would you please complete this sentence?" he asks, and I take another long drag on my smoke. "What road are you taking? The Road of Needles or –"

"– the Road of Pins."

"Why then, I'll take the Path of Needles –" says the man on the radio.

"– and we'll see who gets there first," I reply.

"How many shots did you fire before you were hit?" the man wants to know.

"Like I have told you – however many times it's been now – five or six."

"And that was before the wolves showed up?"

"No, that was after, in the rain."

"The wolves or the dogs," says the man, his voice as flat as hammered shit.

"Isn't it just possible that whatever gleet coded that box Bélanger slipped me wasn't exactly so good with the quality control?"

And he replies, "The possibilities are all but endless."

"And isn't it also possible, just maybe, it was tampered with and the stream corrupted on purpose, because maybe someone – and fuck if I would know *who*, so do not ask – wanted that whole scene to go sideways. Which would be the *why* of all this Heisenbergish bushwa."

"The esteemed Mr. Constantin has many professional rivals," says the man with the Hungarian accent. Which could be him agreeing sabotage is a possibility, or it could be something else altogether. "Ms. Sakellarios, you had a clear view of the target when you fired?" he asks me next. Again.

"As clear as I could manage, what with the rain and the yapping mutts, yeah. I knew it was the best I was likely going to get off, so I took the shot."

"The shots," says the man, correcting me. "You have said you discharged your firearm either five or six times."

I crush out the butt of my cigarette in the ashtray on the table in front of me. Or I miss and crush it out on the table. Six of one, half dozen the other way round.

"Please complete this sentence, Elenore," says the man on the radio. "The better to eat you with –"

"– my child."

"Now come –"

"– and lie beside me."

"And the grenade?" asks the man on the radio.

"That was right after."

"After the fifth or sixth shot."

"Yeah."

"It wasn't raining when the extraction team reached you. You are aware of that, aren't you, Elenore. In fact, the conditions were quite dry. There was not a cloud in the sky. The moon was like a wheel of cheddar, hung up against the velvet night."

"Yeah, I know. And there were no dogs. Or wolves."

"Indeed not," he says.

Then he doesn't say anything for a while, and whoever it is here with me passes me another lit cigarette. I resist the urge to grab hold of their arm. His arm. Her arm. *Its* arm. I smoke and I wait.

There's a burst of white noise, and then the man is talking again.

"Prior to this incident," he says, "your record was, for want of a better word, spotless. Which, of course, is why you were retained. Mr. Constantin had never before been given any cause to doubt your efficiency. But, in light of the discrepancies at hand, concerns arise. I am certain, Ms. Sakellarios, that you understand our position in this matter. I am certain also that you sympathize. Your patience is appreciated."

And then there's more static and this time the man with the Hungarian accent goes away and the room fills up with music made by folks who died before my mother was born. And I sit smoking and sweating and wishing the person standing nearby would open their mouth and say anything at all. One stinking, stingy word would be as good as gold.

4.

Up a flight of stairs so narrow my elbows are bumping the brick walls, and I honestly have no idea what the poor son of a bitch I'm chasing has done to deserve the Turk sending someone like me to end his time among the living. It is not now and never shall be my place to ask those sorts of questions. I am a blackstrap, and I just do my fucking job. I'm taking the stairs two at a time, and then there's the open door leading out into the night, and I pause there just a moment at the threshold to get my bearings. It's a hot night in late January, the mercury pushing seventy Fahrenheit or better, and I'm dripping sweat onto the concrete at my feet. It stinks out there, like every food stall and overflowing dumpster and cut-rate whorehouse in Chinatown. I take a deep breath, breathing the night into me, making of it my ally. It tastes as bad as it smells. I can see that the door does not open out onto the roof proper, but rather it leads onto a rickety-looking catwalk, rusted iron even narrower than the stairwell. I curse and I check my weapon and then I step out to get this over and done with. The mook should be dead and getting stiff by now. He shouldn't have been able to give me the slip down on Cherry Street. And yet he did. My boots on the catwalk sound loud as hammers on tin. And right here it starts to rain pitchforks. Or it has been raining all along, and I just didn't realize through the mist-red haze of adrenaline behind my eyes. And the dogs start barking. It sounds like a whole goddamn kennel has been let loose on the roof beneath me. I wipe rain from my eyes and look down at them. Lips curled back to reveal fangs the yellow white of old piano keys, the bared canines of canines, if you will. I squint, trying to get a better view, because it occurs to me that maybe they are not mere dogs at all. On this side of the river, you get a lot of assholes packing test-tube exotics for guardian angels. I once busted in on a goddamn tiger, if you can believe that. Or even if you cannot. So, maybe they aren't just dogs. It occurs to me they might be wolves. But I am wasting time. They're down there; I'm up here. I have let myself get distracted, and now my mark is getting away. I take my eyes off the snarling, yapping pack beneath me and turn my attention once more again to the work at hand. To my surprise, the mook is standing not more than twenty yards away, just staring back at me. He looks like a goddamn drowned sewer rat, but then, most of a certain, I probably do too. I raise my gun and the laser draws a pretty crimson bead upon his forehead.

"You know this ain't personal," I say, shouting to be heard above the torrential fucking rain and above the hullabaloo of the barking dogs. "Hold still, fella, and let's make it easy. Let's make it fast."

The mook wipes his long, wet bangs from his eyes. He's a stylish-dressed breed, the sort of kid who spends more on clothes and baubles and pomade in a week than I spend on food and rent in six months. And I figure it might just be his taste for fancy duds that has him so far in dutch with the Turk that I'm about to squeeze the trigger and lay him low. The mook looks at me, and then he looks down at the raging cacophony of dogs.

Then he looks back at me again.

"You're Sakellarios, ain't you?" he wants to know, also having to shout to be heard. "Elenore Sakellarios? Yeah, I heard of you. You got glitter. Quelle surprise, that I should rate the likes of you."

"Yeah, you must have made quite an impression," I shout back, and I blink water from my eyes, and I think how, at this range, the blast is gonna rip the mook's head off. I am not taken aback that he knows my name. You work dillinger long enough and with any degree of confidence, you get a reputation. You do it up right, you get T-shirts and fan clubs and goddamn trading cards. You get fortune cookies.

"Funny," says the fancy mook, "how secrets travel."

He smiles.

And me, I fire my gun, and that one shot is all the thunderclap that any rainstorm will ever need. It is loud as the voice of the Lord Jehovah Almighty. *Boom.* The shiny black Heckler and Koch .45 caliber rips a hole in the night, and *that* ought to be *that*, all she wrote, Mister, the last and definitive word on the subject. Or so you would think. But you would be wrong, for the mook is still standing right there, grinning at me, and the dogs are still barking their heads off, and I squeeze the trigger again. I know I did not miss, but I squeeze the trigger again. And however many times again after that. The kid does not move, and also his head does not come apart in a satisfying spray of blood and bone and teeth and atomized fucking brains. He just stands there, watching me.

And all those dogs – or whatever else that barks – have fallen silent as the tomb.

I see the grenade rolling along the catwalk towards me maybe two seconds before it pops and I'm blinded by the flash. That pineapple, it pukes up light like it has serious designs on going full-tilt supernova. And then I realize that I am down on my knees, even if I can't recollect the fall, and I also realize how it isn't raining anymore. I can hear the *whup-whup-whup* of the approaching extraction chopper. And I'm wondering how and why I'm still drawing breath, why it is the mook has not followed through and done for me, even more so than I'm wondering how I could have conceivably blown the hit at twenty yards. Twenty yards and the fancy goddamn mook standing still as a marble statue.

The rotors blow like a hurricane, and all I can see is a hatful of nothing.

5.

Mercedes Bélanger cuffs my wrists before she takes off the bandages. I let her, because she says she has a gun. Also she pokes a lit cigarette between my lips, and I sit there, drowning in sweat and sucking back smoke, and only just then do I realize that it has been her in here with me all along. I might have known. She snips the gauze away, then gently lifts the cotton pads off my eyes. I blink and squint, but there is not a whole lot more than a watercolor blur of colors and shapes, truth be told. Still, I am not blind as a bat, which is what I'd expected.

"It'll get better," she tells me. "There wasn't any retinal or corneal damage, nothing long term. But you're gonna want to avoid bright lights for a bit."

Wrapped up in only the silk robe, I sit here in the stifling room that smells like dust and mildew. I'm looking at the dump for the first time, but I can't tell much more about my surroundings than I could with the bandages on. Mercedes Bélanger is facing me, sitting on the table, and jazz spills loud from the radio behind her. All the lights are down low, but it is sufficiently bright to sting my aching eyes, so I close them again.

"You've been here all along?" I ask, mumbling around the cigarette.

"Not all along, but mostly," she replies and takes the kretek from my mouth.

"So, what's this bushwa then?" I want to know. "You taking me away to the Turk to pay for my ineptitude? If that's it, lady, you could have left the damn bandages on."

"I ain't taking you much of nowhere, Ms. Sakellarios. You'll be on your own when those cuffs come off. Your part in this particular shell game is done, and maybe Constantin don't see it yet – 'cause he can be a short-sighted son of a bitch – but I figure you'll be useful again some day. I don't like waste. My dad, he once told me how, when all is said and done, every evil in the world boils down to a wasteful act."

"You're letting me walk?" I ask. "Don't you think your boss is gonna be a little more than just hot under the collar about that?"

"You let me worry about the Turk."

"Fine, but first you tell me how it is I didn't kill that fancy fella on the catwalk when I had him dead bang, and about the rain and the wolves, and –"

"Used to was," says Mercedes Bélanger, interrupting me, "you did a bitch a solid, and she didn't start right in demanding all the secrets of the goddamn universe tossed into the bargain. Used to was, she'd have shown a jot of gratitude."

I open my eyes, and it seems I can see just a little more than before I shut them. I say to her, "Yeah, well, be that as it might, I am not so accustomed to playing patsy in a grift, and most especially not when that grift involves stealing from men like Constantin Arat, so you'll just have to forgive my lack of gratitude. It was the box, wasn't it? You slipped me a ghost or three in the upload. For all I know, there wasn't only not any rain and not any dogs, there was not even any fancy fucking mook on a catwalk."

And right here Mercedes Bélanger, she taps the side of her nose with a forefinger. Or I think that's what she does. Maybe she's flipping me off and my eyes are still too scorched to know the difference.

"You'll get something for your troubles," she says.

"I just bet I will."

"How about let's get you outta here before the next transmission rolls round," and quicker than I can say yay or nay, she sticks the cigarette back between my lips. She helps me up off the sofa. She leads me from the room and down a long hallway and down enough flights of stairs that I lose count after four. But before too long we're outside. It's night, which is just as well. She puts a pair of cheaters on my face, sets them down on the bridge of my nose, then takes off the handcuffs. There's a cab waiting at the curb. I smell hot asphalt and garbage and the fumes from the automobile's tailpipe.

"Just so we're clear, I'm not happy about this," I say, and she gives me a little shove towards my ride.

"Just so we're clear," she tells me, "I ain't overly concerned with any one blackstrap's dissatisfaction, not even when it's the dissatisfaction of the great Elenore Sakellarios. Got bigger fish to fry and all."

"And if you're wrong and the Turk comes round for my hide?"

"It comes to that," she says, "you'll know he took my hide first. But it ain't gonna come to that. I am a careful girl. Now git," and with that she turns about and marches away and the blur of her vanishes back into the streetlight blur of the tenement building looming before me. I stand there for a minute or two before the driver decides I've stood there long enough and honks his horn. So I get into the backseat, and he asks where I want to go, which comes as a surprise. I expected the Turk's lady would have gone and decided that for me.

"The airport," I say, but when the car pulls away from the curb, I take that back and instead I give him the address of a bordello and shooting gallery across the river in Jersey. Just now, I need to be high and I need to be fucked more than I need to get out of Philly. I have this wounded ego to soothe, I do. And a considerable need to stop puzzling over how one and one isn't making two. The driver tells me it's my funeral.

"Don't I just know it," I reply. "Don't I just."

Estate Sale | *Bentley Little*

The sky was blue, the temperature pleasant, the morning fine. As Ann strolled through the neighborhood on her Sunday walk, she thought about how lucky she was to live in such a community. Year after year, Irvine was ranked one of the safest, cleanest, best places to live in the country. People in inner cities were no doubt awakening to the sounds of gunfire, looking out their broken windows at homeless people camped out on sidewalks and gang members congregating on corners, while here in Irvine Jim was back at home mowing the lawn, the twins were parked in front of the flat screen playing X-Box and she was taking a walk on this beautiful day.

She'd strolled all the way to Woodbridge Park, had followed the trail around the small man-made lake and was heading back on a route she didn't usually take, when she noticed, up ahead, cars parked on both sides of the street. She assumed someone was having a party—birthday? anniversary?—but upon drawing closer, she saw in front of one of the identical peach-colored houses a yard sign: *Estate Sale.*

What was the difference between an estate sale and a garage sale? Ann wasn't exactly sure, but the garage door was closed, and there were no household items laid out on the lawn, so, apparently, an estate sale took place inside the house. Did you have to sign up or register ahead of time? she wondered. Did it cost money? Curious, she walked up the short pathway through the small neatly manicured yard to the open front door. Not sure if she was allowed to step inside, she stood on the stoop and knocked on the doorframe. "Hello?" she called.

An officious young man wearing an expensively tailored suit appeared in front of her. "Welcome! Come in!" he insisted. "There's plenty of room!"

He stepped aside, motioning for her to enter, and Ann saw that the house was filled with men and women jostling for position, some with objects in their hands, others examining the furnishings or belongings of the homeowners. An overweight woman in a loud flower print dress shoved a Precious Moments figurine in front of the young man's face. "How much for this?" she demanded.

"Everything should be marked," he said.

"I don't see any price," she said, turning it over to show him. "How much?"

He took the object from her. "Everything was priced," he said calmly. "You obviously took the tag off. So you are not allowed to buy this item."

"Really!" she exclaimed, acting offended, but her face was red and she quickly faded back into the crowd.

Ann looked at the figurine. It was of two little girls with big heads and big eyes, a quote on the base at the bottom celebrating the importance of sisters. "I have that one," she told the young man.

"Perfect." He withdrew a roll of adhesive labels and a pen from his jacket pocket. "How much did it cost?" he asked.

"I don't know. My sister gave it to me. I don't even like it, really."

"Would you say it's worth twenty?"

"Maybe."

"So I'll put down ten." He wrote the price on one of the labels, peeled it off and placed it on the bottom of the base. "We're selling everything for half of what it's worth. If it hasn't sold by noon, we'll halve that again."

An older man walked up with a small wooden spice rack in his hand. "Where do I pay for this?" he asked.

"On the back patio. There's a table with two women. They'll take your money. You exit around the side of the house."

"I have that, too!" Ann said, surprised.

She looked around the front room, noticing for the first time that the house seemed to have the same floorplan as her own. In fact, whoever lived here had arranged the furnishings in an almost identical manner, placing couches, tables, chairs and television in the same spots she and Jim had.

Not only that, but...

She frowned.

The furniture itself was exactly the same as her own. Their couches had identical patterns. Their tables were the same make. Ditto the chairs.

This was crazy. Ann pushed her way through the crowd of bargain hunters, moving out of the front room into the kitchen. It was like walking through her own house, were her own house filled with strangers attempting to buy all of her belongings. The stove, oven and refrigerator were the same as hers. Even the microwave—white, Emerson—was on the counter under the dish cupboards in the same location as in her own kitchen. On an impulse, she opened one of those cupboards, saw Fiesta flatware of the type on which she served her family's meals.

Was there anything in the refrigerator? She opened it, half-expecting to see last night's leftovers on the center shelf, to find salsa, soy sauce and ketchup adjacent to the butter compartment in the door, but of course the fridge had been cleared out and unplugged in preparation for today's sale.

She closed the refrigerator, feeling relieved that it was empty but still more than a little unnerved.

"Kenmore," a middle-aged Asian woman told her. "That's a good refrigerator. We have one just like it."

"We do, too," Ann said. Politely nodding her head to excuse herself, she made her way through the crowd and down the hall.

The half-bath? Same black and white color scheme as hers, same type of throw rug on the tile floor, same Moen faucets. Master bedroom? She not only recognized the bed but the comforter and skirt, not only the dresser and mirror but the wallpaper behind them.

How was this possible?

She needed to find out who the owners were. It seemed to have gotten even more crowded inside the house, and she turned sideways, making her way between the throng of people in the hall, moving into the living room. In addition to curious neighbors like herself and assorted men and women (mostly women) looking for a bargain, some professionals seemed to have joined the gathering: a man checking prices on his cellphone, a woman flipping through a notebook as she studied an antique china cabinet.

A cabinet identical to one in Ann's house.

Who were these people?

There was no sign of the young man who had ushered her in, but through sliding glass doors that opened onto the back patio, she saw the table he had mentioned, with two well-dressed women seated behind open cash boxes. One of the women was engaged, tallying up the CDs, DVDs and books of a gray-haired man in a faded Pink Floyd T-shirt. The other woman was open, and Ann walked up to her. "Excuse me," she said, "are you the owners of the house?"

"No, we work for the company overseeing the sale."

"I see."

The woman looked at Ann's empty hands. "Are you buying something?"

"No, not yet. But I live in the neighborhood, and I was wondering if you could tell me the name of the owners here?"

"I'm sorry," the woman told her. "I don't know." She motioned for Ann to move aside as a young woman holding a waffle iron stepped up to pay for it.

"But you must know the last name. It's an estate sale, right? And you're conducting the sale. Is this the Jones estate or the Smith estate or what? You must have some name on your paperwork there." She pointed to a stapled sheaf of pages next to the cash box.

Annoyed, the woman picked up the papers, scanned the top page. "It's Lippman. The Lippman estate."

Ann was flooded with relief. She'd been afraid that the owners of the home would have *her* surname, and while "Lippman" was *close* to "Pittman," it wasn't exactly the same, and in her mind the spell was broken. She wasn't sure what she would have done if the people had been named Pittman, but she was happy she didn't have to find out. Tension had been ratcheting up within her ever since entering the house, and the freakiness of the mounting coincidences had made her feel...vulnerable.

Although she'd probably been overreacting. *Everything* here couldn't be identical to its counterpart in her house.

A man emerged into the patio from the garage, pushing a lawnmower exactly like Jim's.

Why was an estate sale even being conducted? she wondered. She still wasn't sure exactly what an estate sale was, but judging by the fact that an outside group had been brought in to sell off every single item in the house, it must mean that the homeowners had died. Although, even if they did die, shouldn't their stuff have gone to a relative?

Maybe it had been an old couple with no family.

These weren't really old people furnishings.

Maybe it had been a young couple with no family who had died in a car accident. Or a single man. Or a single woman.

The possibilities were endless, and she supposed the details didn't matter, but the similarities between this house and her own disturbed her. Identical floorplans were to be expected in a development like Woodbridge, where homes came in only three or four models, but even here in the backyard, there was a bird of paradise planted in the narrow plot next to the garage, and two wire baskets filled with impatiens hanging from the edge of the latticed patio roof, just as at her own house.

She ought to call Jim and tell him to come over here! Yes, that's what she should do. It would make her feel less unsettled to have a witness, and she moved out of the way of two burly men carrying what she would have sworn was her living room end table. If Jim was still mowing the lawn, he wouldn't be carrying his phone, but she could call the house and tell one of the boys to go out and get him. Taking out her phone, she dialed their number.

One ring. Two.

She hoped they didn't have their game cranked up so loud that they couldn't hear the phone.

There was no third ring. Instead, three discordant high-pitched tones sounded, and a recorded female voice robotically stated: "I'm sorry. But the number you have dialed is no longer in service."

Ann frowned. That was weird. She terminated the call and dialed again. Maybe she'd hit a wrong number, accidentally pressing 4 instead of 5, or 3 instead of 2. It had happened before.

No. She heard the same out-of-service message again when she tried to call, and a shiver of cold passed through her as she turned off the phone and put it back in her pocket. She imagined walking home to find that her house had been cleared out, with no sign of Jim or the twins.

Maybe she wasn't even married. Maybe she'd never had kids.

Why would she even think something so crazy? Ann didn't know, but she was suddenly overcome by the thought that her last name *wasn't* Pittman, it *was* Lippman, and this was *her* estate sale. Perhaps she'd suffered some sort of mental breakdown, and after trying in vain to find her, authorities had determined that she had died, leading to the sale of all of her possessions, while her disturbed mind constructed an alternate identity she was now living.

That *was* crazy, and she tried to talk some sense into herself, pointing out to her brain that her house was several streets over—1199 Shearwater—and that she'd eaten breakfast there this morning with her family before taking a morning walk. She looked around. No matter how similar the belongings here might be, they were not hers, and the neighbors and dealers picking up bargains were buying items that coincidentally happened to mirror her own.

Still, she was becoming increasingly uncomfortable. She shouldn't have stopped by in the first place, but even though she had, there was no reason for her to remain. There was nothing she wanted to buy—everything was a copy of what she already owned—and she felt a growing need to ground herself by seeing her family.

The woman who'd purchased the waffle iron was exiting around the side of the house, and Ann followed her. It was as if she'd been holding her breath, as once on the sidewalk she pursed her lips and exhaled, feeling as though she could finally breathe freely. It had been claustrophobic, shoved together with so many people, and here in the open air, the panic that had crept up on her dissipated. She looked up and down the street, saw a late-rising elderly man in a blue bathrobe pick up the newspaper from his driveway, saw a young woman watering flowers, saw two kids on scooters racing. Cars were parked on both sides of the street in defiance of homeowners' association rules—people attending the estate sale—and as soon as the waffle iron woman got into her Prius and pulled out, a man in a Mini-Cooper took the spot.

Grateful to be away from the house, Ann walked up the sidewalk and turned right at the end of the block, once again on her normal track.

Taking her customary route, the estate sale behind her, she should have found herself focused on the walk the way she would on a typical Sunday morning. But her mind kept returning to the estate sale, and she could not deny the fact that, as much as she wanted to pretend the similarities between that house and her own were superficial and entirely coincidental, she knew deep down that the two were identical.

What type of car had the owners driven? she wondered. A Range Rover, she would be willing to bet, just like her family did. Rather than lessening, her uneasiness grew. Each step that took her further from the estate sale brought her closer to her own house, and in her mind she saw a crowd of people sorting through her own family's possessions, to the point that when she reached their street, she almost expected to see a sign announcing an estate sale at *their* house.

There was no sign, but there did seem to be too many unfamiliar vehicles parked along both sides of the street, and she increased the pace of her walking. She was nearly running by the time she reached their yard.

And there, to her relief, was Jim. He had finished mowing the lawn and emptying the bag of grass clippings onto the compost pile on the side of the house, and was just starting to reattach the bag to the mower.

Thank God!

"Jim!" she said gratefully. She couldn't wait to tell him about her little adventure, about the house that looked just like theirs, but when he looked up at her, she saw no recognition in his eyes.

He was joking. It had to be a joke. "Jim?" she said tentatively.

"Yes?" And she recognized the generic smile he gave to sales clerks and mailmen, people he didn't know. "Can I help you?"

Twisted Hazel | *Stephen Gallagher*

From the window I can see them coming and going. They're not the same people as before. Most of them are men, though I've counted two young women. They're working in the marked space in front of the house, the safe space, the space inside the ropes. Where the big lawn used to be, and where they won't get blown up. First they laid out poles on the ground, and then put them together into a low framework. Then they dragged a big canvas all the way over; it took ten of them to do that. Now they're all at the corners, winding at handles and calling out to each other. And as they wind the big marquee is slowly rising up, like a circus tent.

So much happening. Nothing ever happens here. It's no wonder I can't take my eyes off them.

I'd love to get closer, but I can't. I can't leave the house unless it's to go into the garden at the back, which has a wall around it. I can't go past the walls. Don't ask me why. If I ever knew, I don't remember.

So I watch.

Everything started the day the soldier and the woman came. They arrived in a Land Rover. He was in uniform, she very elegant, with perfect hair, and carrying a leather folder. I looked at her and saw everything I dream of being. Strong and gorgeous and she just didn't care. She stepped down onto the weeds and gravel as if the driveway was a red carpet. While the soldier was sorting out his big bunch of keys she was looking all around, taking everything in. I ran down the stairs to be there as they came in through the door.

She took a few steps into the gloom as he closed the door behind them, and when the floorboards creaked she turned and said, "Is it safe to walk around?"

"On tiptoe, yes," he said. And I think he was making a joke that didn't quite work because then he said, "No, we're fine."

It's a big hallway, with columns and a big wide stairway. The only light is from a glazed dome in the roof, high above the upper landing. There was a click and I saw that in her free hand she had a flashlight, not much bigger than a pencil, and she was directing its beam onto a lacquered cupboard with Chinese figures all over it.

She clicked off the light and said, "Your Colonel wasn't wrong. The house is a real time capsule. Who's had access?"

"Since they sealed it up?" he said. "I couldn't tell you. I do know that only three of us can lay hands on the keys."

"An empty manor and you've had no break-ins. That's rare."

"I'd say it's largely down to being surrounded by a minefield."

They moved on through into the first of the rooms. The one I call the Horse Room, because of the picture over the fireplace. The furniture in here had all been moved over to one wall, and some of it was covered over.

She lifted a corner of the sheet and said, "Is there a plan of the floors?"

"'Fraid not," the soldier said.

"I'll have to make one."

The soldier had crossed the room and was standing in front of the fireplace, shining his own light up on the horse picture. The picture was mildewed along the top and sagging in its frame. The fireplace had more carving, all fruit and violins.

He said, "I don't know what the Colonel told you about the contents, but I wouldn't get my hopes up."

"I never do," she said, and let the dust sheet fall. The soldier was now tugging at a corner of hanging wallpaper alongside the fireplace, peeling it away from the wall like a piece of skin.

He said, "See what I mean? This is what happens when the damp gets in."

She glanced back. "But there's always room for surprises," she said. "Glass and fine china don't spoil. Metal and marble clean up. And a good enough picture can be worth the restoration."

He returned his beam to my horse picture. "What about this one?"

"Maybe not. Look, give me a chance to get my bearings. I'll call out if I need anything."

He got the message. "Yes, ma'am," he said.

"What do I call you? Captain? Adjutant?"

"Harry."

"Olivia."

"I'll be unlocking the cellars," Harry said, and went away.

I followed Olivia around. She fascinated me. She was so focused, so organised. She used the leather folder as a rest for her notepad and worked up a map of the ground floor as she went from room to room, inspecting all the things and making notes. She didn't see me. No one sees me.

Then I ran ahead of her upstairs. It had been so long since I'd been around anyone new. Some men had come once and boarded up the windows. For a while the army had used some of the bigger rooms to store boxes and equipment, but much of what they'd brought in had been cleared out again. Mostly the days were long and empty and to be honest I seem to prefer them that way. I might spend my time yearning for company, but whenever there are strangers around I get all excited and then after a while I can't wait for them to go.

Olivia would be different, I thought. I'd taken to her. She was making a second diagram of the upstairs rooms beginning with the one with the stuffed animals and the doll's house. I wished that I could tell her how this was my favourite but it would be pointless, she wouldn't hear me. She picked up the bear and sniffed it, made a face. She seemed more interested in the framed alphabet pictures around the room. She lifted one away from the wall to look at the back and then wrote something down.

The four-poster in the biggest of the bedrooms took her interest as well. She pulled on the heavy cover until she'd dragged it onto the floor and completely clear of the bed, and then she took hold of the frame and braced herself against it, trying to make it wobble. It didn't even creak, and she seemed impressed. She didn't replace the cover but she made a note.

Captain Harry was waiting at the foot of the stairs when we were done. He was still dusting cellar dirt off his hands when we reached him and he said, "There's a big wine collection. Wish I'd known."

"Most likely undrinkable," Olivia said. "Which may not deter a collector."

"I know plenty of chaps it wouldn't deter," Harry said.

Olivia's work here was all done, it seemed. She now began to gather her notes into the folder and said, "You say the building's safe?"

"The sappers looked it over and gave it the all-clear."

"Sappers?"

"Royal Engineers. They reckon the timbers are too rotten for saving but nothing's about to fall down. Did you see everything you wanted?"

"Enough to get my colleagues in and make a proper inventory. Can we get those windows unboarded? Maybe a generator and some lights?"

"You think it's worth the trouble?"

She zipped the folder. "I think it's worth doing the diligence."

"How long can I say will that take?"

"A couple of days at least. We'll go through all the rooms, tag and photograph everything that isn't nailed down, and make a spot valuation of each item for the catalogue. I'm thinking we should have the actual sale on-site."

"How would that work?"

"A country house clearance makes quite an event. We put a marquee on the lawn and open up the house for the viewing. Bidders get to see the lots in their original situation."

Harry seemed doubtful. "That could be tricky."

"It's an unusual venue. I can see it getting a lot of attention."

"A public auction on a firing range?"

"Your Colonel's the one who suggested it," she said.

"Then I'm wholly in favour," Harry said without hesitation.

Olivia indicated that she was ready to leave, and they made a move toward the door. She said, "How do I arrange access?"

"Through me," Harry said. "I'll sort you out with whatever you need."

I watched them leave. Captain Harry locked the big door from the outside. They seemed nice.

Something must have been set in motion, because some days later an army truck came down the long road from the trees on the hill. Along with the driver came a dozen squaddies and a sergeant. They unboarded the windows and then set about spraying weeds and roping off a safe area in front of the house. On other visits I'd heard them talk about all the 'live ordnance' that might still be lying in the fields hereabouts; people wandering outside designated areas might step on something that could explode, which is why the marked road is the only way in or out.

Olivia came back while the yard work was going on, and she didn't come alone. She arrived with her team in two escorted buses. Captain Harry opened up the house and then went off to talk to the sergeant. Olivia gathered everybody in the hallway and stood on the third stair to give out her instructions. Everyone, Olivia included, was wearing a security pass today. I was able to read their names, which is how I learned the rest of hers.

Olivia Lloyd. I like it. I wish it was my own.

She said to them, "I've been told the building's sound, but go carefully. The West Wing and the ballroom seem to have suffered the least."

The ballroom was obvious but I never even knew we had a West Wing. An older woman named Geraldine Logan asked, "Is the kitchen range to go?"

"Everything's to go," Olivia told her, and then they all dispersed off to their assigned parts of the house.

I wandered from room to room for a while, watching different people work. At this stage the presence of company was still a novelty. They made careful notes and took lots of photographs and left paper tags on everything. I could tell they'd done this many times before. They were in the attic, they were down in the cellar with portable lights. Out in the walled garden, two of them were pulling down ivy and cutting back bushes to reveal urns and statues long untouched by daylight. One tried to open a door in the wall to see what was beyond, but a gnarly corkscrew shrub had grown wild and spread across and there was no shifting it.

I went back in to look for my new friend, and found her talking to one of the men.

"Christopher," she said to him. "You look excited."

Going by his security pass his full name was Christopher Holland, and if he was excited, the signs of it were too subtle for my eye. He said, "There's one picture in the study I'd like moved today."

"The Stubbs copy?"

He chose his words carefully. "Let's call it that for now."

Shortly after that, two of them put on cotton gloves and carried my horse picture out to their bus. There was nothing I could do about it.

Geraldine Logan told Olivia, "There's some local interest to be found in the books, but they're all in a bad way."

"Pick out anything saleable and box up the rest in job lots," Olivia said, and so it went on.

They worked until the light faded, then came back the next day and the day after that and worked some more. Just as I was beginning to get used to them, they stopped coming.

Left alone again I wandered from room to room, looking at the notes and the labels they'd left on everything. Most of the notes meant nothing to me. I'd seen the people cleaning off some of the objects with soft brushes but otherwise they'd left everything dusty. *In context,* they called it.

I no longer had to go up to the attic to look out of a window. The view up there was limited but sometimes the sky beyond the trees would light up with explosions to the sound of distant gunfire. There was no firing tonight. Just clouds and stillness and stars.

It was quiet for a while and then all the activity started again. The tent people turned up this morning. The marquee is raised now, and they're setting out chairs under the canvas. There must be a hundred of those. They've got a generator, lights, loudspeakers. And now more strangers, different strangers, bussed in on coaches down the safe road, swarming over the house, catalogues in hand, poking into everything. There's a member of Olivia's team in every room to answer questions and forbid any handling. I'm already liking this part less.

I find Olivia with Captain Harry. He's always around somewhere, keeping an eye on everything, staying out of it.

He says, "Well, my boss is happy. What about yours?"

"He's Swiss," Olivia says. "So I never quite know."

I MIGHT AS well admit it, I'm miserable. It's auction day and there are men in brown coats and those same white cotton gloves moving to and fro, carrying everything out of the house and across to the marquee, one piece at a time. I hadn't understood their plan. I think I'd imagined they were here to bring the house back to life. I can hear the loudspeakers over there, but not well enough to make out what's being said. Every now and again there's a small ripple of applause from the tent.

They're dismantling my world and there's nothing I can do.

I try to stay close to Olivia but she's constantly on the move, only in the house for minutes at a time. I look for her upstairs and find two of the men carrying my doll's house out of my favourite room.

My doll's house!

I ask them to stop and they don't hear. I try to get in the way but that doesn't work. I'm just driven on before them, down the stairs, paper label on the dollhouse flapping while they navigate with care. I can't obstruct them, I can't get their attention. They've a special trolley waiting to take it across to the sale. They're setting it down on the trolley and again I beg them to stop.

Once it leaves the house, I can't follow. What can I do? I have to do something.

I get right into the face of the older man and I scream as hard as I can. Really loud. There's no response. He doesn't hear, he doesn't see.

But behind me there's a crash of porcelain hitting the floor.

I turn.

It's Geraldine Logan and she's looking straight at me, pale as the white figurine she just dropped.

I move toward her. She sees me. Her eyes show it. Her gaze stays on me as I move. She takes a step back and then turns and runs before I can make my appeal. Within seconds she's out of the door and I can't go after her.

I stand there in the doorway, hoping she'll look back and relent. She does, she looks back from the driveway; but it's in fear, and I can tell that she no longer sees me.

Whatever the moment was, it's over.

My doll's house passes me by.

From behind me inside the house I hear Olivia call out, "Who did this?"

You did, Olivia, you did. You and your people. Why are you doing this to me? I have so little and you're taking my life apart.

For the rest of the afternoon I just sit on the stairs while the house empties around me. Things I don't treasure, some things I even hate, but that's not the point. It's my world.

Geraldine doesn't come back. From what I overhear she's left the site, and hasn't said why. Everyone thinks she's embarrassed by the breakage. She's the books and manuscripts person, I hear them saying. She shouldn't even have been handling china.

When they stop for the day, the house empties out and eventually there's only Olivia and Captain Harry left. She goes around all the rooms with her big list, checking things off. He waits to lock up. I've heard her say that she's worried about security now that the public have had a chance to look the house over. There are gangs that target country houses. They use auction catalogues and *Country Life* magazine as shopping guides.

She says to him, "I asked for someone to keep watch overnight."

"That would be me," he says.

"Oh," she says. "Sorry about that."

"I've had worse billets."

We're in my Horse Room, the one I've heard them call the study. Though the work's over for the day, neither of them seems in any particular hurry to leave.

Captain Harry says, "Can I make a confession?"

"Do I look like a priest?"

"Before your people took the inventory, I picked out a bottle and hid it."

"From the wine cellar?"

He nods.

Olivia is shocked. "You didn't."

"Army property," he says. "At least at the time."

"But still…"

"It was fair game," he says. "Your lot had a chance to find it."

"Where?"

He goes over to the big wooden desk where there's a bronze of a Greek lady dancing or tripping along or something. The statue's about two feet high. Olivia winces as she sees him take hold of it and tip it at an angle. She tries to say something but it's already too late, he's got it tilted. The inside of the bronze is hollow. He reaches in and slides a wine bottle out of it.

"I don't believe this," Olivia says.

Captain Harry blows some of the dust off the bottle and holds it up to the light. Then he sniffs around the cork, but you can see that he doesn't really know what he's doing.

"I know you deal in this kind of thing all the time," he begins, "but haven't you ever wondered..."

"I should stop you right there."

He reads her tone. "But you won't."

She takes the bottle from him and inspects it. My Olivia, she does know what she's doing. Even though she's brought disruption into my home, she's everything I want to be.

"Chateau Montrose, 1939," she says. "A high to mid shoulder fill."

"Is that good?"

"Wine loses volume through the cork as it ages. The less that it's lost, the better its chances."

He digs around in his pocket and brings out a pocket knife; opens it up and it's a corkscrew.

"Join me?" he says.

"You're kidding."

"Think of it as army surplus."

"The rest of the case went for six thousand pounds."

"But this one didn't."

She shakes her head in disbelief. I don't even know how many bottles make a case but I can see that, to her mind, what he's proposing is something outrageous and unimaginable.

Then she says, "Oh, fuck it. Yes."

She goes looking for some glasses. He clears off an old chesterfield and sets a low table in front of it. Then he hunts around and I think he's looking for a silver tray that he may have noticed in here one time, but that's gone.

Olivia comes back with two long-stemmed crystal glasses that I can't recall seeing before. They sit, and he strips the end of the bottle to get to the cork.

"I feel like a criminal," Olivia says.

"Exciting, isn't it?"

All three of us are transfixed as the first glass is poured. I don't know what I was expecting but to me it just looks like wine.

Harry takes a good mouthful and sits there holding it for a while, considering. I'm watching, Olivia's watching even more closely, and I don't think either of us can tell what he's thinking.

Eventually he swallows and gives his verdict.

"I've had worse," he says.

Now it's Olivia's turn. She swirls the wine, breathes in from the glass, then takes a sip. She gives it a few moments, then shrugs.

"'Salright," she concedes.

They both relax back. Captain Harry says, "So what's after this?"

"We'll move all the lots to our warehouse in Northolt," she says. "Buyers arrange collection from there."

"Hmm."

"That's not the 'after this' you had in mind."

He made an open-hands gesture, a plea of innocence. "Most people reckon my mind is a blank."

"Will you patrol the place like a watchman or do you plan on sleeping tonight?"

"You'll laugh."

"Try me."

Glass in hand, he stands. Picks up the unfinished bottle and indicates for her to follow. They go upstairs with me right behind them.

He's laid out a sleeping roll and made a camp on the four-poster bed.

"That's it?" she says.

"All I need," he says.

She laughs and pushes him and then the mood goes all strange and they start wrestling, except that it's actually hugging and kissing while they pull at each other's clothes.

I don't understand but it stirs something in me. Not so much like something I've forgotten, more like something that I've been trying to forget. Now they're on the bed and squirming around and she's making noises like he's hurting her, calling out and scratching at his back, and I want them to stop.

I don't know why, but I'm afraid. I can't take my eyes away but I really, really need them to stop. I can't be sure but I think I'm starting to sob.

Then suddenly she's looking straight at me and I know she can see me, just like the woman who dropped the jug.

She scrambles back up the bed, right up against the headboard. She hits it with a bang. He doesn't know what's wrong. He thinks it's something he's done. I take a step back. She's looking all around the room and now I can tell that she can't see me any more.

"What is it?" he says. "What did I do?"

"Nothing," she says.

"*What?*" he presses.

"I said, nothing."

He keeps asking but she won't tell him. She's pulling her clothes back on and she keeps looking around the room as if she fears seeing whatever spooked her again, but now she's looking in all the wrong places.

The mood is broken. When Olivia's dressed, she leaves in her own car. Captain Harry spends the rest of the night walking around the house, drinking the rest of the old wine, flicking at the paper tags on everything.

I walk with him, for the company. He seems sad.

Today is the second day of their sale. The final day, if I've heard it right. More people have turned up and they say that's because they've been holding back some of the more popular things. That doesn't include my horse picture, by the way. That's going to be sold in New York when they've finished fixing it up. I'll never see it again.

The desk and the sofa and the bronze lady, all gone. There are men taking measurements in the kitchen to get the old stoves out. They'll be sizing up the fireplaces next, and who knows what else. They were even looking at the stairs, but decided that the wood's no good.

Again, when Olivia's in the house, I stay close. She's looking out of a window at the back, into the walled garden. The statues are gone but there's a man out there on his own.

Straight-faced Christopher sees her by the window, and he stops to look out as well.

She says, "I'm keeping an eye on that one. He's registered as a buyer but he's made no move to the bidding tent."

"That's the head gardener's lad," Christopher says. "He won't be bidding. He told me he only signed up for the sale so he could see the house again."

"He's a bit old for a lad."

"Then imagine the state of the head gardener."

Olivia finds his name on her list. Then she goes out into the garden to speak to him. He's looking at the gnarly bush, the one that's grown over and blocked the gate. He's pretty gnarly himself.

"Mister Gilbert?" she says.

I can see that he's wearing a hearing aid, but he seems to hear her all right. Without actually looking at her he gestures toward the shrub and says, "There's nothing left of the garden. This is all I can recognise and it's the one thing they'd never let us touch. It's tragic," he says, "what's happened to the estate."

"You lived here?"

"My dad had one of the cottages." Another gesture, to somewhere vaguely beyond the walls. "Over there. Before the army took it on. That's gone."

"So you'd be just a boy."

"I was."

She glances back at the house and then picks her next words with care.

She says, "Was there ever talk of a ghost?"

Well, now he looks at her. His eyes are very pale, like they've been boiled. He doesn't give a direct answer but says, "Have you seen her?"

"Have *you?*"

He returns his attention to the old tree, growing out of control along the wall. "No one knows who she was," he says. "Just that her bones were under the twisted hazel. I bet if you dug there you'd find nothing. But you can imagine how we all stayed clear."

Then he smiles to himself, as if at some old folly.

"Twisted Hazel," he says. "That's what we called her."

Olivia stays for a while after he's gone. I try to work out what she's thinking. She's just standing there, stroking her upper lip with a forefinger, looking at the shrub without really seeing it. The same way that, apart from that one moment in the bedroom, she always looks through me.

She starts shaking her head. I realise that she's quite upset.

"I'm so sorry," she says quietly, and goes inside.

I look up, and see Harry watching from the window.

It's all over. The marquee team begin taking down their canvas even as the last of the visitors are leaving. There was a smaller tent selling lunches and that's gone already. With its rooms mostly stripped bare, the house seems twice as big as it did before. I can't settle anywhere. I stand in one room or another and screw my eyes shut and summon it all back, reassembling in my mind one piece at a time, but when I open my eyes nothing's changed.

I stand at the window where Captain Harry stood, looking down into the garden as he did. When I see the twisted hazel I think of the old man and his silly stories. I've been here all this time and I've never seen any ghost.

Captain Harry's walking through the house. I follow him. He's looking for Olivia and he finds her in the morning room, counting rubbish sacks. There was a lot of debris and litter left scattered and not all of it's been gathered up.

I think he's been waiting to get her alone. He's nervous and doesn't know how to begin.

He says, "Are we…?"

And she immediately catches his meaning and says, "Yeah, we're fine. I'm sorry. I never meant for that night to get weird. Can we just forget it?"

"As you wish." I can't tell if he's relieved or disappointed. I think it's some of both.

She says, "We're all but done, here. What happens when everything's gone?"

"You mean, tonight?"

"I mean in general. What's the army's plan for the house?"

I can see that he's happier with the change of subject. He says, "There was talk of using it for urban warfare training. You know, dressing the place like an embassy and putting in a squad to practice room-to-room clearance and such. But then they'd have to fix it up for health and safety, which is kind of absurd."

"So it'll be left empty again?"

"Not for long. Artillery can always find a use for a new target."

"You're going to bomb it."

"Not me, personally. But yes. Come back in a year and chances are there'll be nothing to see."

She looks around. "It seems a shame."

"It is. But what can you do?"

"Lend me your knife," she says, but she won't tell him why.

That isn't quite the end of it. There's a gap of a few days and then men come in and start smashing through walls in the kitchen to get the oven ranges out. That takes them most of a week. The fireplaces go, and one entire three-part window at the top of the staircase. They lift the whole thing out of the wall, leaving the house wide open to the wind and the rain.

I don't keep track of them. I've no interest in who they are, or what they do. Mostly, I hide.

At nights I go and stand where the window was and look out toward the trees on the hill. With the window gone, it's almost like being outside. They've started their night firing again and it lights up the sky like fireworks. It takes my mind off things for a while.

Before she left for the last time, Olivia went down to the garden. She looked around to be sure no one was watching and then used Captain Harry's knife to take a cutting from the twisted hazel.

The night fireworks seem to be getting closer every evening, but I think that's just my imagination.

I don't know where I'll go.

I know there's a place for me somewhere.

If Olivia ever comes back, perhaps I can go with her.

There's always hope.

Death Comes for the Rich Man | *Robert McCammon*

ONE
LORD MORTIMER HOPES

When December had reached the doorway of the new year of 1703, a sallow white-haired man in a black suit, black tricorn and black fearnaught coat also reached the doorway of Number Seven Stone Street in the town of New York. It was the middle of the afternoon, yet the blue light of evening lay upon the hills and streets. The sallow man began his climb up the stairs, and to his meeting with the problem-solvers above.

His ascent reached the realm of Hudson Greathouse and Matthew Corbett. They had been waiting for him, alerted by his letter of the past week posted from the New Jersey town of Oak Bridge. Thus by the blue light that fell through the windows, by the eight white tapers that burned in the wrought-iron chandelier above their heads and by the polite flames that crackled in the small fireplace of rough tan and gray stones, the two associates of the Herrald Agency sat side-by-side at their desks as the sallow man removed his coat, hung it upon a wallhook and then seated himself in a chair at the center of the room. He removed his tricorn and held it between his gnarled hands, and he looked at Matthew and Greathouse with sad and watery gray eyes. He had signed his letter *With Most Hopeful Regards, Jesper Oberley.* Without further hesitation he answered Hudson's first question, which was *How may we help you?*

"I am servant to a very rich master. Lord Brodd Mortimer," said the sad-eyed man. "I have been so these past eleven years. It pains me to say it, but Death is coming for him."

"True for everyone, isn't it?" asked Greathouse, with a quick glance at Matthew. The great one was yet hobbling about on a cane after the incident at Fort Laurens in the autumn, and what pained Matthew was hearing him struggle up the stairs and then a further struggle for breath at the top before coming to his desk. Matthew had to wonder if Hudson would ever again be the rakish and adventurous hell-hound of a man he'd once been. Of course he held himself to blame for that, and nothing Hudson could say would shake from his burdened mind the thought that he'd failed his friend.

"Lord Mortimer," said Jesper Oberley, with the faint trace of a smile that did nothing to alter his expression of solemn finality, "is nearer Death's hand than *most*. His physician predicts the end will come within a few days. Lord Mortimer has been ill for some time. It is consumption. Nothing can be done."

"Our condolences," Matthew said. He was studying Oberley's face, with its hanging jowls and furrowed fields. Matthew thought that Oberley resembled a loyal dog that had been much mistreated but always came back to lick the master's hand, because that was the nature of a loyal dog. "Such an illness is a tragic thing. But…as Mr. Greathouse has asked…how may we help?"

Jesper Oberley spent a moment staring into space, as if the answer to this question hung there like a spiderweb in a corner. Finally he drew a breath and said, "My master believes…very strongly…that Death will come for him in a physical form. The form of a man. My master believes that Death, in this physical form, will enter the house and come into his bedchamber. There, Death will not hesitate to take my master's soul and leave the husk of the body behind. Therefore, kind sirs, my master wishes to hire you to…shall we say… cheat Death."

"Cheat Death," said Hudson Greathouse, in a graveside tone. He had spoken it an instant before Matthew could.

"Yes sir. That is so."

"Hmmm." Greathouse tapped the musket-ball cleft in his chin. "Well…*usually*…one has not the power to do what your master is asking. I mean to say… Death is his own master and eventually master of all men, isn't he?"

"Lord Mortimer *hopes*," said Oberley, "that you might use your powers of persuasion in this instance. For certainly this would be a problem to be solved, would it not? The result being that Death—when he arrives at the manor—can be persuaded to allow Lord Mortimer a little extra time? A few days, perhaps, or even a few hours? It would be of great importance to my master."

"May I ask *why?*" Matthew prodded.

"Lord Mortimer's daughter Christina is a teacher at the school in the town of Grainger, some six miles from Oak Bridge. He moved the household from England five years ago, to be near her. But... there has been difficulty between them for many years, gentlemen. She is thirty-two years old and unmarried. She is...a free spirit, one might say."

"Must run in the profession," said Matthew.

Oberley of course did not pick up on this comment concerning a certain red-haired young woman who often bounded into Matthew's world and thoughts with no warning. Oberley simply nodded as if this made perfect sense. "Lord Mortimer," Oberley went on, in his dry and quietly raspy voice, "wishes to make peace with his daughter before he passes from this world." The watery eyes moved from Matthew to Greathouse and back again, seeking empathy and understanding. "It is of vital importance, to the resting of his soul. *Vital*," he repeated. "That Lord Mortimer sees his daughter, and settles some issues disturbing to him, before Death takes the bounty."

Neither Matthew nor Greathouse moved for a moment. There came the sound of a creak on the staircase, which Matthew thought might be one of the office's ghosts curious as to how this situation might turn out, and perhaps a little jealous that he had not been so valued.

At last Greathouse cleared his throat. He said, "I have to wonder if we are up to this task."

"If you are not," came the reply, "then who might be?"

"The daughter," Matthew ventured. "Possibly she might not wish to visit her father?"

"I have spoken with her, four days ago. She is still pondering the invitation."

"But the visit is uncertain?"

"Uncertain," Oberley allowed. "Which is why you gentlemen are needed so urgently."

"It would probably do better to use our powers of persuasion on Christina, and not any vision or illusion of Death," said Matthew. "I would think a real ear should be more likely to listen."

"Vision?" Oberley's white eyebrows went up like signal flags. "Illusion? Oh, sir...my master is utterly convinced Death will come wearing the costume of a man, and that this man will not hesitate to end Lord Mortimer's life. I should say...it has been a fitful life, both for himself and others. He has many regrets." A thin smile surfaced. "He *should*." The smile faded. "Nothing I, any of the other servants nor Vicar Barrington can say will change his mind or alter his belief. He is convinced Death will come in this fashion, and—gentlemen—he greatly fears the moment of his reckoning."

"I suppose you're saying he's not only rich," said Greathouse, "but less than saintly?"

"His riches have sprung from the fountain of his greed," answered Oberley, his face displaying no emotion. "Many others have drowned in it."

Matthew and Greathouse both glanced at each other, but neither commented on this damning statement.

"I am empowered to offer you money." Oberley reached into a pocket of his velvety black waistcoat and brought out a leather pouch. "One hundred pounds, sirs. I should hope that Christina will come to the house tonight or tomorrow. Later than that will be, I fear, too late." Greathouse made a sound between a grunt and a whistle. Matthew knew that one hundred pounds for two nights' employ was quite the golden sum, and yet...it was a preposterous deed to be done. Intercept Death on his way to Brodd Mortimer's bedchamber? Convince such a tenuous phantasm to allow a few extra hours of life? It was absolutely—

"A fine problem to be solved," said Greathouse. His face was as serious as granite, but Matthew could sense the wolfish smile beneath. Greathouse's black eyes sparkled. "We'll do it. Or...rather...let me say that Mr. Corbett will do it, as I am not yet able to travel comfortably and this wet cold in the air tells me trouble is coming."

"Oh yes," said Matthew tightly. "Trouble *is* coming."

Greathouse's laugh was not merry. He kept his focus upon Jesper Oberley. "We accept this worthy challenge, sir. And may we have delivery of the money now?"

"Fifty pounds now," Oberley said, as he leaned forward to put the pouch into Greathouse's outstretched hand. "Fifty pounds when the task is done."

"Well done," said the great one.

"Burnt to a crisp," said Matthew.

"A few papers to be signed." Greathouse retrieved them from a drawer of his desk and pushed forward the quill and inkpot. Done way too eagerly, Matthew thought. Oberley got up from his chair and gave his signature on the necessary forms. "I have a coach down the street." His attention was fixed upon Matthew. "If you'd care to pack a bag for one or two nights, I will have the coachman take you to your house."

"That would be fine, thank you." Matthew also stood up. Oberley retrieved his fearnaught and began to shrug into it. The black tricorn went atop his head and the fearnaught's bone buttons were fastened. "Mr. Oberley," said Matthew, "may I send you down to your coach and spend a moment speaking to my associate?"

"Of course. I shall be waiting." The sallow servant departed the room and a moment later came the sound of his boots on the stairs.

Are you insane? Matthew started to ask, but Greathouse's voice was there first: "Calm down, now. Settle yourself."

"Settle myself? You're sending me on a trip to have a talk with *Death?* On behalf of a dying man who *must* be at least half as moonstruck as you are!"

Greathouse was already opening the pouch to inspect the gold coins within. "Nice. Look how they shine in this light."

"I've been blinded by such glitter once before. Hudson, are you *serious?* This is like…highway robbery!" A job for which Greathouse seemed to be well-suited, Matthew thought.

"Wrong." Greathouse aimed his black gun-barrel eyes at Matthew. "It's a worthwhile task to be undertaken on behalf of a dying man. Put yourself in his position."

"I'd rather not."

"For the *moment.*" The great one found the temptation too great not to spill the handful of coins across the green blotter on his desk. "You—being Lord Mortimer—fear the coming of Death in physical form. You wish to speak to your daughter, to correct past ills. It will be a comfort to you in your last hours, Matthew, to have yourself there at your bedside." He frowned and shook his head as if to clear his ears of cotton wads. "You know what I mean. Anyway, you have experience with lunatics. So go heap pride upon the banner of the Herrald Agency."

"I think it's wrong to—"

"Tut, tut!" came the reply, along with the aggravated wave of a hand. "Off with you!"

Being dismissed had never pleased Matthew's hackles. He therefore felt the rising of said hackles as he put on his gray cloak, black woolen gloves and black tricorn hat with a thin red band. He was aiming himself toward the door when his more mercenary associate said, "Getting colder outside. Ice may be coming. Guard yourself so you don't have to speak to Death on your own behalf."

"When I get back from this," Matthew said with a little crimson heat in his cheeks, "I'll be going to dinner at Sally Almond's as your guest. From wine to crumble cake."

"A pleasure. Now stop whining and go crumble the problem."

TWO
THE BEST MAN

THE BLACK COACH with its seats of fine dark red leather rumbled along the road, as cold rain swept in from the west and began to ice both earth and trees. Matthew was untouched by the weather, the coach being enclosed and having its own candleflame lamp attached to the wall beside his head, and yet he did feel the heaviness of the dark clouds above New Jersey. Across from him sat Jesper Oberley, half-dozing in spite of the jarring ride. The suffering driver was a man so wrapped in coats and shawls that only his eyes could be seen and these squinted behind ice-frosted spectacles. The four horses sometimes slid on dangerous patches, but they blew gouts of steam and righted themselves and muscled forward into the gathering night.

"Surely," Matthew said as the coach rocked back and forth and ice cracked at its seams, "Lord Mortimer can't really believe Death will come to him in human form."

The servant's eyes opened, and if he had been half-dozing a moment before now he was fully awake. "You would not be here, Mr. Corbett, if it was otherwise."

"It's a delusion. From his condition, I'm sure."

"He's nearing the end, but he's not raving. His mind is clear."

"Hm," Matthew said. He frowned in the yellow light. "I have to say, I feel I'm robbing a dying man."

"Lord Mortimer can afford to be robbed." The eyes had slid half-closed again. "He has robbed so many himself."

Matthew had no response to this rather cold statement. It seemed to him that Oberley both cared for his master and yet also reviled him. "Lord Mortimer has made his fortune at what concern?" Matthew asked.

The eyes closed. There was no response for perhaps ten seconds, and then: "Many concerns. Mining. The building trade. Logging. Shipbuilding. Money lending. He has made several fortunes. And held onto his money with an iron fist, save for his own desires."

"A selfish man," Matthew offered.

"He would say he was a self-directed man. I would say he has the ability to..." There was a pause as the thought was formulated. "Use others, on behalf of that self-direction," Oberley said at last.

Matthew let both the subject and Jesper Oberley rest. The coach jubbled over a stony path. Freezing rain whipped against the black window curtains. Matthew felt the oppression of storm and winter, a treacherous combination. At one point he felt the coach wheels slide to the left for a precious two seconds of terror before the horses pulled onward. He realized his hands were clamped to his knees so hard there would be ten bruises. It was difficult to relax, on a night when Death was roaming. But there *was* a silver lining to this very black cloud: for a while he would count himself lucky to be away from New

York and the presence of the two shadows in his life, the devilishly-handsome Dr. Jason Mallory and the doctor's beautiful wife Rebecca. Those two seemed to be walking at his heels these days. Wherever Matthew went—to Sally Almond's, to Trinity Church, to the Trot Then Gallop, or just covering the distance from his converted dairy-house to the office—those two made an appearance, casting their dark eyes upon his progress. Matthew knew that the lady Mallory wished him to come to their house for dinner, and that it had something to do with a certain professor of crime, but...

...what did they *really* want?

He was sure that time would tell the tale.

Matthew pushed aside one of the black curtains to see where they were and was rewarded with a scattershot of sleet in his face. When he got his eyes clear, he saw they were still on a forest road, rutted and ill-travelled. The horses were heroic, to be pulling weight on a night like this. Then suddenly the road came to a covered bridge across a rush of water—the Oak Bridge of the town's name, Matthew assumed—and the sound of the hooves echoed between roof and planks. The sides of the bridge were open save for a plank railing, and ice was beginning to form even on the rough boards. It was not a night for man nor beast, Matthew thought. Certainly even Death would not wish to be wandering on such an eve.

Just beyond the bridge was the town, which passed in nearly a blur: it seemed to Matthew to be several stores, a few whitewashed houses, a church, a cemetery, a stable, a tavern throwing lamplight from its windows, and a long building with chimneys that might be some kind of workshop. In any case, the place was there and gone in a moment.

The coach went on. Jesper Oberley was awake now, and also peering out the window. "Not very far now," he said to Matthew's unasked question though it was indeed about to *be* asked, for even the richly-padded leather seats could not cushion an ass from a rocky road. And Matthew certainly felt himself to be an ass in this situation. The robber of a dying man, as well, even though in Oberley's opinion Lord Mortimer was robber enough.

In another moment the coach took a curve and began to attack a steep incline. The attack, however, was thwarted, for Matthew both heard and felt the wheels slip on icy gravel and the horses strained to obey the whip even as their own hooves slid one way and the other.

"Go on! Go on!" the driver hollered through his shroud. The whip cracked and the coach shuddered but there was no forward progress. Then the driver evidently gave up and eased the team backward, for the coach was sliding back down the incline and when it stopped there was the *thunk* of the brake's sharp end being speared as far as possible into frozen earth.

"*Well*," said Oberley, his voice heavy. "It appears we're—"

"Can't make the grade, in *this* stuff!" The driver's swathed head had appeared, frighteningly so, through a window. "Team can't pull it!"

"It appears we've arrived," said Matthew, to finish Oberley's statement after the driver had withdrawn to tend as much as possible to his horses.

Bundled up against the biting cold and carrying his belongings for two nights in a leather bag, Matthew followed Oberley up the incline. Their boots crunched through a crust of ice. The bitter rain was still falling, making tapping noises on the curled rim of Matthew's tricorn. His boots slid and threatened more than once to drop him on his reputation. As they reached the top of the hill, Matthew made out through the trees the shape of a huge—one might say monstrous—mansion, candlelight showing from some windows but many others—indeed, most—absolutely black. A dozen stone chimneys rose from the peaked roofs, but only two spouted smoke. If the mansion was akin to a monster, it was indeed a dying beast. As Matthew and Oberley got nearer, the problem-solver saw that withered trees stood around the mansion, and the wet dark stones of the place were matted with dead and leafless vines that resembled brown cobwebs spun by an equally monstrous arachnid. Matthew decided he might spend one night in such a house, but the second night? No.

They reached the front door. Oberley beat twice with a knocker shaped like a lump of coal. The icy rain continued to fall, crusting Matthew's coat. At length a bolt was drawn, the door opened, and a slim woman with a tight bun of gray hair and sad but cautious eyes peered out. She wore a black dress laced with gray and was holding a triple taper.

"I've brought someone," said Oberley. This simple explanation seemed to speak volumes, for the female servant with a face like a wrinkled purse nodded and stepped back to give them entry.

"Sir? I'll carry that," said another serving-man, who came forward from the gloom with his own burning candle and took Matthew's belongings. He helped Matthew shrug from the coat and also took his tricorn before he retreated.

"How is he, Bess?" Oberley was addressing the woman after the door had been closed and the bolt thrown.

"Failing," replied the woman, whose thin-lipped mouth moved only enough to squeeze the word out.

"We'll see him, then. Shall we, Mr. Corbett?"

"Yes." Did he have a choice?

"Bess, make Mr. Corbett some hot tea. And I think a platter of corncakes and ham. I'm sure our guest is needful." As the woman moved away across the foyer, Oberley picked up a burning taper in a pewter holder from a table and said, "Follow me, please." It was spoken less like an invitation than as an act of solemn and dread duty.

Matthew followed Oberley through a hallway lined with suits of armor. Their helmets and breastplates reflected the single candleflame. It occurred to Matthew that such suits were constructed to protect the bodies within from crushing and cutting blows. No such protection could now be offered to the body of Lord Brodd Mortimer. Matthew felt the heaviness of dread illness in this house. He felt a kind of hopelessness here, like a contagion. He did not fail to note the mounted heads of stags and wild boar, the display of crisscrossed swords upon the wall and the collection of muskets in a glass case. At one time Lord Mortimer had been a huntsman, a vibrant man of action. Now, though, a gilded grandfather clock ticked in a corner and the sound of each passing second seemed as loud as a gunshot.

The hall widened to a staircase. Matthew followed Oberley up, and in another moment a door was reached and a knob turned and the two men entered a room where even the softest candlelight was the harshest cruelty.

A few candles burned about the chamber. It was a large space, its floor covered with a red carpet accented with gold trim. The furnishings were dark and heavy. The ceiling was high, with exposed beams from which hung flags that might have been emblazoned with the symbols of business ventures and money-making industries. Huge paintings adorned the walls. Here a three-masted ship battled the waves against a moonlit sky, there a quartet of gentlemen sat about a table engrossed in some game of cards with a pile of gold coins at their midst. The chamber's four-poster bed stood so far from the door that it seemed a coach must be called to reach it. Beside the bed in a spill of candlelight was a black leather chair, and from this chair a silver-haired man in a gray suit stood up as Matthew entered behind Oberley.

"Dr. Zachary Barker," Oberley said to Matthew. "He has been at my master's side these last few days."

They approached the bed. Barker, about sixty years of age, wore square-lensed spectacles and had a trim, straight-backed figure. His silver hair fell about his shoulders. He had a strong jaw and the clear blue eyes of a youthful mind. No country physician this, Matthew thought. Likely from Boston or perhaps even brought over from England.

"Good evening," said Barker, nodding at Matthew. The eyes were inquisitive but not rude. "And you are...?" The hand was offered.

"Matthew Corbett, at your service." Matthew took the hand and felt a strength that ten years ago might have put a man on his knees.

"Ah. Come from New York, brought to confront Death, I'm presuming?"

"As I understand my task, yes."

"So be it." A quick glance was speared at Oberley. "Nonsense and double sham, but here we are."

"*Corbett?*"

And again: "*Corbett?*"

The voice that had rasped the name was like the sound of dry reeds blowing in a wind. It was like a lonely echo in a barren room. It was like the rattle of bones at the bottom of an empty bowl of broth. It was like the saddest note of a violin, and the sound of the whimper before the sob.

"Speak to Lord Mortimer," said Dr. Barker, and he motioned toward the bed.

Matthew had not looked upon the bed as yet, for he was consciously delaying that action. He had been aware that *something* was lying amid the sheet and red coverlet, but his mind hadn't yet let his eyes go there.

Now, though, he turned his head a few inches to the left and he looked upon the rich man.

Could flesh become liquid, while it still clung to the bone? Could it become puddled, and glistening, and mottled with dark splotches like an overripe pear on the edge of rot? Indeed, it appeared so. And then there were the plasters covering what must be open sores, and there were the open sores that were so large no plaster or healing cloth could contain them. And there were too many of those, it seemed, to be counted.

Lord Mortimer had surely thinned since his last hunting excursion, for sticks such as those could never hold a musket nor indeed a handful of musket balls, and legs skeletal as those could not hold even such a frailty aloft. Spidery hands were folded upon the bony chest, and above the chest was the veined neck and the cadaverous face grizzled with beard. Upon that face the nose seemed already to be collapsing inward, the lips were whitened with some kind of salve to deaden the pain of those raw red sores at their corners, and below the spriggins of sparse white hair and the sweat-sparkled forehead two eyes peered up at Matthew with an expression of both terror and hope. The left eye was dark brown, the right lost under a pale oyster-color film of blindness.

The smell of sickness, which Matthew had already caught upon entering the room, was as strong here at the bedside as if a plate of spoiled and worm-eaten beef had been offered for his delectation. He wondered about his mettle, as he looked into the ruin of Lord Mortimer's face. He couldn't help but wonder if he might end his days in such a fashion, and God forbid he live one moment as damp and dissolving flesh with the odor of illness and piss and excrement rising up from the bed like a foul green miasma.

"Help me, Mr. Corbett," whispered the rich man. "I know you can."

It took a moment for Matthew to find his tongue. "I'll do my best, sir." At what? he asked himself. The heartless robbery of a wretch such as this?

"Your *best.*" There was a twist in Barker's voice. "Oberley," he said to the servant, "I protest this...this travesty. Going to New York to bring this *boy* here? Look at him! Wet as water behind the ears!"

"Zachary!" Even so near his end, Lord Mortimer could still summon a faint rumble of thunder. "I trust...that Oberley has done as I asked. Brought...the best man here. I know..." He had to stop, to breathe for a moment. If that wheeze could be called such. "I know your objections. They have been noted."

"This is a farce, Brodd. *Paying* anyone to—"

"Objections," said Lord Mortimer, "*noted*."

And *that* voice was near the thunder of distant cannonfire. It caused the good doctor to look down at his shining black boots and then examine his well-manicured fingernails.

"Mr. Corbett," the dying man said, "I just need you...to *be* here. To help me...to give me time. To speak to Death on my behalf...when he arrives at the door."

"Oh my God," said the doctor, but it was muffled by his hand.

"She will be here." The face nodded. "Yes. I think she will come tonight. I think...she will come."

"In this weather, sir?" Oberley moved forward to adjust the coverlet. "It's very foul. I'm not sure Miss Christina—"

"She will *come*," Lord Mortimer said, and that ended the discussion. For all his sickness, the rich man still held command in his castle.

"Yes sir." Oberley did his work with a mannered hand. His face was solemn and somber; he was a loyal dog who knew his place. He withdrew and stood a respectable distance away, there if needed.

One of the spidery hands moved. Slowly, as if in agony. The hand came up, trembling, and motioned the best man nearer.

"Dr. Barker," said the dying man to Matthew Corbett, "doesn't *believe*. He doesn't...know. What I know." The single eye blinked; there was still a red spark of fire at its center. "Are you *listening?*"

"I am, sir," came the firm reply.

"Death will arrive here. In human form. As it did...for my father. For my grandfather...as well. Yes. I am certain of it."

Matthew said nothing, for nothing was required of him to say. He had taken the measure of the doctor's bag open on the table beside the bed, and arrayed around it all the gleaming instruments and bottles of potions and herb packs and liniments and little jars of mysteries. Alas, no human hand or medical creation by even a London physician could stay the impending moment. It seemed to Matthew, from the labor of Lord Mortimer's troubled lungs, that the moment must be very near.

"*Listen*," said the voice from the bed, as if his instinct for reading people was still as strong as it had been when he was striding God-like through the fields of industry. "Hear me," he insisted. "Death came as a man for my father. My father...saw the same...with *his* father. My *poppa*," came the soft breath. "Always...always, so busy."

"Brodd, you should rest," said the doctor.

"*Rest?* For what occasion?" This was spoken with near vehemence, and for a while Lord Mortimer had to breathe slowly and steadily to, Matthew assumed, hold his tenuous grip upon this world. "Mr. Corbett," came the voice when it was able, "I saw a man enter the room...where my father lay dying. When I was ten years old. A young man...well-dressed. He entered that room...and when he left it, my father was dead. Did anyone know that man? Or...from where he came? No. I was standing outside...in the rain...when he passed me. And he looked at me and smiled...and I knew...I *knew*...this was Death, passing by. It was the man my father always knew was coming. Oh, yes...I heard him many times...speaking of the man he saw enter the room of his own father. A young man...well-dressed. Confident, he said. Walking away...no coach or carriage, and no horse. The same as I saw. The same who will be here...very soon." The hand reached up for Matthew's sleeve. "You must speak to him. Give me time...to make my peace with Christina." A sob rose up and nearly overcame the voice, but Lord Mortimer pushed it down. "My daughter," he said feebly, losing ground. "I *must* see my daughter."

Oberley came forward. "The weather, sir. It's so wretched."

"She will come," said Lord Mortimer drowsily; his strength was leaving him. "I *know* she will...by however means she can get here."

Matthew looked at Oberley, who sadly shook his head. A glance at Dr. Barker brought a shrug.

Across the room were long windows covered with heavy red curtains. Matthew went to one of them, drew aside the curtain and peered out. The window was glazed with ice. There was nothing to be seen but darkness. He sensed someone coming up behind him and knew who it would be. "Might she arrive tonight?" Matthew asked quietly. "She lives six miles from here, yes?" It was a hard distance to be made on a night like this. He considered that he'd answered his own question. "Perhaps she'll come tomorrow."

"Perhaps," said Oberley. "But tomorrow may be too late."

Matthew nodded. Brodd Mortimer must surely be a man of great strength and determination, but his clock was running down. Matthew crossed the room again to be near the bedside, and that was when he heard the distant, hollow *thump...thump...thump.*

He realized it was the lump of coal. The doorknocker. Someone had come to call.

Suddenly Lord Mortimer lifted himself up on his elbows. His glistening face with its agony of sores contorted. The single eye found Matthew.

"I beg you!" His voice was harsh even in its pleading. "Help me! If it's her, show her up to me! If it's him...for the love of God...talk him into giving me a few more hours!"

"Sir, I—"

"Please! Now is the moment! *Please!*"

"All right," said Matthew. "I'll go." He turned away from the bed and the ruin of a rich man and started for the way out, and suddenly Dr. Barker was walking at his side and the doctor said in Matthew's ear, "The consumption has taken his mind. You *know* that, don't you?"

"I know I've been paid to perform a task. Which I shall perform to the best of my ability." Matthew reached the door. With taper in hand, Oberley came up beside him and opened it, and together they left the room and went downstairs to greet the night visitor.

THREE
SINS AND ABOMINATIONS

The grandfather clock began to strike as they descended the stairs. It ended on the ninth bell as Oberley told Bess to stop on her progress to the door. Matthew pulled the bolt, opened the door and was pelted by icy rain and a bone-chilling wind.

"I've come," said the figure wrapped in a hooded black cloak, "to see him."

"Oh...please." Oberley, in his eagerness, pushed Matthew aside. "Please come in, Miss Christina."

She crossed the threshold, and shivered. Oberley closed the door at her back.

"Your cloak. May I?"

She shook her head. "No, not yet. I'm very cold. Not yet."

"The tea and corncakes are made," Bess offered.

"Neither thirsty nor hungry," Christina Mortimer answered. Her voice was tight and clipped. "I just want to get this over with...and then I'm going home."

"I'll take some tea, thank you," Matthew told Bess. "A little sugar, if you don't mind." He then focused his attention fully on the rich man's daughter, who stood rubbing warmth into her arms with what seemed to be nearly desperation.

"I've never been colder in my life," she said. Her eyes, the same brown as her father's, scanned the foyer. "Dear God, what am I doing in this house?"

"The right and proper thing, I think," said Matthew.

Which caused Christina to look at him as if she were first seeing him, and he had been a moment before only a shade barely illuminated by candlelight. She frowned, her brown brows knitting. "Who are *you?*"

"My name is Matthew Corbett. I've come from New York."

"That tells me nothing. How do you know my father?"

"He has hired me."

"For what purpose, sir?"

There was no use in hiding such a thing. "For the purpose of cheating Death. Or, rather...asking Death to give your father more time to speak to *you.*"

"Oh...*that* old story." Christina gave him the faintest and most disdainful half-smile. "You are here, then, on a madman's errand."

"An errand, none the less."

"Hm," she said, and they seemed then to take the measure of one another.

Christina Mortimer shrugged out of her hood, perhaps the better to let Matthew see who he was dealing with. Her thick reddish-brown hair tumbled about her shoulders. Her face was pale, her jaw firm, her eyes intense. She was of medium height and solidly built, a formidable wall of prideful intent. Something about her put Matthew's nerves on edge. He could see how father and daughter might shatter the world between them. Her stare into his eyes was unyielding. "You don't think this is nonsense, sir?"

Bess came with a brown mug of tea. Matthew sipped it before he answered. "My opinion doesn't matter here. Your father's does."

"I see." She started to remove her black gloves and then, blinking, seemed to think better of it. "*Cold*," she said quietly. "I should never have come out this night."

"I thank God you have," Oberley said. "Would you not want some tea to warm you?"

"There is no warmth in this house," she answered. "I should suffer a chill here even with a belly full of fire."

"But you *are* here," Matthew said, and she gave him her piercing and unsettling stare again. "You braved the elements to come. That means you are at least interested in hearing what your father has to say."

She was silent. Her mouth opened and then closed once more. Her head took on a crooked angle. "The elements," she said, and seemed for a few seconds to be drifting. Then: "Yes. Pardon me...my mind is..." She shook her head. "I don't care for this place. I have passed it before, in daylight. It grieved me then. At night it just..." A gloved hand came up and stroked the back of her neck. "Wounds me," she said.

"Shall we go see Lord Mortimer?" Oberley asked, in a quietly apprehensive voice.

"Yes. All right. I am here...for how long, I don't know, but I am here."

"Long enough, I trust," said Matthew, "to honor a dying man?"

"*Honor*." She made it sound ugly. "You, sir, must not know the meaning of the word. Take me to him," she told the servant.

They started toward the stairs. "Your horse made the incline?" Oberley asked.

"My horse?" Christina frowned in the candlelight. "My horse has... run away, I think." Her eyes had frosted over, like ice on glass. "I tried to...catch the reins, but...I think he has run away."

Oberley and Matthew glanced quickly at each other. "Miss, aren't you feeling well?" Oberley asked.

"I'm feeling...I don't know. I think I...shouldn't be here. I think this is wrong." She stopped at the foot of the stairs and peered up, and Matthew saw her tremble.

"It will be all right," Matthew said.

"It is *wrong*," she repeated, with some force. "Wrong. Everything is..." She put a hand to her forehead and staggered, and when both men tried to steady her she shrank away and said, "Don't touch me! I don't wish to be touched!" with such ferocity that both Matthew and Oberley immediately drew back.

Matthew thought this woman must be either on the edge of madness or she needed something much stronger than this sugared tea to calm her nerves. In fact, he was beginning to crave some courage juice himself, in the form of a rum toddy. With less toddy and more rum.

"I can go on," Christina said softly yet with grit in her voice. "I can go on." And, so saying, she started up the stairs.

Almost to the top, Christina staggered again and looked wildly about herself. Both Matthew and Oberley stayed a few risers behind.

"Miss Christina?" Oberley prompted.

"Did you hear that?" the woman asked. "That *noise*."

"Noise, miss?"

"Yes, that one!" She seemed to be searching all around, her face pallid and eyes full of fear. "I heard...a breaking noise. Like... I don't know." She caught Matthew's gaze. "Didn't *you* hear it?"

"I'm afraid I didn't," Matthew replied, thinking that the rich man's daughter was in need of a penny's worth of sanity.

She nodded and seemed to be getting a grip. Then she started the ascent again, and her followers came up afterward.

Oberley opened the door for her. She slid in. The figure in the bed was already sitting up with expectation against the sodden pillows. It was, Matthew thought, an incredible feat of decaying mind over decayed matter. He finished his tea and, feeling somewhat fortified, put the mug aside on a table. He watched Christina walk quietly across the carpet. The doctor moved back to give her room, and his chair if she needed it. She reached the bed and looked at what lay there, as Matthew and Oberley came up alongside.

There was no sound but the wheeze of the rich man's breath. The moment seemed as icy and treacherous as the earth beyond the windows. It hung on an uncertain air.

"Daughter," Lord Mortimer rasped.

She gave no reply. Once more a gloved hand rose and pressed against her forehead, and she weaved back and forth on her feet. She looked around the room, at the walls and the ceiling, with what Matthew thought was the expression of a trapped animal with nowhere left to hide.

"Speak to me." The voice was near begging. "*Please.*"

She did not speak.

"*Christina,*" said Lord Mortimer, as if kneeling before the Cross.

Matthew saw her gaze fall upon her father. He saw her flinch. He saw her gloved hands ball into fists at her sides. But she was of his blood and perhaps of his nature, and she held herself firm.

"Of what shall I speak?" she asked quietly, her voice eerily controlled. "Shall I speak of my mother...your wife...and the suicide you forced upon her? Shall I speak of how Morgan was broken by your displeasure? Shall I speak of all the times I and Morgan reached out for you with love and you turned your back upon us? Because... Poppa, you were always, always so busy?" She didn't wait for a response, but continued along this headstrong and crushing path. "Shall I speak of the hundreds of people—perhaps thousands—who suffered in your mines and workhouses, in your fields and sweatboxes?

"Shall I speak of the shame we felt, when we discovered how you used people...and how you *enjoyed* doing so? Shall I speak of the Nance family, and the Copelands, and the Engelburghs? Friends of our family...until your needs led you to destroy their fathers in business and ruin any dream those children might have had? Shall I speak of the Wittersen building, and the workmen who died? And of the lawyers you hired to year after year block any payment of what you *must* know to be right? What shall I speak of, then? All these, or other sins and abominations? Other hurts and misdeeds? You tell me."

The dying man shivered. Matthew thought he might be contemplating the fact that Death had not yet come for him, but Truth had.

Christina Mortimer plunged the sword deeper. "And you *dare* to follow me here? To send your hired man to woo me? To make me forget all the horrors of being your daughter? Of seeing you destroy my mother, my brother, and most everything I held dear?" She blinked, and a wild terror leaped into her eyes, and she looked around and around the room and nearly wailed it: "Why am I here? What am I doing in this place? I don't know...I don't *know!*"

"Miss Christina," said Oberley, and he reached out to touch her shoulder but she recoiled. "Please. Have a *little* mercy on him."

"No," said Lord Mortimer, in almost a clear, strong voice. "*No,*" he repeated, with a crooked smile on his grim-lipped face. "*Not* mercy. That's not why...why I asked you here, daughter. I have shown no mercy in my life...I ask for none." His single good eye glittered wetly. "None was ever shown to me. I don't understand it. I have no use for it. Weakness. A crutch. It is kill or be killed...and that is what I have ever known, all my life. Even my father...it was a death battle against him... for he tried to destroy me...to find out what I was made of. Locked me in a closet. You talk about a sweatbox, daughter? Locked me in a closet...for some piddling infraction of his rules. And I could not come out...could not be fed or watered...until I would beg his forgiveness. Do you know how long I stayed in that closet...in the dark? With my piss and my shit all around me? Do you know...how long?" He nodded, as if still proud of his childhood triumph. "The butler told me...it was five days and fourteen hours. They took me out over my father's wishes. And when I was well enough...he put me right back in again. This time...I nearly made a full week. But I learned, daughter. I learned...a man—a boy, let us say—cannot survive on a good heart. He survives only on the strength of will. Yes. That is why I am living today. This moment. For I have wished to see you...to speak with you, and hear you speak...and I will not die until that is satisfied within me."

"Kill or be killed?" she asked. "What did Mother do to you that made you so angry? What did Morgan do? Dear God, Father..." Her voice cracked. "What did *I* do?"

Lord Mortimer did not answer. Perhaps, Matthew thought, he could not.

"Were we not good enough for you?" she asked. "Were we not *strong* enough?"

The answer at last came, with a harsh and hollow rasp. "You were too good for me. I know that now, through the backwards mirror... of time. And I was too weak...to let those things...inside me...go. Too weak. And here I thought...I was so very, very strong. Now look, daughter...at what I am, and what I have...*look*," he said, addressing Matthew, Oberley and the doctor, "as a warning of what a man may become...who never fully emerged...from that dark little room...and who lives there, in terrified silence...*still*.

"I will not ask for mercy," said the sore-covered mouth in the glistening face, "but I will say...as I would never say to my father or to any other human on this earth...I am sorry." The eye closed and he sank back against the pillows. "I am sorry," he breathed. "I am sorry."

Christina stood without moving. She stared fixedly at her father, with eyes that Matthew thought might melt iron. She was as difficult to look at as he was. Something moved in her face. Or something moved *under* her face. It was hard to tell. Matthew wondered if what was in her mind could ever be eased, for she was just as confined by the terrors—and errors—of the past as was Lord Mortimer. They were, indeed, a matched pair.

From downstairs there came the *thump...thump...thump* of the doorknocker.

The rich man's eye opened. He gasped. He searched for Matthew, and found him.

"He has come," Lord Mortimer whispered. "Please. I beg of you... detain him. Just a short while. We are not done here. Not done. Are we...daughter?"

She drew a long and ragged breath. She was a soul in the deepest agony, yet there was something in her—some strength of will—that was trying to swim up from the deep.

"No," she answered, also in a whisper. "No, Poppa...we're not done."

"Please...Corbett...detain him, just a while longer..."

Matthew said, "Yes sir," and he turned away and left Oberley and Dr. Barker in the room, and he went downstairs thinking he would meet the vicar or some other personage from Oak Bridge but there in the foyer stood the young and handsome man Bess had just let into the house, and the young man in his dark cloak and tricorn with a purple band smiled at Matthew and said, "Hello, sir. I've come to see Lord Mortimer."

"Lord Mortimer is ill."

"Oh, yes. I'm aware of that."

"Ill unto death," said Matthew.

"Aware, also, of that. Time is urgent, sir. Might you take me to him?"

"And your business *is?*"

"My business," said the young and handsome man with the affable smile, "is the end of suffering."

FOUR
I AM NO ANGEL

MATTHEW MAY HAVE taken a backward step. He didn't remember if he had or not. The young man—possibly only two or three years elder than Matthew—had a friendly, open face and a light demeanor. He removed his tricorn with black-gloved hands. His hair was pale blonde and as fine as silk, his eyes the color of smoke. He unbuttoned his cloak to show a well-tailored black suit and a dark purple waistcoat.

"You're not afraid of me...are you, Mr. Corbett?"

"*What?*" Matthew asked.

"You took a backward step. Did something I say disturb you?"

"My name. How did you...?"

"From New York, yes? A beautiful town. Industrious. No, I'll hold my cloak and hat," he told Bess. "But thank you, all the same." The smoke-colored eyes focused again on Matthew. "The hour is late, sir. I do have other appointments. Please take me to Lord Mortimer."

Matthew felt the breath stuttering in his lungs. "Who *are* you?"

"I am but a lowly messenger. A bearer of tidings. Now...I *have* travelled a distance. I would like to conclude my business with Lord Mortimer and be on my way as quickly as possible. These things should not be drawn out."

"These *things? What* things?"

"Errands such as mine," said the handsome man. His smile had lost none of its brightness, though Matthew thought his eyes had darkened. "Really, sir, this is a business matter to me. I regret Lord Mortimer's condition, but..." He shrugged. "This too is part of life, is it not?"

"A terrible part," said Matthew cautiously. He didn't know which might go first...his knees or the top of his head.

"Not at all!" came the spirited response. "Freedom from life's duties, trials and tribulations is *terrible?* The view beyond the glass is *terrible?* Throwing off the yoke of enslavery to pain and all the many faults of flesh is *terrible?* Oh, Mr. Corbett...you and I should someday drink a glass of ale and have a long discussion about the value of release from this world."

"I think...not anytime soon," said Matthew.

The smile became a grin. "As you please. Now, really...are you trying to detain me?"

"Uh..." He was totally jawsocked and rumpunched. His stomach was doing slow flipflops. Everything north of his border felt heated and everything south was in a frozen state. He could not—could *not*—believe he was speaking to Death in human form. Could *not.* It was just impossible.

"You came from where, sir?" he managed to ask.

"My place of origination."

"Where is that?"

"A long ride from here."

"You came by horse?"

"Well, yes. Did you expect me to spread my arms and *fly?* I have been called many things, but I am no angel. *Please*, sir...it's best we get this over with. Have some pity on a solitary traveller, won't you?"

"Where's your horse?"

"I left my horse at the bottom of the hill. Where the coach is. All that ice...very nasty. My horse's name is Somnus, if you care to know."

"What is *your* name?"

"All these questions...should have been expected, from a problem-solver. Oh, all right! My name is Clifton. First name Kenyard. Does that suit you?"

"Is that your real name?"

"As real," said the man, "as you wish it to be. Honestly! It does no good, putting this off! I have business with Lord Mortimer!" A small frown rippled across the face. "The night is passing, sir! I have many miles yet to go. Now...I am patient...but I don't like being toyed with. I don't like being denied, when this is something that *must* be done. As I said, to end suffering! I am here for a *good* purpose, can't you understand that?"

Matthew wished for a wall to put his back against, but there was nothing. At least Kenyard Clifton or whatever he was calling himself was substantial, for the candlelight threw his shadow large upon a wall.

"Lord Mortimer is with his daughter," Matthew managed to say. "He wishes only a short while longer. Will you allow it?"

"How short?" Irritation flared in the voice, and at last the smile went awry.

"I'm not sure. He's fading, but holding himself to..." Matthew couldn't fathom the moment, and suddenly it seemed almost absurd. "Listen, sir! You're not who you say you are! You *can't* be!"

"And sir, you are a pennynail short of enough to seal Lord Mortimer's coffin, if I may be so bold. I said I'm Kenyard Clifton! That's my name! Out on the road in this weather! Looking to get home to a wife and two children at least before dawn! Won't you have some mercy on me and let me see him before he passes?" A frown forced the rest of the smile away. "Very well, then! *Here!*" A hand went into the coat and brought out a brown envelope. "Deliver this to him yourself, but by law and the dictates of my employer I must be present when it is put before him!"

Matthew was further dumbstruck. Had Death just said he had a wife and two children? Matthew stared at the offered envelope. "What is that?"

"Legal papers. If you must know. Concerning a lawsuit that has gone on for many years. I am out by the order of my employer, the law firm of Pierce, Campbell and Blunt. Based in Boston, an *awfully* long way from here. My understanding is that there's been an agreement between lawyers to settle this case, and the workers who suffered injuries will be fully compensated. Plus widows who lost husbands, equally compensated...if that is at all possible."

It struck Matthew what the man was talking about. "The building accident. The Wittersen building."

"Correct. Several weeks ago Lord Mortimer informed his lawyers he would no longer contest the case, and as I understand it he has given over a sizeable amount of money to take care of the workers' needs. Therefore I am here to have either him or his designated representative sign the final papers."

"Oh," Matthew said. It was a stunned sound, barely audible. He regained himself in the next instant. "But...how did you know my name? And my profession?"

"Simple. I asked the coachman at the bottom of the hill who he had brought to the mansion tonight, in this weather. Poor wretch is down there determined to stay with the horses. Interesting, isn't it, how men of extreme wealth always want to build their mansions at the summit of the highest hills? Unfortunately they must often pay a price for that lofty height. Now...would you please show me to—"

"*Mr. Corbett?*"

Matthew turned toward the voice, which had come from behind him.

Jesper Oberley stood there, holding a candelabra with three burning sticks. His face was long and drawn and deep-shadowed. His eyes ticked toward Kenyard Clifton, held for a few seconds, and then returned to Matthew.

"Lord Mortimer," said Oberley, "has a few moments ago passed away. Miss Christina was at his side. I am happy to say...that Miss Christina offered forgiveness to her father during his last few breaths... and that at the end she was holding his hand. I think it was a great effort for her...to speak to him so, and to touch him...but she performed that gesture with perfect calm and perfect grace. I have shown her to her room for the night." His eyebrows went up. "And this gentleman is...someone we've expected?"

"He represents a Boston law firm," Matthew said. "He's brought papers to be signed. *Important* papers, I might add. Having to do with...an end to suffering," Matthew decided to say. He had a sudden thought. "Perhaps it would be fitting for Miss Christina to sign them?"

"She has complained of feeling faint, and of her head...as she put it...swimming. She wanted neither food nor drink, only to be left alone. I think she's been drained by this experience. But I thank God she came. Lord Mortimer may not have had the brightest soul, but perhaps even he has earned a little rest and the forgiveness of a daughter." Oberley held the candles forward to further illuminate Kenyard Clifton. "I regret you have missed Lord Mortimer, sir."

"I also. But...I do need these to be signed before I can go. Is there a representative who can sign? The papers are very straightforward in the amount of money set aside for compensation of workers injured in the collapse of the Wittersen building in London eight years ago. It's a large sum, and greatly needed." Clifton offered the envelope to Oberley. "Might you sign, sir?"

"Me? No, sir. I am not able, as regards my station. But...Mr. Corbett is an employee of Lord Mortimer. *He* might sign, I think."

"Oh, I couldn't!" said Matthew. "Not for something as important as this. I still say Miss Christina should sign."

"I wouldn't want to bother her again, sir. She said she wanted very greatly to rest." Oberley reached out, took the envelope from Clifton's hand and put it into Matthew's. "If you'll follow me, gentlemen, I'll take you to a room where pen and ink are available."

Before his signature was applied, Matthew took the time to carefully read the document. It was, indeed, straightforward and allowed for an amount of money that might well have been half the rich man's fortune to be divided among fourteen workmen and three widows. A duplicate document was signed, and given to Oberley for safekeeping. Then Kenyard Clifton wrapped himself in his cloak, put on his tricorn and said goodnight.

"Safe travel," Matthew said to the young man who might have been Death, but was in actuality a new Life for many who had suffered under Lord Mortimer's will.

Clifton left the house, Bess closed the door behind him, and the grandfather clock ticked on.

"I can offer you and Dr. Barker dinner and wine, sir," said Oberley as he and Matthew walked back along the hallway. "Bess is an excellent cook, and Lord Mortimer has some very fine wine in the cellar." He gave a smile that was still sad-edged, yet genuine enough. "I think Lord Mortimer would appreciate that you have the best vintage in the house."

Matthew nodded. "I accept. And I shall drink a toast to Lord Mortimer's spirit...and the fact that if Death had really shown up here tonight I would have been reduced to a pile of jibbering jelly."

The dinner was indeed excellent and the wine flowed. The doctor excused himself to go to bed as the clock struck eleven, and soon afterward Matthew also asked to be shown to his room. Thus he settled down to sleep on a comfortable four-poster bed and listened to the icy rain peck the windows, and though a dead man lay in a room not far along the hallway there seemed to be peace reigning over the household tonight...a certain rightness of things...a satisfactory conclusion...and therefore Matthew had no trouble at all falling away from this world.

He came back to it with a knocking at his door. The knocking became more insistent.

"Sir? Sir?" It was Oberley's voice, not a little bit...the word would be *unnerved*.

Matthew got up. Gray light showed through the windows. It appeared the rain had ceased. Outside the trees gleamed. Matthew opened the door and squinted in the servant's candlelight. "What *is* it?"

"Would you come with me, please?" came the request, which carried a note of urgency.

Oberley escorted Matthew to a room past Lord Mortimer's chamber. He opened the door to show an empty room and a four-poster bed similar to the one Matthew had slept in.

"All right," Matthew said. "I see this. What is it?"

"This," Oberley replied, "is Miss Christina's room. You will note, sir, that the bed has not been slept in. There is no evidence of anyone disturbing that bed. I have searched the house for Miss Christina, and not found her. I thought she might have slept in a chair, at her father's side, but no. I have gone to the bottom of the hill to see if her horse is there. It is not. She has gone. Why...I don't know. Perhaps it was all too much for her. But...I was up most of the night, sir. I never saw Miss Christina leave, nor did anyone else. No one heard the door open and close. She has gone, yes... but *when?* And how did she leave without anyone *hearing* her?"

"It's a big house," Matthew said. "No one was watching the door all night, were they?"

"No sir, no one was. But still...I have a strange feeling about this."

"A strange feeling?" Matthew wiped grains of sleep from his eyes. "What feeling?"

"Just that…Miss Christina was so *different* from when I visited her in Grainger. I can't put my finger on it…but different. And she so willingly and completely forgave him, and grasped his hand at the moment of his last breath. It's just that…well…I am beginning to think…" Oberley trailed off.

"Beginning to think what?" Matthew urged.

"To think…that might not have *really* been Miss Christina."

A silence fell. One of the candleflames hissed in its burning progress.

"Say *again?*" Matthew asked.

"That…what appeared to be Miss Christina…was not. *Sir,*" he added. "That we were expecting a man. And…sir…Death *did* come in human form for Lord Mortimer, but was dressed as a woman."

Matthew was momentarily stunned speechless. He recalled something Christina Mortimer had said with ferocity at the foot of the stairs: *Don't touch me! I don't wish to be touched!* "You're wrong!" he managed to reply. "Utterly wrong!"

"Yes sir, I may well be. But where is Miss Christina *now?*"

"Home, possibly. Or on her way there. I think she…she was simply overcome by her father's death and she had to leave the house. I don't know why she wasn't seen or heard, but I'd think a person could slip out without making too much noise if they really wanted to. I repeat… no one was *watching* the door, were they?"

"No sir, they were not."

"There you are, then!" Matthew made a motion as if to brush Oberley away. "Nonsense is what you're talking! The heated imagination knows no bounds!" He decided he wished no more of this house. His job was done. It was time to get dressed, pack his belongings and go home where he belonged. "I'd like to be taken back to New York within the hour. Can that be arranged?"

"It's early, yet, but…yes, sir. It can be arranged."

"You needn't go with me. I am content to ride home by myself."

"As you wish, sir. I have to take care of the funeral arrangements anyway. Vicar Barrington must be notified. I'll pay you the rest of your fee." Oberley started to walk away and then stopped. It seemed to

Matthew that the sad-eyed servant drew himself taller. "I am pleased that you would come to do this duty, Mr. Corbett. I know...this whole idea was an affront to you, but I think—or I would like to think—that your presence gave Lord Mortimer some comfort. I will not say he was a good man. I will not say I know where his soul is now. All I know is...he was my master." So saying, he moved along the hallway with a deliberate pace and out of Matthew's sight.

Matthew had to walk down the slippery slope to where the horses and coach had spent the night. The driver had stayed with his team and warmed them with blankets and himself with hot tea and corncake biscuits supplied by Bess. He grumbled a bit when Matthew announced he was ready for the several hours' return trip, but in a few minutes Matthew was inside the coach and the wheels were turning...if only slowly, due to patches of ice still whitening the road.

They were not very far along when Matthew felt the coach slow almost to the speed of a man's walk. He looked out a window and saw they were approaching the oak bridge.

"Some trouble ahead!" the coachman announced through his muffler.

Matthew craned his neck for a better look. The coach had nearly stopped. On the bridge stood a group of men, and on the floor of the bridge was...

...something covered over with a white sheet.

The coach did stop. A man approached the window Matthew was looking out of. He was tall and slim, and had a florid face reddened by the cold. He had deep-set brown eyes under a high forehead and whorls of white hair curling out from below a green woolen cap.

"Sir? I'm the vicar Barrington," said the man. "Do you live around here?"

"No, I'm from New York. Going back there today. What's the trouble?"

"A tragedy, I fear. A young woman, killed."

"A young woman?" Matthew's heart jumped and pounded. "What happened?"

"The watchman heard it. He thinks a branch snapped with the ice over the bridge and struck the roof. The noise must have frightened her horse. She was thrown, and broke her neck on the railing. Her body is here because...no one seems to know who she is. I'm trying to find someone—anyone—who knows her. Would you take a look at her, young man?"

"I will." He started to get out. If it was indeed Christina Mortimer, then her journey home had been a tragedy indeed, especially after she had made—and found—some kind of peace with her father. "What time did this happen? A few hours ago?"

"Oh, no sir," said the vicar. "The watchman says it was just before nine o'clock."

Matthew froze, halfway out of the coach. "Nine o'clock? This *morning?*"

"Sir, it's only half past eight. It happened just before nine o'clock last night."

Matthew held himself where he was. He stared at the sheeted figure that lay only about twenty feet away. He recalled the grandfather clock chiming at nine o'clock last night...a few minutes after the knock on the door. *Impossible*, he thought. *Impossible.* No, the watchman had to be wrong. It had happened this morning, not last night. And besides... it most likely wasn't Christina Mortimer, anyway.

"We can't understand what she was doing out in such weather," said the vicar, as he too stared at the figure. "Whatever her purpose was, it must have been very important to her. Come, sir! Please have a look! It's not a bad sight. She must have died instantly, for she only appears to be sleeping."

Matthew remembered, as if in a fevered dream.

Neither thirsty nor hungry, she'd said. *I've never been colder in my life*, she'd said. *I heard...a breaking noise*, she'd said. "No," Matthew whispered. His breath, ghostly, drifted away on the chill breeze. "No," he repeated, as if he might alter history.

"Am I to take it that you're wishing not to have a view?" asked the vicar.

"I want..." He didn't know what he wanted. He had to focus his mind and try again. "I think you should send a man to the Mortimer house. Lord Mortimer passed away last night, so your services are needed there. But..." He could hardly speak, his mouth was so dry. "But ask Jesper Oberley to come view this...this very valiant young woman. This...very noble...*essence*," he said, as if that made any sense to Barrington. "He might know her."

"You won't look then, sir?"

"No," Matthew said. "I won't. Would you move her a little—carefully, please—so we might be on our way?"

"As you wish," the vicar answered. "Good day to you, then."

"Good day," Matthew said. He eased back into his seat and closed the door. He remained staring straight ahead at the opposite wall of the coach until he felt the wheels moving and they were off again, and it was a long time before he relaxed from that position and, taking off his tricorn, ran a hand across his forehead.

It seemed to him that...if one believed such things, which he did not...Death had delivered two souls from their cages of suffering. Had slipped into one and taken the image of its body, and who could say which part was Death and which part was Christina Mortimer?

If one believed such things, which he did not.

But it seemed to him that on this day Death was a benevolent shade. There were accidents in this world and there were diseases. There were things no father could fully undo, and no daughter could fully forget, and yet...some measure of peace had been offered, and taken, and perhaps that was all that could be asked for. And that alone had to be appreciated.

If one believed such things.

Matthew pushed aside the black window curtain. The sun had emerged from milky clouds. The sky was turning blue again. The world was thawing out, as the world eventually did after every storm of ice.

He settled back into his seat, determined to tell Hudson Greathouse that this indeed had been a matter of no consequence. Better that than to let the great one think he believed in such things as Death coming for a rich man in human form.

"*No*," he said to himself, but he was aware that a table at the Trot Then Gallop and a mug of ale were calling his name for a long communion with the spirits of silence and the realm of the unknown, to which he was a mere child. Onward rattled the coach, breaking wet ice under its wheels. Sometimes as confused and uncertain as any human being on this spinning globe but very often the best man for the job, the problem-solver was on his way home.

At the Threshold of Your Bedchamber on the Fifth Night | *Sarah Gailey*

It didn't happen the way you think it did.

Stop crying, please, you don't need to—I'm not going to die. I know you think I'm going to die if you let me in, but I won't. I'll live, and I'll marry you.

Let me explain. Your father told me. He told me the first night, the first banquet, the one where you welcomed me to your dinner table with those big beautiful sad eyes, and you looked at me with all the pity a butcher shows a goat. It's alright, my love, my Amalia, don't cry, I know you didn't mean to look at me like that. I know you didn't mean any of it.

Are you sure you won't let me in?

Your father told me that night. He didn't really tell me, but he was trying to tell me, I know that now. He got drunk and after the banquet was over, after you'd gone to prepare for bed, he took me aside. No, not like that—he took me aside to tell me a secret, the way drunk people do. His eyes were glassy and his teeth were purple with wine, and he grabbed my arm and pulled me over near that tapestry of Queen Edith and the hunt, the one where she's carrying a spear that represents...something, I remember you explained it to me on the second day. Empire? Courage?

Anyway, your father. He bumped over a candelabra, almost knocked it right into that damn tapestry. I caught it before he noticed, though. I saved Queen Edith's life.

(It's good to see you laugh. I love you.)

He leaned in, and he told me that he liked me. He said that I reminded him of you—I know, yes, he really said that. I didn't think he meant it, except as a compliment. How could I remind him of you? We're so different, you all legs and me all shoulders, your eyes so dark, your hair so long, your mouth so full and soft and—

I'm sorry, I'm getting distracted. You have that effect on me. I promise not to kiss you again until I've finished explaining everything. And I promise not to kiss you at all if you don't want me to.

Your father. I was telling you about your father. He pulled me aside, and he told me that I reminded him of you, and he said that he wanted me to survive. I was shocked, of course. He's developed something of a reputation since your nineteenth birthday. Twenty suitors dead, just for the crime of failing to stay awake for five nights in your bedchamber. Why should he feel differently about me?

But now I think I know what he meant when he said that I reminded him of you. All the others, they were loud, swaggery boys, weren't they? Thought they had a claim to you, to the crown, to the seat at his right hand. That's what you told me on the second night—you told me about all those boys boasting at the banquet, talking too loudly about how they'd brought potions and tricks to stay awake, all of them murmuring to you in the dark about how you could help them stay conscious that whole time.

But I was something different. I wasn't a boisterous, terrified boy, looking everywhere but at you, whistling into my own open grave. I was a girl. I was quiet and fearless and ready to die, and I was staring at you because I kept catching you staring at me.

Your father told me that I reminded him of you, and I think that's what he meant. And then he told me that he wanted me to survive. And then he told me his secret.

Tessia, he said, *I didn't kill a single one of them.*

Yes, love. He told me. I didn't understand then—I thought he was drunk, or confused, or maybe lying. But he told me that I was in danger, and that he wasn't the danger, and he told me not to sign the contract.

Did you know that was an option? I didn't. Any eligible suitor can accept the invitation from your father, have a lovely feast, and then turn the contract down. He gave me the option, just like he'd given all of them, and he tried hard to convince me to take him up on his offer. He tried hard to get me to escape.

He didn't understand one thing: I arrived at this palace ready to die rather than return home. All your other suitors had something to lose; if he'd warned them away, I'm sure they would have run. But not me.

I signed my name at the bottom of that contract, underneath twenty other names, each one of them crossed out by your father within a few days of their arrival at the palace. He made me read through all the terms, even though everyone everywhere knows them by heart already: five nights in your bedchamber, five nights without sleeping, five nights wide awake, and at the end of it, your hand in marriage. But a single lapse into sleep, and my life would be forfeit.

When I'd signed the contract, your father shook his head at me, rested a heavy hand on my shoulder. He wished me a good night. I don't think he expected me to make it to dawn.

I remember being amazed by your bedchamber. By how welcoming it was. The chair—my chair—can I come in and sit in my chair?

That's alright. I can sit here. I don't mind. Can I lean my back against the doorframe, at least? I'm very tired, love, and a little dizzy.

Thank you.

The chair beside your bed was covered in a pile of furs that first night. They were so soft that I could barely stand to touch them, could barely stand the comfort of it—but I was so tired from the journey that brought me to you, and from the banquet, and from the years I'd already lived. I sank into the chair, and the fire was at my feet, and you handed me a glass of wine, handed it to me yourself, and you smiled at me and asked me if I'd had enough to eat at the banquet.

I drank the wine, just a small sip. It was bruise-dark and sweet, hot in my throat. I watched your eyes track my hand as I raised the glass to my lips, and I wondered if you were poisoning me.

I wondered if it could be so easy as that.

You asked me—do you remember?—you asked me what I brought with me, what my plan was, how I intended to stay awake all night. You watched me with those big dark eyes of yours, and you twisted a curl around your finger, and the sadness was gone. I'd been watching you all night—the sorrow, yes, but also the sweet smooth curve of your hip, the melting slope of your décolleté, the full lush ripeness of you.

When you asked me how I intended to stay awake, all that softness seemed to evaporate. You had become a single continuous edge, a bone and a blade.

You looked hungry, love. Just like you look now.

I promise I'll finish telling you my side of this story as fast as I can. Could I have a glass of water? It will help me go faster, if I can stop pausing to cough quite so often.

You asked me what I was going to do to keep myself awake all night, and I asked you what you usually did to stay awake all night. Your lips went pale, and I apologized, I thought I'd implied something inappropriate. I thought you were offended. Your knuckles were white as you asked how I could possibly know that you'd stayed awake all night with the other suitors.

I thought you were embarrassed. And I was right, wasn't I, in a way? You thought I somehow knew about what you'd done with them on those long nights.

I know, love. I know it wasn't that. I know you wouldn't, not with anyone who talked to you the way they did, looked at you the way they did. I know you just wanted them to go away.

You asked how I knew. *Well,* I told you, *it's only the two of us in here. How else would the King know who to kill, without you watching to see if your suitor dozes off in the night? You certainly don't have to stay awake with me,* I added, *but I wouldn't mind having someone to talk to. And,* I added, bold, *I especially wouldn't mind talking to you.*

You sat on your bed, your bed with too many pillows and a linen coverlet, your bed with firelight glinting off the brass. You sat on your bed and looked at me, looked right at me, and you didn't seem sad but you also didn't seem quite so hungry anymore. You rang the bell on your bedside table. Penelope came in, and you asked her to bank the fire, open the window, bring strong tea for us.

Don't drink that wine, you said. I raised my eyebrows and you answered without me having to ask: *It's not poisoned, but it will make you sleepy.*

We stayed awake until dawn, talking. The cold air and the tea helped, yes, but talking to you was the thing that really kept me awake. You told me about the other suitors, and god, you were so funny—your impression of the Archduc d'Hamponign snoring made me laugh so hard that I thought I was going to suffocate.

Do you remember? I was gasping for air, and I looked up at you, and that hunger was back in your eyes, flashing bright as an arrow's tip. Your eyes were on my throat. Did you see me seeing you? I coughed a little extra to give you time to cover, if you needed it. And you did. When I looked back up at you, you'd composed yourself again. You looked concerned. You handed me water, asked if I was okay.

I haven't faked a cough since then, in case you're wondering. I haven't faked the bruises or the weakness or the fatigue. That was the only time I pretended. That was the only time I let you hide.

The thing I haven't told you—I am sorry to have kept a secret, love, I know we promised we wouldn't: I was planning to fall asleep that night. This, you, all of it was supposed to be a gracious way for me to absent myself from the world. Answer the King's summons, eat a nice meal, enjoy a conversation with the famously beautiful Princess, fall asleep. Never wake again. I had planned to chat with you for an hour, then give myself over to fatigue and have one last nightmare before the end.

It should have been easy.

Instead, you tricked me into staying awake until sunrise, and then you rang the bell for breakfast, and we began our first day together.

Yes, thank you, I will take a blanket. I know it isn't cold out here for anyone else, but—you understand. I haven't been able to keep warm for days, except when I'm beside you.

The second night was much the same. I was exhausted from a sleepless night, and from a day spent walking the grounds with you, touring your home. That day, I met no one. I suppose it makes sense; after twenty failures, I'm sure you learned not to waste anyone's time with introductions. But you showed me your secret places that day. You looped your arm through mine when we were in the garden, walking through that abandoned briar maze. We stumbled upon a huge, beautiful mushroom, one that branched into twenty caps, each one the size of your fist. You stroked the top of one of those mushroom caps and you told me that mushrooms don't fear death. You told me that decay is an extant form of life.

I remember.

When we left the garden, you took my arm again. I felt the cool weight of your fingers on my wrist, and I could smell the rosewater you'd combed into your hair—it is rosewater, isn't it? Or is that just your skin? I know that's a silly question, but maybe the smell is part of it. Part of you. You don't have to answer now, but I would like to know the details later, if you feel like you can tell me.

The second night, I was so tired, and again there were the furs and the fire and the wine. The fire cast shadows over your face, and I could see the hollows under your eyes. It was like someone had scooped chunks out of you with their fingertips. Your collarbones stood out stark enough that I wanted to take them between my teeth—gently, you understand, just to see how they'd fit.

I thought you were tired, the same way that I was. I smiled at you, and I drank a little wine, and I said that you could sleep if you wanted to.

The wine was good, even better than the night before. It was blood-black, thick and heavy on my tongue, and I thought: *tonight will be the night. I have feasted well, and I have spent a wonderful day with Amalia. I have smelled the rosewater in her hair, I have touched the softest part of the inside of her wrist, I have listened to the song that is her laughter, and that is enough happiness to see me through to the end of this. I will watch her fall asleep—she must be so beautiful when she sleeps—and I will finish this wine, and then I will let myself fall asleep, and then it will all be over.*

I told you to rest; you shook your head and rang the bell on your bedside table. Poor Penelope looked as though she'd been getting ready for sleep herself, but you asked her to bank the fire and open the window and bring strong tea, and she did, and you arranged your pillows so that you could sit up and look at me.

Tell me about yourself, Tessia, you said, and my stomach clenched. I had not anticipated this.

You were meant to be—forgive me for my early assumption, my love, you must know how unusually wonderful you are for your station—you were meant to be a selfish, arrogant Princess who cared nothing for the people who were summoned to die on her behalf. I never thought I would have to tell you much more than my name. But you saw through me. You looked at me, hunger tucked into every shadow on your face. *All day, you've been asking me about myself, what I like and what I want and who I am*, you said, the way you do when you know someone has been trying to fool you. *It's not fair. Who are* you?

You have to know that I never intended to make it to the next morning. I never would have told you so much about myself, otherwise. I never would have told you about my childhood, about what home was really like.

I have never told anyone else, Amalia. I have never told anyone what it feels like to be the only surviving child of a father like mine. I have never let myself—I never want to complain, you understand. I am very fortunate to have survived. But there were supposed to be twelve of us, and it's hard.

You already know all of this. I'm sorry, I'm just tired, and getting distracted. I know you're hungry. I'll try to go faster.

We talked, and we talked, and we talked, and then I dozed off. I didn't realize I'd done it until you were shaking me awake. I didn't even dream, just closed my eyes, and then there was your hand on my shoulder, rosewater smell from your hair brushing my arm, sunlight through the window, an ache in my chest.

Your face was so close to mine. Your eyes looked brighter than they had in the night, and those shadows under your eyes were gone. I assumed that you must have slept, too. You smiled at me, and I smiled back because how could I not smile at you?

Then I realized what I'd done—I'd fallen asleep. And I felt the strangest thing. I felt disappointed.

For years, my love, I felt disappointed upon waking because I hadn't died in the night. But that morning, the morning of the third day, I felt disappointed because I knew what it meant. It meant that I would not get another night talking to you.

It meant that I would die, and for the first time in years, that did not feel like a relief.

But then you leaned in even closer to me, and I felt your breath on my ear, cool and sweet, and all I could smell was rosewater and fresh-turned earth, and you whispered to me that you wouldn't tell anyone if I didn't.

You offered me a secret.

You offered me one more night with you.

I will confess that I was more than a little overwhelmed. I'd shared my biggest secret with you, my deepest shame. I'd told you that I knew I was not supposed to be the sibling that survived, that I knew about my father's mistake—and yet you wanted me to live.

You wanted to save me.

You had seen the shameful, awful, poisonous part of me, and you had decided that you wanted to know more.

Do you see what I'm getting at, my love? Do you understand? Will you let me come in yet?

I will keep going, then.

On the third day, you introduced me to your work. Your correspondence, your study. You told me about the different diplomatic relationships you were trying to set up now so that you could rely on them later, in months and in years and in decades. I don't think you ever showed any of my predecessors that, did you? Everyone who saw us together in your study did a double-take. I don't know if you noticed, because you were so excited to tell me about cartography, about the mythology of borders, about the fluidity of your own kingdom's boundaries. My chest ached all day, and I kept coughing, interrupting you to try to shift that ache up out of my lungs. You rubbed my back once—it seemed automatic, a reach and a touch—and when I looked up at you, your brows were furrowed tight with worry.

You are brilliant, my love, and kind, and passionate, and I very much wish you would let me come in. Will you at least drink some water? You look so parched.

That night, the third night, you told me about your childhood, endless lessons on the people you'd thought of as friends, tutors showing you how to think of them as connections. You told me what it had been like, learning about the levers of power and the weight you could lean upon them. You told me about how much that hurt, and then you told me about how you did it, how you planned to be the kind of Queen who used her weight to move that lever toward Good.

You never rang the bell for Penelope that night. The fire was warm, and the wine was sweet, and the furs were soft. The ache in my chest had nearly subsided, leaving a deep fatigue behind it.

When my skull started to feel too heavy for me to keep holding up, you invited me to lie down in your bed. It was, I think, two hours before dawn. I hesitated, because I was falling in love with you, and I hardly knew what to do with the feeling of *wanting to live* but I couldn't help it, I wanted to live, I wanted to know you for just one more day if I could.

And if I wanted to know you for one more day—if I wanted to live—I knew that I must not lie down in your bed. I knew that I must not sleep.

But you smiled at me. You moved to the far side of the bed. You promised me that you wouldn't tell anyone. You fluffed a pillow for me, and you whispered that I could rest until dawn, and you promised me that you would keep my sleep a secret.

Your bed looked so soft, my love, and the fire was warm on my skin and the wine was warm in my belly, and you looked at me the way you're looking at me now, pale and hollow, your lower lip between your teeth, your breath coming fast, your eyes so bright, and I knew that you needed me to say yes.

Of course I did.

I fell asleep the moment I breathed in the rosewater scent of your pillow.

I woke up on my own. I woke up so tired. I woke up ravenous, and my chest hurt and my limbs were heavy—but there you were, bright-cheeked and smiling, your hand smooth and cool on my clammy forehead.

You asked me if I'd had a nightmare.

I lied, and said yes.

The fourth day, you introduced me to the staff, all of whom were astonished to see me still alive and at your side. I sat next to you, because I couldn't stand for very long without getting lightheaded. It's hard to breathe deep, with the ache in my chest. Not too hard, love, just hard.

You told me the names of all the members of your staff, and their jobs. You also told me about their families, their kindnesses, their ailments. I don't think any of them suspect how much you know about them, how closely you watch. I don't think they know how much you care about them.

But I do.

You let me see how much you want them to be whole and happy and well, how much you want to be kind to them. It's why none of them spend the night in your bedchamber, even though a woman of your station should have bedfellows and chambermaids to watch over her in the night. You just want them all to be safe.

The fourth night—last night—there were no furs on my chair. There was wine on the bedside table, and the bed was turned down, and you sat on the side of the bed furthest from the chair. You tucked your legs under the covers, and I sat on top of the covers, and we sat far apart as we could, but we couldn't help drifting together, could we? We waited so long to let our fingers touch, to let our shoulders brush. At long last, you rested your head on my shoulder, and I let my nose fall to the part in your hair, and I breathed you in.

You asked me to tell you about what kind of Queen I wanted to be.

I felt a tickle at the nape of my neck and at my collar, at the base of my skull—but when I looked down, nothing was there. Your hair was loose, cascading down across your chest. Does it hide you? Did you do that on purpose? I'm only curious, my Amalia. That's all.

You laced your fingers through mine, and we dared to plan a life together. Children and travel and policies and peacetime. The fire was warm, and the bed was soft, and your voice was low as you murmured about a future we could share. You told me that I was the first suitor you'd ever had who seemed to want a future with *you*, instead of a future with a crown.

I told you that I thought I was starting to fall in love with you. I was lying, of course. I didn't *think*. I wasn't *starting*.

I knew.

You told me that you were starting to fall in love with me, too. Your hands were trembling. You lifted your head from my shoulder, so I could see the firelight playing across the plane of your cheek, the soft skin of your throat. You tilted your chin up at me, and your eyes flashed, and I know I shouldn't have, but I did.

I kissed you, my Amalia. I kissed you, and you kissed me back, and I could taste the hunger on your lips.

Two hours before dawn, I stopped kissing you and told you that I was tired. I told you that I needed to sleep a little, if you didn't mind keeping another secret for me. You smiled and said yes. You looked so hollow. You looked so sad.

I put my head on your pillow and I closed my eyes and I waited for you.

This morning, the fifth morning, the last morning. You woke me, and you took me to meet your family. Your brother, your father—you were right, talking to him when he's sober is very different from talking to him when he's drunk—your mother's crypt. All the walking was hard, but you were so patient with me when I got dizzy and had to sit down. You were so kind to me when I kept stopping to eat.

You kissed me in the courtyard where we'll be married, and I felt that tickle at the nape of my neck again, and I held you tight as I could, because I remembered what you were, and I knew what you needed.

Amalia, I didn't sleep last night. Not at first. I just couldn't let you wait any longer. You were so hungry, and I knew you needed me to sleep, but kissing you sent so many bright sparks through my veins that I could have stayed awake until dawn. So I put my head on your pillow and I closed my eyes and I waited for you, and you came.

I opened my eyes just a sliver when I felt the tug at my collar. I saw you.

Don't cry, love.

I saw the pale skin of your throat flutter open into countless soft folds, like the gills under a mushroom, like the tulle petticoats under your banquet gown. I saw the silk-fine tendrils that drifted out from those folds. They're white as moonlight, thin as hyphae, luminous as your smile. They tucked themselves around me so tenderly, found their way to the base of my skull and my collarbone and between my ribs. When you began to drink, I saw your cheeks flush and your eyes brighten, and in the moment before I blacked out, all I could think of was how beautiful you were.

Do you see? Do you understand? I know. I know what you are. I know that you have been going hungry, taking only a little of what you need from me at a time so that I could stay with you. You haven't drained me all at once, the way you did with the other suitors who have come to drink your father's wine and make jokes about you keeping them awake. You haven't kept me at a distance, knowing that you mustn't befriend your food.

You've let me know you, and you've let me nourish you.

I know who you are. I know *what* you are. You are an extant form of life, Amalia, and I am not afraid to love you.

I arrived at this palace ready to die, but now—for the first time I can remember—I feel ready to live. I want to spend my life with you, if you'll have me. I would want it even if there wasn't a crown waiting for me when your father dies. I would want it even if it meant sleeping right here, on the floor outside of your bedchamber.

I want it even if it means dying a little sooner. You've only been feeding a little each night, and I know you're leaving yourself hungry, but Amalia, my Amalia—if you can stand to be a little bit hungry for the rest of your life, I can stand being a little bit sick for the rest of mine.

It's almost dawn of the sixth day, love. Our fifth night is almost over. Please help me stand up. Please invite me in. You must be so hungry, and I am so tired.

Final Course | *C. J. Tudor*

"Daddy, I'm scared."
"Don't be. There's nothing to be scared of."
"There's something inside."
"It's just the dark."
"I don't like it."
"It's okay. The dark can't hurt you."
"Promise?"
"Promise."
"Now open your eyes."

Invitation:

You are cordially invited to the 20th anniversary reunion of the Infamous Five. Bring scones, jam and lashings of booze!

Date: Saturday the 26th of October
Venue: Berskow Manor, Barley Mow Lane, Hambleton
Dinner Theme: End of the World as We Know It

"Are we nearly there yet?"

Some things never changed.

The skies could fall. Oceans boil. Eternal darkness descend upon the earth...but somewhere along a journey a child will sigh, kick their feet against the back of your seat and mutter those immortal words, closely followed by:

"I'm bored."

"It's not much further."

"How much further is 'not much further?'"

He glanced at the clock. 1:37 p.m. They had set off just before 10 a.m. Before, it could easily take over four hours to drive from the Midlands to Sussex. But there was less traffic on the roads these days. People didn't like to travel too far in the darkness. Not least because the demise of Sat Navs meant no-one knew where the hell they were going anymore.

"Half an hour. Maybe less."

He raised his eyes to the rear-view mirror. Millie sat in the back, idly staring out of the window.

"Want some music on?"

"*Your* music?"

Only eight and already Daddy's music was deserving of derision. They grew up so fast.

"No, you can choose."

She debated. "Okay. Can we listen to Mary Poppins?"

He groaned. "Really? Again?"

"You said I could choose."

"I know, but I was hoping you might choose Metallica."

"Da-ad."

"Metallica can be 'feel good' too."

"Yeah, right."

He sighed. "Okay."

He turned on the CD player and Julie Andrews's twee tones floated through the car, singing about a spoonful of sugar helping the medicine go down. Good old Mary, able to sort out everyone's troubles with a saccharine song and a talking umbrella. Back in the days when the world wasn't supercalifragilistically fucked, and the scariest thing lurking in the shadows was Dick Van Dyke with a British accent.

He tried to tune the songs out as he navigated the winding lane. The headlights only illuminated small patches of road ahead of them. In places, where the darkness was thicker, swirling in the car's beams like inky fog, he could barely see more than a few feet. He kept his speed low, hands gripping the wheel tightly, alert for anything else moving in the blackness.

He knew it was a risk to have accepted the invitation. Travelling itself was a risk and he and Harry had hardly been the closest of friends at uni. Harry Fenton was one of those privileged young men that Tom, from his working-class background, found it difficult *not* to despise. Popular, sporty, good-looking (in the ruddy-cheeked, thoughtless way that all the moneyed upper-class seemed to share), Harry Fenton glided through life effortlessly, his path gilded with money and good fortune. Tom was pretty sure, if Harry stood in front of the sea for long enough, it would part for him.

He had always tried to quell his resentment for the sake of the group, but after they left university, while he kept in intermittent touch with Alex, Michael and Josh, he deliberately let his contact with Harry slide.

And now he had accepted an invitation to stay at Harry's country pile for the weekend. Hypocritical, he knew. But needs must, and he needed to get Millie out of the city. Things were getting worse every day. Riots, looting, burning cars on almost every street corner. That was the problem with scared people. Ultimately, they became more dangerous than the thing they were afraid of.

Well, almost.

The countryside was safer. Everyone said so. Plus, Harry had told them that they were welcome to stay as long as they liked.

"I've got plenty of spare rooms, two massive generators, a wind turbine, electric fences. I'm completely self-sufficient out here."

Of course. Good old Harry. *Student most likely to land on his feet during an apocalypse.*

A white wooden sign drew into view ahead. *Hambleton, 1 mile.* Tom signalled left and pulled onto an even narrower lane, not even wide enough to fit two cars, which was a pain in the backside because a large stag was blocking the entire road in front of them. He hit the brakes.

"Shit!"

"What is it?"

"A deer—a stag."

It was a beautiful creature. At least six foot, with a proud head and elegant furred antlers. It stood for a moment regarding the car. No fear. Not of them anyway. And then it bounded across the hedges and into the field. A thunder of hooves and the rest of the herd followed, bursting from the hedgerow and springing delicately across the road, a dozen or more. And finally, a straggler. Older, slower. It stopped in the road, panting, disorientated. *Run*, Tom thought. *Run*. But the deer just stared around, eyes terrified orbs.

"Daddy?"

"I know."

The shadow swooped from their right. Black, amorphous. The deer screamed, hideously human. Something wet spattered the windscreen. Tom hit the full beams, illuminating a vague blur of tentacles and bulbous eyes. The creature hissed at the light and retreated, dragging its prey back into the darkness.

Tom let out a breath. He glanced in the rear-view mirror. "You okay?"

Millie nodded. "I'm hungry."

Tom pressed his foot back down on the accelerator and flicked on the windscreen wipers. In the distance, illuminated by floodlights, he could just see a glowing spectre of grey stone. Berskow Manor.

"Almost there."

THEY WERE THE last to arrive. Tom pulled in through the electric gates and trundled along a winding private road to find four other cars parked outside the turreted building on an expansive gravel driveway. He guessed that the battered Defender was Harry's, the Land Rover belonged to Michael and his wife, Amanda, the Volvo was probably Alex's and the yellow Mini had to be Josh and his partner, Lee. Tom pulled up alongside the Mini.

"We're here," he said to Millie.

"Cool."

The floodlights provided a wide area of illumination around the building. Coming from the grid-dependent, power-rationed cities, such a wanton use of light seemed a bit excessive. The have-watts and the have-nots. He tried to stamp on the green worm of envy wriggling in his gut, climbed out of the car and opened Millie's door. The October air was brisk and fresh. Fresher than the city, he thought. But then, anything was an improvement on the smell of burning rubber. He breathed it in, relishing the clean feeling in his lungs. This was the right thing. A good thing, he told himself again.

The door to Berskow Manor suddenly swung open.

"Tom!"

Tom stared at Harry Fenton. When he had checked up on him on social media, he had looked pretty much the same as he remembered. But those must have been old photos. Because this was not that Harry. Gone were the polo shirts, smart jeans and loafers. Gone was the floppy, foppish side-parting. This Harry wore his dirty blonde hair long, tied back in a scruffy ponytail. He sported baggy jeans, a loose hessian shirt and battered Converse on his feet. A stud glinted in his nose. If old Harry could have walked straight off of the pages of *Tatler*, this one could have stage-dived right off the cover of *Kerrang!*

"Hi," Tom stuttered.

"Man, it's so good to see you."

Even the plum wedged in his mouth had softened. Before Tom could move or stop him, Harry stepped forward and embraced him in a tight, incense-scented hug. Tom resisted the urge to squirm. Harry released him with a warm smile and turned his attention to Millie.

"And this must be your little girl?"

"I'm not little. I'm eight."

Harry chuckled. "Sorry, my bad." He held out his hand. "Good to meet you."

Millie continued to stare at him through her red, heart-shaped dark glasses, arms at her side.

"She's a little shy," Tom said.

"Sure." Harry lowered his hand again, still staring at her. "Cool glasses, kiddo."

"The rest of the gang are already here."

Tom and Millie followed Harry across the huge hallway. Tom had been half-hoping that inside, the manor might be slowly falling into a state of disrepair. But his mean side was disappointed. The hall was shabby certainly, but still beautiful. Huge lamps lent the space a warm glow. The stone-flagged floor was softened by a worn but obviously expensive Persian rug. In front of them, a wide staircase wound up to the second floor, and a giant chandelier drooped sparkling crystals overhead.

He felt a small hand creep into his. "It's huge," Millie whispered, and he knew she was conscious of her voice echoing off the walls.

"It's an old manor," he told her. "They built them big back in the day."

"Yeah," Harry said. "I rattle around here, to be honest. In fact, I've sealed the whole east wing off. No point heating and lighting it when I never use it. Got to preserve the power, right?" He gave a small laugh. "That's why it's so cool to have you guys here. Add a bit of life." He glanced down at Millie again. "I've often felt this place could do with a few children running up and down the halls."

For a moment, a sadness seemed to sweep across his chiselled features. Then, he gathered himself. "So, anyway, the others are just through here in the drawing room."

Tom could already hear the sound of conversation drifting from the open door. Or, more to the point, he could hear the sound of Josh's voice regaling the others with a lewd and, no doubt, imaginatively embellished story.

Harry led them through into another beautiful room. Tasteful art and carelessly scattered shabby-chic furniture. Although, Tom noted a few bare patches on the walls where pictures had obviously been taken down. Maybe the family money wasn't stretching quite as far as Harry had made out.

He turned his attention to the five people standing around, a little awkwardly, holding drinks. He hadn't seen them in twenty years. Not in person. As Harry had proved, pictures on Facebook and Twitter aren't the same as seeing people in the flesh. Normally, you could add ten pounds, a few chins and a lot of laughter lines.

And then sometimes, it's the familiarity of old friends that's as shocking as the changes. Josh stood, centre stage as always, a glass of champagne in his hand. He may have lost the glossy mane of dark hair which had earned him the nickname *"Boy Josh"* at uni but he was still just as striking with a shaven head, dressed (almost) in a fitted black shirt undone to his skinny jeans.

His partner, Lee, looked younger by a good decade and the total opposite to Josh's overt flamboyance. His curly brown hair was unkempt. He was unshaven and dressed in baggy cords and a shapeless jumper over his shirt. Rather than champagne or wine, he clutched a pint of beer. Tom had never met the young man before but found himself instantly warming to him.

Michael and Amanda stood, as always, shoulder to shoulder, stiffly clutching glasses of wine. At uni they had been inseparable. "The Siamese Twins" people often called them, which was a little creepy as they were the sort of couple who could, actually, have been brother and sister. They shared the same short stature, thick dark hair and striking blue eyes. Both looked a little stockier than before, although that might just be the matching padded windbreakers, but otherwise they were barely changed. Again, kind of creepy.

Last, but by no means least, his eyes came to rest on Alex. He wished she had aged badly. But Alex never did anything badly. He remembered her sashaying around campus in ripped fishnets, Docs and baggy jumpers that hung off her shoulder, revealing a tantalising glimpse of scarlet bra strap. She had worn her thick, brown hair in semi-dreadlocks and Tom used to dream of it brushing his face as she kissed him.

It never happened. And now the dreadlocks were gone. So was the long hair. She sported a sharp pixie cut that suited her small features, and wore skinny jeans, heavy boots and a loose, striped jumper. His heart still did a little forward roll.

"Hi everyone, look who's here," Harry said.

Josh whirled around. "Tommy. Darling." He grinned, revealing an expensive row of gleaming veneers.

Josh—student most likely to look fabulous at the end of days.

"I always knew you'd grow into those features," he said. "Come here."

Tom didn't really have a choice as Josh swooped in and enveloped him in a waft of skinny limbs and expensive aftershave. Lee held back and then sauntered over and proffered a hand. "Good to meet you."

Tom shook his hand. "You too. Josh, you haven't changed a bit."

"Liar, but I'll take it!"

Michael and Amanda walked up together. "Lovely to see you, Tom."

They exchanged air kisses. Tom noted a large silver crucifix glinting around Amanda's neck.

"Hey-up, Tom," another voice said.

The warm burr of the Midlands accent still did something to him. Alex pressed her body to his and softly kissed his cheek. He felt it flame red.

"I, err, like the hair," he said. "It suits you."

She grinned. "Which is what men say when they mean they preferred it long."

"No, really. It's nice."

They stared at each other and then Tom felt a small tug on his hand.

"Oh," he said. "And this is my daughter, Millie."

Millie edged out from where she had been lurking behind him.

Alex's smile only faltered slightly. "Hi Millie," she said.

Tom waited, holding Millie's hand, looking around at the rest of the group.

Michael broke first. "What's with the glasses?"

"I love them," Josh said blithely. "A real fashion statement."

"Really?" Amanda asked, voice tight. "Is that what they are?"

Tom met her gaze. "Actually, no. Millie is blind."

He felt the atmosphere in the room change. A stalling of the conviviality.

"And you brought her *here?*" Amanda spluttered.

Michael laid a hand on her arm. "Mandy—"

She shook him off and turned to Harry. "Did you know?"

"No, but…Millie is welcome here. You all are."

"She's *blind.* You know what that means. You know what they're saying."

"Hysterical claptrap," Josh said. "I thought you and Michael knew better than to listen to that nonsense."

Michael coloured. "You still should have told us, Tom."

"She's just a little girl," Tom said. "She deserves to be safe too."

"Safe?" Amanda looked around at them all and clutched her crucifix. "None of us are safe now."

THEY UNPACKED. MILLIE remained silent. The bedroom was large and airy, but cobwebs collected dust in the corners of the high ceiling and there were more bare patches on the walls. Still, the huge king size bed looked comfortable. Tom would have collapsed in it right away, but he wasn't sure they were stopping that long. He had a feeling—well, more a certainty—that downstairs, he and Millie were the subject of heated discussion.

He had hoped that the suspicion and intolerance might have been confined to the more ignorant members of society. But he should have remembered that liberalism was just a veneer, the first thing to fall away when the world went to shit; when darkness fell.

History had an unfortunate habit of repeating itself, over and over again. Human beings didn't learn, or rather, they conveniently forgot. The massacre of the Jews in Nazi Germany, the wall between Mexico and the US; the hatred and segregation of the Muslims in the UK. It didn't take much for society to fold in and start devouring itself. Usually at the expense of the most vulnerable.

People always needed someone to blame, a scapegoat, especially when they were facing things they didn't understand. Things that had the politicians blustering and the scientists scratching their huge, intelligent heads. The sun hadn't gone out, the earth still turned, flowers still grew, and the temperatures hadn't plummeted.

But the earth had gone dark. For almost a year now.

The power shortages and managed power cuts came first. "Just like the seventies," people who remembered the seventies grumbled. Government infomercials advised people about preserving power, safe use of candles, remembering to wear fluorescent clothing when travelling to school or work. Sales of solar panels plummeted, and, in response to public demand, wind turbines began to sprout up everywhere. As did the religious loons declaring the end of days. *We're all doomed.*

Still, people could have coped with that. People *were* coping with that.

But then, with the descent of darkness, came something else.

"We are going to stay, aren't we?" Millie asked him.

"Yes, it will all be fine."

"That lady didn't sound fine."

"Don't worry about her." He sat on the end of the bed next to her. "You know what we talked about? About fear?"

She nodded. "It can make people do stupid things, things they wouldn't do if they weren't afraid."

"That's right."

"Like Jonas at school, who called me names. And Mrs Masters—who didn't want me to come into class anymore."

He felt his throat tighten.

"For the safety of the rest of the children. Obviously, it's just a precaution."

And that was how it started. Exclusion. Isolation. Suspicion. Whispers between parents at the school gates, unfounded stories in the press, Twitter hysteria-mongering.

They act like magnets to those things. They can communicate with them. I'm not prejudiced but...we can't trust them, they need to be contained, monitored.

Next came the name-calling in the street. Attacks. The mobs with their burning torches. And he only wished that statement was metaphorical.

"You said we'd be safe here?" Millie said.

"We are. We will. It will all be—"

"Fine?"

A knock at the door. Tom rose and pulled it open.

Harry stood there with a tray, upon which he had placed a flute of champagne, a glass of orange juice and a plate of biscuits. Iced party rings, bourbons, custard creams. Tom felt his stomach gurgle.

"I come bearing gifts." He laughed weakly.

"Thanks," Tom said.

Harry put the tray down on the chest of drawers by the door. "I'm so sorry about before."

"Not your fault."

"But I invited you here. You're all my guests. I didn't realise that Amanda would be so, well, you know—"

"Bigoted? Offensive?"

Harry shrugged, ran a hand through his hair. "I don't know what to say...you know what she was like in uni."

Tom did. Michael, like Harry, came from a well-off farming family. Traditional, conservative. Despite that, Michael was a decent enough bloke; easy-going and good-hearted...until he met Amanda. A horsey-type of girl, brought up in a strictly Christian household, she set her sights upon Michael and the pair quickly became inseparable. Michael started attending her church, spouting all sorts of religious nonsense, even spending less time with Josh who he had always got on well with. Tom had never liked her, and always hoped that Michael would grow out of his infatuation. Sadly, it never happened.

"Anyway, I hope you're not changing your mind about staying," Harry said. "It really is good to see you and…I think it would be good for Millie here."

"What about the others?"

"We've always gotten over our differences in the past. The Infamous Five, remember?"

He clapped Tom on the shoulder. Tom smiled.

"Right," he said.

But they weren't. That was the problem. They hadn't been for a very long time.

Harry was staring at Millie again.

"Does she always wear the glasses?"

"I have to," Millie said.

"It's too dangerous otherwise," Tom said.

Harry nodded. "Of course. I understand."

But he didn't.

"Anyway," Harry continued. "I said I'd give the others a tour of the place before dinner, if you fancy it?"

"Well, we're a bit tired—"

"I'd like it," Millie said suddenly.

Tom glanced at her. "Well, okay, if you're sure?"

"I am."

"Right then. Count us in."

"Great. Catch you back in the Grand Hall at five."

Grand frigging Hall, Tom thought as he pushed the door closed. Right.

FIVE OF THEM were waiting in the "Grand Hall" when Tom and Millie came downstairs: Harry, Josh and Lee, Alex and Michael.

"No Amanda?" Tom asked.

Michael cleared his throat. "She's got a bit of a headache."

"Right. Shame."

For a moment, there was an awkward pause and then Michael said: "It really is good to see you again, Tom—and your daughter."

Hardly convincing, but at least he was trying. Tom smiled back. "Thanks."

"So, Lord of the Manor, are you going to show us around your ancestral money pit or what?" Josh drawled.

For a fraction of a second, Harry's grin faltered. He shot Josh a look, one Tom couldn't quite read. Then the grin was back up to full wattage.

"Of course. This way."

They filed behind him like day trippers following a tour guide. Grand room followed grand room. Tom described them to Millie in a low voice, trying not to let the bitterness creep into his voice, consoling himself by noting more bare patches on the walls. Still, it was insane that just one person lived here.

"How do you manage?" Alex asked Harry, as if reading his mind. "Do you have staff?"

"Well, I have a girl and her mother who come from the village to clean and help with the cooking."

A girl and her mother. Too inconsequential to name.

"No Mrs Fenton going insane in the attic?" Josh asked as they climbed the grand staircase.

"No," Harry said evenly. "Just the odd rat." He smiled. "Come on—you must see the observatory in the west turret."

Observatory. Of course.

Harry led them along the landing, past the bedrooms and then up a winding staircase. At the top they found themselves in a large glass dome. Tom imagined that once, you would have been able to see for miles. Possibly all the way to the coast. Not anymore. Darkness caressed the panes and below, charcoal countryside petered out into densely shadowed woodland. To their left, a short distance away, a large white wind turbine slowly turned. Below it were two more hulking structures.

"What are those?" Josh asked.

"One houses the generators—main and back-up—the other is just an old barn."

"How much land do you have?" Michael asked.

"Around five acres."

"How come you've never farmed it?"

"I'm not much of a farmer, I'm afraid."

"I thought you said your family were farmers," Josh said. "Or don't you like getting your hands dirty?"

Tom glanced at him. Josh could be provocative, but he seemed to be deliberately needling Harry today. He wondered why.

"We have lots of farms nearby," Harry said pleasantly. "And they need the income. I think it's important to help others in these dark times, don't you?"

"Oh, absolutely," Josh said. "That's why I took in Lee, out of pity for the poor thing."

"I'm eternally grateful," Lee deadpanned.

"You have electric fences around the whole estate?" Alex asked, peering out of the glass.

"Entirely. Nothing gets in here," Harry said. "Nothing." He looked around at them meaningfully.

"Does anything try?" Alex asked.

"Occasionally I have to scrape a mess off one of the electric fences. But that's another beauty of the countryside. We're far more prepared for this type of thing. Used to dealing with vermin."

"Any guns?"

"A couple of shotguns. For what it's worth. Bullets don't have much effect on the buggers."

"What about looters?" Michael said. "After all, you do hear about gangs coming over from London, killing land owners for their homes."

Harry offered a steely smile. "Like I said, nothing gets in here."

"Are you two still in London?" Alex turned to Josh and Lee. "I heard things are getting pretty bad?"

"Oh, you'll never drag Josh out of London," Lee said.

"Unless it's by my cold, dead hands," Josh added. Then he glanced at Tom and coloured. "Oh God. Sorry, I didn't think…"

"It's okay."

Alex laid a hand on his arm. "We were sorry to hear about your wife."

"Thank you."

Harry offered his best sympathetic smile, blue eyes crinkling around the corners like a favourite uncle. "Well, it's getting a bit chilly up here. Let's go back downstairs and warm up."

They filed back down the stairs to the first floor. Tom went last, leading Millie carefully by the hand.

"What's that way?" Lee asked, gesturing down the landing, to where the corridor ended abruptly in a sturdy-looking door.

"Oh, that's the east wing. It's just used for storage. I keep it shut up to save heating and lighting the whole pile. No point wasting energy, right?"

Except it hadn't stopped him illuminating the rest of the place like a fairground, Tom thought. There was something else. The door. It wasn't the same as the others in the house. It was new. He frowned. If the east wing was just used for storage, why put on a new door?

They reached the staircase. Millie was very quiet. He let the others go ahead and then asked quietly: "You okay?"

She shook her head. "They're lying."

"Who?"

"All of them."

The human mind has the wonderful capability to put aside things that it doesn't want to think about, to neatly store away troublesome thoughts and concentrate upon the moment.

There were plenty of moments over the last year when Tom had found that useful. His wife's death. Fleeing their home. The things that had happened since. Survival.

And then sometimes, your brain gets a worm. Much like an ear worm. A train of thought that just won't go away, however hard you try.

The door. The bare patches on the walls. They're lying.

Something here was wrong, in a way he couldn't quite put his finger on.

Millie dozed on the king size bed. Tom had been convinced that, the moment he got a chance for a nap, he would join her. But he had been lying here for the best part of an hour now, trying to get to sleep. His brain worm refused to let him.

He sat up and swung his legs off the bed. His throat felt dry and scratchy from the dust in the room. He needed a glass of water (*and a snoop around,* a small voice whispered).

With a final glance at Millie—he wouldn't be long, he promised himself—he padded across the room and slipped out of the door.

He walked back along the landing. The others had also retired to their rooms to rest and get ready for dinner. He wondered if Amanda's headache would be better by then. He hoped not. He hoped it turned into a migraine.

He paused at the top of the staircase and stared down the corridor, towards the door that barred the way to the east wing. He walked over to it and tried the handle. Locked. Why lock the door if the east wing was only used for storage? You didn't lock a door on junk. You didn't lock a door to save on heating and lighting.

He turned and walked down the stairs. Maybe he was just being paranoid. Maybe the events of the last months had made him overly suspicious of people and their motives. The problem with darkness was, once you let it in, it lurked in the corners of your mind, filling them with shadows.

He reached the hall—sorry, the *Grand* Hall—and turned left, towards the kitchen. He half-expected to find Harry, in an apron, busily preparing food. But the large space was empty. Pans filled with chopped vegetables sat on the hob. French loafs were laid out, ready to be cut. There was a little detritus of food preparation, but mostly it was clean and tidy. Organised, Tom thought. Everything about this reunion was meticulously organised. So, why did that just add to his uneasy feeling?

He pulled open cupboards, found a glass and walked to the sink to fill it. Cookbooks lined the windowsill in front of him. "Vegan and Vegetarian Recipes". No surprise there. But also, "Cooking for Your Family" and "Healthy Food for Kids". He frowned. Harry didn't have a family, or kids. Of course, perhaps the books had belonged to his parents, when they had been alive—or their chef. He reached out and opened one. The inside page was inscribed:

"To Lucy, love Dave."

Dave and Lucy. He couldn't remember what Harry's parents were called but he felt pretty sure it wasn't Dave and Lucy. He closed the book carefully and put it back on the windowsill. A door creaked behind him. He jumped and whirled round.

Alex and Lee stood in the doorway. Alex looked worried. Lee looked more dishevelled than ever.

"Christ! You made me jump."

"Sorry," Lee said. "What are you doing in here?"

"Getting a glass of water. What about you two?"

They exchanged a look and it struck him what was wrong with this picture. Alex and Lee. But what about…

"Where's Josh?"

"That's the thing," Alex said. "We can't find him."

THEIR FEET CRUNCHED on gravel. They wore thick jackets and clutched heavy-duty torches. Darkness pooled at the edge of the spotlit area. Despite Harry's assurances about the electric fences, Tom felt the hairs on the nape of his neck bristle.

"We went back to our room to have a shower," Lee said. "Josh said he was just going outside for a cigarette. I laid down for a nap. I woke up to find someone knocking on the door. I thought it might be Josh, but when I opened it, it was Alex."

"I wanted to borrow a charger for my phone," she explained.

"How long has he been missing?"

"Over an hour."

"Perhaps he's just stretching his legs, getting some fresh air?"

Lee gave him a look. "This is Josh. A man who regards a Marlboro Light as a health kick."

True.

"Plus, no-one just goes for a stroll to stretch their legs. Not these days," Alex added.

Also true.

They rounded the corner of the house to a courtyard area. In one corner stood a dilapidated block of wooden sheds that Tom presumed were once stables, the first sign of disrepair around the place. But then, horses were not exactly a useful commodity these days. They didn't produce things, you couldn't eat them, although that hadn't deterred some people. They were an expensive luxury that most people could no longer afford. Many had just been left to run wild. Ahead of them, where the land rose, the huge wind turbine sliced at the air. Beneath it, a modern steel building that Tom presumed housed the generators. A little further back was the old barn, all shuttered up.

"Are you sure he came out here?"

"We checked everywhere inside," Lee said.

"Except for the mysterious the east wing," Alex added. "But that was locked."

They looked back at the house. Tom spotted something he hadn't noticed before: the first floor shutters on this side of the building—the east wing—were all closed. He felt that primeval shudder of fear again.

"Did you ask Harry?"

Lee hesitated then said, "Josh doesn't really trust Harry."

"Why?"

"Back in uni, he found out that Harry's background wasn't quite as upper crust as he made out. His parents had money but the whole 'Lord of the Manor' thing was a bit of an exaggeration."

Tom thought about the cookbooks again. *Dave and Lucy.*

"What were Harry's parents called?" he asked Alex.

Her forehead creased. "Julian and Annette, I think. Why?"

"When I was in the kitchen, I found a cookbook inscribed '*To Lucy, love Dave*'. A family cookbook. And did you notice the bare patches on the walls?"

"I did," Lee said. "Like paintings had been taken down."

"Or photos? There are no photos of Harry, or anyone, in the house, not that I could see."

"So, what are you saying?" Alex asked. "This house doesn't belong to Harry?"

"And if so," Tom said, "where are the owners?"

"And where's Josh?" Lee added.

They stared back at the house. Then they turned the other way, toward the hulking old barn.

"Only two places we haven't looked," Tom said. "And one's locked. C'mon."

They traipsed through the overgrown grass towards the dilapidated old structure, flashlights illuminating a narrow path of light. The turbine whirring overhead made it difficult to hear anything. But Tom's nose was working overtime. A smell. Actually, more of a stench. Rich, tangy, metallic. Getting stronger and stronger as they approached the barn doors.

"Jesus!" Alex pulled her coat up over her nose. "I can't go in there."

Tom looked at Lee. He was a greener shade of pale, but he nodded resolutely. Tom shoved the barn doors open.

Inside, it was dark, but just normal dark. Tom tried to breathe through his mouth, but the smell seemed to clog in his throat, making him want to gag. Beside him, Lee pulled up his jumper to cover his lower face. They pointed their torches around. Rusting machinery, rotting wooden beams, mouldy hay and in front of them: the source of the smell. Two dead and decomposing horses, their carcasses busy with a shifting mass of white maggots, wriggling in the ruined flesh.

"Fuck!"

Lee turned away and promptly threw up. Tom managed to wrestle the contents of his stomach down, but he had a feeling that it was only a temporary reprieve. He walked carefully around the dead animals, trying not to step in putrescent flesh or bodily fluids. There were two stalls towards the back of the barn. He approached them with a growing trepidation. Lee straightened and followed, making muffled noises of disgust.

Tom peered into the first stall. A mass of rotting black and yellow fur that he guessed had once been the family dogs. He backed out again. A heavy dread weighted his limbs. Horses, dogs and one more stall left for a full house. He turned slowly and trained his torch inside. Then he reeled away again. This time his stomach had its way. He vomited biscuits and cheap champagne all over the rotting hay.

He heard movement behind him and turned, gasping for breath. "Don't."

Lee looked at him through red-rimmed eyes. "Not—?"

Tom shook his head. "But I think I found Dave and Lucy." He swallowed bitter bile, wishing he could erase the image that had branded itself on to his brain. "And their children."

LIGHTS BLARED FROM the house. As they entered the Grand Hall, Tom could hear classical music tinkling out from the dining room. The three of them looked at each other.

"I say we leave right now," Tom said.

"I can't," Lee said. "I have to find Josh."

"Besides," Alex added. "We need Harry to open the electric gates."

"Did I hear my name?"

They turned. Harry walked into the Grand Hall wearing a formal dress suit, his shaggy blond hair loose around his shoulders.

He smiled. "Guys, you're not dressed for dinner? What gives?"

Lee stared at him. "Where's Josh?"

"Josh? I've no idea. I thought he was with you."

"No," Alex said. "We've been out looking for him."

"We went to the barn," Tom said.

"Ah." Harry's smile slipped. He nodded. "Okay. Look, I can explain—"

"There are *rotting bodies* in your barn, Harry. At a wild guess, the rotting bodies of the family who lived in this house. How do you explain that? You fancied being the lord of a real manor, so you killed them for it?"

Harry's eyes widened. "Jesus! No! Christ." He ran a hand through his hair. "Okay, I admit, I may have exaggerated about my past. And yes, I have recently been 'between properties.' But this place was empty when I got here. I *found* the bodies in the barn. They'd shot the animals, their kids and themselves. They were already dead. What was I to do?"

"Bury them," Lee said coldly.

"You're right. Yes, I should have but I just couldn't bring myself to touch them. It was all so horrible…" He sighed. "Look, I made a bad call but please don't let this ruin our night."

Tom barked out a laugh. "No. Why should a few rotting corpses ruin dinner?"

Harry gave him a keener look. "These are different times, Tom. Don't tell me these are the first dead bodies you've seen? Don't tell me you haven't had to make some hard decisions, to look after yourself and your loved ones? All of you?"

Tom wanted to retort but found he couldn't reply. Neither Lee nor Alex would meet his eyes.

Harry nodded. "I saw an opportunity and took it, before someone else did. We all do what we have to do in order to survive. So, why don't we sit down for dinner and talk about this, like grown-ups? I have a proposition I want to discuss with you. The others are waiting in the dining room. Michael, Amanda, Millie..."

"Millie?" Tom advanced towards him, fists clenched. "If you've hurt Millie—"

Harry held his hands up. "For God's sake. I found her wandering the corridors upstairs looking for you. She was upset, so I suggested she join us downstairs to wait for you. I thought I was looking out for her."

Tom's cheeks flamed, with anger and shame. He shouldn't have left her. Not here. Not in this house.

Harry turned to Lee. "I don't know where Josh is, but he was quite drunk. Alex, remember that time at uni he wandered off after a party and we found him the next afternoon, asleep in the middle of a roundabout?"

Alex nodded reluctantly. "Yeah."

"Please guys," Harry said. "Just hear what I have to say and then, if you still want to leave, I'll open the gates for you, and you can be on your way."

Tom smiled thinly. "What a generous, unconditional offer."

"Do we have a choice?" Lee asked.

Harry grinned his big, shit-sucker grin. "Not really."

The table was dressed in crisp, white linen. Crystal glasses sparkled. Overhead, another large chandelier dripped with sparkling glass, although Tom was pleased to see that, next to it, there was a large discoloured patch on the ceiling stippled with lines and sagging a little. The cracks were showing, he thought, quite literally.

Amanda and Michael sat at the far end of the table, Michael in a suit and Amanda wrapped in some sort of stiff, patterned curtain. Millie sat beside them, in her pretty party dress. The one they had chosen because every little girl loves sequins, even ones who can't see them. Tom's heart swelled.

Don't tell me you haven't had to make some hard decisions, to look after yourself and your loved ones?

"Millie!"

"Daddy!"

She pushed her chair back and ran to him. "I woke up and you weren't there."

"I know and I'm sorry. But I'm here now. It's all fine."

"Nice of you to join us," Amanda said coolly.

"We're not stopping," Tom said.

"Oh, don't be like that," Harry said. "Come on, help yourselves to a drink."

The three of them sat stiffly and pulled out chairs. Millie sat beside Tom.

"What's going on, Daddy?"

"I think we're about to find out, sweetheart."

Lee poured himself a hefty red wine and passed the bottle to Tom. He hesitated and then did the same. Alex held out her glass. He filled it with a slightly shaking hand. A few red splodges hit the white linen.

Harry gazed around the table benevolently and raised his glass. "First, I would like to propose a toast."

Alex rolled her eyes. "For Christ's sake!"

"To the infamous five, back together at long last. Here's to our future adventures."

Amanda raised her glass. Michael followed. Tom, Alex and Lee looked back at Harry, glasses resolutely lowered.

If Harry was disappointed at the lack of enthusiasm, he didn't let it dent his sales patter.

"Okay, I have a confession to make. I have an ulterior motive for inviting you all here tonight…to this beautiful house, in this beautiful setting and most importantly, free and safe from the troubles of the cities." He looked around the table, face a picture of practised sincerity. "We have an opportunity here. To create a sanctuary. Not just for us, but others who would like to join us."

"What are you suggesting? Some kind of cult with you as our wondrous leader?" Lee asked.

Harry's eyes gleamed. "Not exactly. Sanctuary comes at a price."

And there it was, Tom thought. "You want people to pay to come here?"

"Of course. Look at this place. We have the land, this huge house. We're secure, self-sufficient. We can build and expand, I'm thinking another turbine, indoor pools, a spa. A place people can quite literally escape from the horror of the cities. A safe place. Sanctuary. That's what I plan to call it: The Sanctuary."

"You're crazy," Tom muttered. "What makes you think people will come?"

"You did."

"And who's going to build all these amazing things?" Lee asked. "Who's going to run it—you?"

"That's where you all come in. Lee—you and Josh have experience in advertising. You can get the word out through social media. Alex, with your architectural experience, you can help with building and Michael and Amanda, well, they have offered a very generous investment."

All eyes turned.

"You knew about this?" Tom said. "Before?"

Michael looked down. Amanda held Tom's gaze. "Yes, we were in touch with Harry before we came, and we think it's an excellent idea. Someone should make something out of all this."

"Commercialising the apocalypse," Lee said drily.

"Someone has to."

"Isn't the whole point of an apocalypse that money and possessions are all useless?" Tom said.

"Only for the losers," Amanda said. "There are always people who survive and profit from a disaster. The ones with the money, the land. We'll be in charge."

"And what about what's out there? In the dark? Are you going to be in charge of that too?"

"Like Harry said, we're protected here."

Tom snorted. "Right. Just like the family in the barn. Did Harry mention them? The former occupants of this house. They felt so safe and protected they killed themselves and their children."

Tom waited for the look of horror, confusion, shock on Michael and Amanda's faces. It didn't come. They looked down at their napkins. Realisation dawned.

"You knew about that too," he said flatly. "You knew and you didn't care."

"They were already dead," Amanda said.

"Jesus!"

"Don't judge me, Tom. You came here too. For your daughter. Without even considering the rest of us."

"She's right, "Michael said. "Let's not pretend we just wanted to catch up. I'm sure most of us would have happily have never set eyes on each other again. We're all here to escape from something, aren't we?"

Tom reached for his wine. Anther splodge of red hit the table. He frowned. Brighter red. Not wine.

Lee shoved his chair back. "I'm going to find Josh. Then we're leaving."

Another splodge. And another.

"Shit," Alex said, as one hit the table near her. "Is that...blood?"

They all looked up. The stained patch on the ceiling had darkened. As they watched, it bubbled and swelled and more drops of red fell, hitting the table below.

Lee's face paled. "Oh God."

"Harry?" Tom asked coldly. "What's above here?"

Harry tipped back his wine. "The east wing. Used to be the children's rooms. But I really wouldn't advise you to look in there."

Tom grabbed him by the arm and forced him to his feet.

"Show us. Now."

THEY FILED UP the stairs, Harry in the lead followed by Lee then Alex, Michael and Amanda. Tom brought up the rear, holding tightly to Millie's hand.

"Stay back, Keep safe. Remember what I told you?"

She nodded. "Yes, Daddy."

"What is all this, Harry?" Amanda huffed. "I thought you said the east wing was used for storage?"

"It is. I just didn't mention *what* was stored there." He sighed. "I wasn't lying when I said the fences keep everything out. But sometimes it can take a minute for the generator to kick in when the power goes. I think that's when it happened."

"When what happened?" Michael asked.

They reached the first floor. To their right, the door to the east wing hung open. Darkness swelled ominously inside. Noises came from within. Faint, wet, squelching sounds.

"*When what happened?*" Michael asked again.

"It got inside. Damned if I know how and damned if I can get rid of it."

Like he was having a problem with rats or mice.

"One of *them* is in there?" Tom clarified.

"Afraid so. I didn't realise until I moved in, and by then, it was too late. Obviously, I can't let it out, so I've tried to keep it contained. But I'm running out of ideas. And food."

"Jesus, you've been feeding it?"

"I started with some stray dogs. Then there was the occasional trespasser, lurking around the lanes."

He stuck his hands in his pockets and stared down the corridor.

"I really didn't expect Josh to be next. Damn. He must have found the spare key."

"Christ, no," Lee moved forward. Tom laid a hand on his arm. "You saw the blood. It's too late."

"I'm not leaving him in there. With *that*."

"Lee—"

But Lee yanked his arm free and walked to the door. The corridor yawned, bristling with tenebrosity. The noises were louder now. A hideous slurping. Lee turned on his torch and advanced into the darkness.

"Shut the door," Amanda said.

"And shut him in?"

"If he wants to commit suicide that's his choice."

"LEE!" Tom called.

But it was too late. A sudden movement of shadows. Black tentacles whipped around his body. His mouth opened, but before he could scream, they squeezed. There was a pop, a sound that made Tom think of the time he ran over a pigeon. Lee's head flew off like a cork squeezed from a bottle. Mercifully, the torch went out.

"Shut the door!" Amanda screamed.

This time, Tom obliged. He ran forward and yanked the door shut. Something silver fell to the ground. A key. He snatched it up and fumbled it into the lock. Behind the door, in the corridor, he could hear the creature eating, absorbing Lee. It couldn't help it. It was just an animal. Just trying to survive, like they all were. The sounds still sickened him.

He turned back to the group who looked shaken and shell-shocked, apart from Harry, who still stood with his hands in his pockets, looking contrite but composed. Tom fought the urge to smash a fist into his face and pummel it into putty.

"What the hell have you done?"

"I'm sorry. This wasn't supposed to happen."

"Right. And what exactly did you expect to happen?"

"It's just a small setback."

"A small setback?" Michael spluttered. "This…this ruins everything. How can we create a sanctuary here with *that* in there?"

"Just hear me out. I told you, I invited you *all* here for a reason."

"What? To become the next course?" Tom said.

"Not quite. Didn't you wonder why I invited you?"

"I don't care."

"I *knew* Millie was blind. I did my research on all of you."

Tom felt something curdle in his stomach.

"So?"

"I did a lot of reading about the empathy the blind have with the darkness and what lives in it. Particularly those born blind. Their connection seem to be the strongest."

"I've told you, it's all rubbish."

"Is it? Millie was a pupil at Elmwood Primary. The school wanted to exclude her as a precaution. You refused. The school was attacked while the children were in the playground. Millie was the only one to survive. Untouched."

"She was lucky."

"I don't believe in luck. I believe Millie can save us."

"You're crazy."

"If she can communicate with what's in there and get it out, we'll all be safe."

Tom glanced at Amanda and Michael. "You're surely not buying this?"

Michael shook his head helplessly. "We've left everything. Harry promised us a fresh start here. Peace, security. What choice do we have?"

"You're not using Millie as some sort of guinea pig." He grabbed Millie's hand. "We're leaving."

He turned. Cold metal grazed his neck.

"No. You're not."

He swivelled his head. Alex stood beside him, pressing a small handgun to his neck. His heart crumbled.

"And what did he promise you?"

She smiled bitterly. "Like Harry said, we've all done things to survive. You think you have it tough? Do you know how hard it is for a single woman out there? It doesn't take much for men's veneer of civilisation to slip. I need this."

Something dropped in Tom's mind with a dismal thud.

"Earlier you said the east wing was locked. But it can't have been. Josh must have already been inside."

She shrugged. "Josh shouldn't have gone poking around in stuff. He brought it on himself."

"How compassionate."

"Practical. Now, it seems to me we have a situation here, and if you and Millie can help to get us out of it, then that would be a good thing for everyone."

"Please, Alex. She's all I have."

"We all have to make sacrifices."

"No one is going to *sacrifice* Millie," Harry said. "We just want her to help us."

"You're like a bunch of scared peasants wanting to burn the witch to save the rest of the village. I won't let you hurt my daughter."

"Fine." Alex cocked the gun. Tom tensed.

And then a small voice said: "It's okay, Daddy." Millie let go of his hand and stepped forward. "I'll do it."

He looked down at her, tears in his eyes. "You can't."

"I know what to do."

"It's dangerous."

"I can handle it."

"Are you sure?"

"Yes."

"Good girl," Harry said.

Tom stared at him. "Remember, you asked for this."

"And I *always* get what I ask for."

"Oh, you will." Tom smiled. "Millie, take off your glasses."

IT WAS DONE in seconds. Just like at school. Just like the other times it had been necessary.

People thought they understood the darkness. But they didn't. They didn't understand how it had found a home inside Millie. Ever since the first day it fell. Even before it birthed the creatures. It filled her. It spoke to her. It protected her and gave her strength.

But it needed to feed.

MILLIE'S EYES BULGED, tumescent black orbs. They swelled and swirled, pregnant with blackness, and then they burst. The darkness poured from her sockets, surging forward, wrapping itself around Harry, Michael and Amanda, so fast they couldn't even scream.

It squeezed them tight, caressing them like lovers' fingers, probing their soft flesh, plunging into inviting moist orifices, pushing into the deepest parts of their bodies, filling every organ and artery and then, in one quick moment, as though dissatisfied with what it had found, it split its hosts open like rotten fruit, tearing them asunder, body parts flying across the landing.

Alex tried to run but the wispy tentacles flicked out and snagged her feet, dragging her backwards. More found her arms, stretching her into a human star shape. The gun slipped from her fingers. Panic lighted her brown eyes.

"Tom! Please! Help me!"

He regarded her sadly. "I'd like to."

"Please, Tom! I know you still care about me."

"I do...but we all have to make sacrifices."

Four wet snaps and her arms and legs were torn from her body. Her limbless torso hit the floor with a thud. Momentarily, her head snapped from side to side, mouth open in a blood-choked scream and then the tentacles reached forward, ripped it off and tossed it carelessly over the banisters.

"Millie," Tom said. "That's enough."

The darkness slowly retreated, seeping back into her. Millie blinked a few times as though dislodging a stray eyelash. Then she placed the glasses back over her eyes.

Tom stared around at what remained of his old friends. Reunions, he thought. They always got messy.

"Did I do good?"

"You did good, sweetheart."

"Those people were bad."

"Yes. We did the right thing."

"Like with Mummy."

"She didn't understand your gift. We couldn't let her take you away."

"And my friends at school."

"They shouldn't have picked on you, called you names."

"And the other people."

"Sometimes, if people won't help, you have to hurt them."

Millie yawned. "I'm tired."

"It's been a long day. You should get some sleep now. Ready?"

She laid her head down on the pillow, slipped off her glasses and Tom deftly placed the sleeping mask over her eyes, securing it tightly.

"Are we there yet?" she whispered dozily.

Tom considered, thinking about the house, the grounds. Harry was right. It was beautiful, secure. You could charge people to come here. And if some disappeared, well, nothing was completely perfect. Not even Mary Poppins.

"Yes." He kissed her on the forehead. "I think we are."

LAMAGICA | *Ian R. MacLeod*

1

IT WAS ALREADY hot down at the port in Verarica on the morning when the vessel arrived from the Old World. Vendors, hawkers and luggage porters surged forward as the gangplank lowered and the sails fell flat as the last breeze summoned for the voyage dissolved. Shouts. A reek of bilge. Wafted hands and voices amid the shadows of the bondhouse cranes. Chests and suitcases teetering on handcarts as barefoot children darted here and there to pilfer, peddle and deal. The best maps, the best tools, the best señoras. Or simply grabbing and tugging as the new arrivals struggled by.

For Dampier, as an experienced prospecting guide—*experienced* in this context meaning he still felt just about sane, whole and alive—the scene recalled many others he'd witnessed. The faces of these new arrivals were seasick pale, and their clothing and preparations almost comically naive. Clutched phrasebooks and the kind of prospecting handbooks that were hawked off barrows on the streets of Lisbon, Paris and London, although he could have told them they could have saved themselves the expense. That, and that those fold-out spades were of cheaply magicked tin, and would snap at the first hit of rock. Most of this latest batch would probably never make it out of the back streets of Verarica, and those that did would soon come to regret that they had. Then he noticed a woman in a broad-brimmed white hat raising her face as she looked about her, peering over heads into the sun's full blaze.

2

"I DON'T HAVE any money for the services you seem to be trying to offer. And I wouldn't pay even if I did. It's clear to me—and I'm not some babe-in-arms—that this whole place is infested with rapscallions such as yourself."

Rapscallions? Dampier didn't bother to smile as he set his beer down on the scarred table between him and Clemency Arbuthnot in the bar of the Casa del Conde hotel. "If that's your problem, Miss, you might as well quit right now and go back to wherever it is you've come."

"That would be London, England," she snapped, "via Paris, Nantes, Toulouse and Bilbao. A journey of several months and not a little inconvenience. And I'm not leaving this...this..." She waved a hand in a gesture which seemed to encompass not only this run-down bar with its circling flies, or the men sunk into their drinks at the counter, but this whole town, and the jungles, mountains and deserts of all New Spain beyond. "...dreadful place until I find out exactly what happened to my brother."

"I can save you the trouble—he'll be dead. Best thing you can do is get back aboard the *San Salvatore* before the captain calls up the evening winds. Perhaps before winter, you'll make it back home to... to London." Even more than speaking his native English, the name of that city set off strange echoes in his head.

"I'm not someone who gives up. And, as I've already told you, Mr... Mr—"

"Dampier."

"—I don't have the money to pay you for your services, and I don't trust you one inch. So you may as well push off."

Not a bad idea, to say such things as loudly as she was, Dampier thought. But *no money* to her probably still meant a lot of money here in Verarica, or at least that was how she'd be judged from how she acted, dressed and spoke. Plainly a high-born English guildswoman, here in a place where even the kids and the whores were tougher than the hardest men almost anywhere else.

"But seeing as you still seem to be sitting opposite me, Mr Dampier, and the staff here are so wilfully unhelpful, I might as well do what I've come here for, and ask if you happen to have seen my brother."

"I told you. He'll be dead."

"I do wish you'd stop saying that."

"New arrivals don't survive, Miss. They stay here in Verarica for a day or two, then head out into the jungle looking to strike aether, and they're either forgotten—never heard of again—or they come back deranged, changed, starved or seriously ill. Or if not the jungle, it's the—"

"But you don't know that for sure, now do you, Mr Dampier? My brother left this town almost two years ago, and the last letter I received from him was written in a room in this excuse for a hotel. He seemed excited, and he'd done his research, and I can assure you he was well-prepared. He was going upriver just as soon as he'd sorted out the necessary equipment. I have his letter here with me now..."

Clemency Arbuthnot lifted off her hat and hooked it to the back of the chair. Then she leaned down toward the bag she'd kept close to her feet, a many-pocketed brown canvas thing that she'd probably imagined would be practical for these climes. "It's *definitely* here... Somewhere..." Trickles of light played across the thin silver chain that circled her neck.

3

THE PRESENCE OF the Company in Verarica was as ubiquitous as the peeling letters which spelled out *Calahorra & Calante* across the raw brick of its many offices, brokers, agents and warehouses. The Company was everywhere; it ran the quarries and owned the harbour and took by far the biggest share of the riches the province had to offer, which it then shipped on to the Old World at immense profit. And it always wanted more.

Gold and silver, obviously. Gum and tobacco, for sure. And emeralds, yes, and obsidian and turquoise. Zinc, copper and lead, too. That, and maybe a few servants of what was left of the native Mayan race, although they were notoriously unreliable and illness-prone. All of this was taken, but were mere distractions compared to the thing that the Company, that Calahorra & Calante, wanted most of all.

Aether—being the fifth element Plato had named, after earth, air, water and fire—which an English alchemist named Wagstaffe had isolated and purified in the year 1678 by the old calendar, and which had granted mankind the ability to manipulate the material world merely through the power of his will. Crops became more bountiful, messages could be sent across great distances, winds, even, could be summoned to fill a ship's sails, and all through casting the appropriate spell. The Old World blossomed, and its guilds prospered and its cities grew in all their magicked smokestack glory, and the first of the Ages of Industry began.

For several centuries, the new lands discovered across the Atlantic had seemed little more than a distraction; places of bizarre geographies and brutal beliefs where fortunes were far more likely to be lost than won. But as the Ages of Industry continued and the aether seams were exploited in the Old World by companies such as Calahorra & Calante, it became apparent that, just like iron, gypsum or coal, and for all its incredible properties, aether would eventually run out.

4

A fine grey-white haze of dust hung over most of Verarica that afternoon. It swirled in the streets. It clung to the skin, chafed the eyes and clogged the lungs. Borne with it came a dull rumbling, punctuated by louder crashes and booms. It seemed as if an army of conquest was forever on the march.

Some of the men who worked the Company aether quarries spoke Spanish and some spoke English, and some were either French or German, but all of them looked like ghosts. Halfbreed Mayans also laboured there, at least in the more menial capacities, and Dampier also did his best to convey what Clemency Arbuthnot was saying into their tongue.

Her brother was, or had been, Benedict Arbuthnot, and he was a recently qualified Master of the Galvanic Guild. As well as that last letter, she also had his likeness trapped inside a locket on a chain around her neck. The tired and grizzled men clustered around the glowing image which she conjured in the cup of her hand. Benedict Arbuthnot hung before them in a tight black evening suit with hints of lamplight, music and good living drifting out from the scene beyond. He had much of his sister's look about him, the same wide green eyes and lightish red hair, but broader at the chin and nose. And, despite the affluence of his surroundings compared to this sweated place of grinding heat and noise where they were standing, he somehow looked less at his ease than his sister did.

Dampier could have explained to Clemency Arbuthnot that these men were looking as much at the gap in her loosened blouse as the summoned image, and that most would have told her they remembered her brother just for the sake of an hour or two of her company, if he hadn't been standing close by with a gun at his belt. It was much the same up at the railhead, and then beside the giant crushing engines, where broken rock and other artefacts were sorted and ground to powder, and she had to shout to be heard. Then on amid the quickening pools, where the aether-rich dust was allowed to settle before being filtered and refined by increasingly delicate devices, until there was nothing but the pure, precious, dangerous fluid itself which was then sealed into vials, and packed inside padded lead-lined cases, and borne on across the Atlantic to feed the magic-hungry industries of the Old World.

5

"So how does this work? You keep following me for the sake of a few pesetas until you eventually give up?"

"How it works, Miss, is that you don't know where places are here, or how things work, or even how to speak to most of these people in their own tongue..."

They were walking uphill toward a cross-topped bell-tower rising above a high greystone wall. Beneath them, Verarica was revealed in glimpses through the curtaining dust. The harbour at the mouth of a great lagoon and a long isthmus fanned by white-edged, turquoise waves. The streets a chaotic sprawl that slowly gave way to the jungle, although its green continued to be scarred by mine-workings, engine house chimneys and lines of railroad until, further off, reaching toward cloud-hung mountains at the horizon, it became one shimmering mass.

Another much grander spiritual edifice had once stood not far from the humble mission house that lay ahead. Back when he'd still nursed his own dreams of making a fortune here in the New World, Dampier had read and re-read the Conquistadors' amazed descriptions of the vast, many-stepped pyramid that rose at the heart of this once-great Mayan city. Now, it was just another opencast sore.

The iron knocker boomed, an eye peeked out from an iron-grid, and the mission house door screeched ajar.

"I don't know how we manage sometimes," said Sister Bernadette in a light German accent, after she'd given Dampier a brief look of dry surprise, and as they followed her along an arch-roofed corridor with peeling whitewashed walls. "The well seems to be running dry and the boiler in the laundry has just blown. But..." She glanced back at them, a wearied face framed by a white wimple. "...I'm not asking for sympathy or money, although I do have one small request." She held open the door to a room filled with shelved lines of folders and scrolls. "If you should ever get back to the Old World, Miss, will you tell the people there about the work of us Grey Sisters? I sometimes think we're forgotten. Now, let me see... What was that name you said again?"

"Benedict Arbuthnot."

"Arbuthnot... Arbuthnot..." She ran a finger down dusty lists. "I don't think so, I'm afraid, and I pride myself on having a good memory for the names of our patients. Do you have anything else...?"

Clemency Arbuthnot opened her locket.

"A handsome figure. But, if I may say so, not your typical prospector."

"I just need to find out what happened to him. He was, is, wearing a locket just like this one, but bearing my own image instead of his."

Sister Bernadette studied the glowing likeness floating before her a moment longer, then shook her head.

"But might he still be here in this mission house? Confused or injured, perhaps, and without a name?"

"I suppose there is a chance." She looked doubtful.

"Can I look in the wards?"

She gave a slow nod. "Although I must warn you, you might not like what you see."

The wards lay on the far side of a central courtyard where a few men with hollowed cheeks and yellowed skin sat out on wheeled wicker chairs in patches of shade. Most were recovering from malaria, the sister explained, although, and as Dampier himself could attest, the disease would probably return. Another patient hopped past on a crutch, being one of the many who'd suffered a minor wound that had festered and spread. He was lucky to have lost only the one leg.

Clemency Arbuthnot spoke her brother's name to those who seemed capable of listening in the fetid warmth of the wards, and Dampier observed how these diseased and shrunken men reacted to a woman who plainly wasn't a nun, with wide green eyes, an untarnished complexion and loose copper-gold hair, peering down at them. Some called or reached out. Others fell silent. A few, perhaps imagining she was some messenger from another life, cowered or muttered protective spells. Some of the men here coughed up a phlegm thick and bloody with the dust of the Company quarries, or had sustained injuries from explosions, landslides and rockfalls.

"It seems to us," the sister said, "that the Company destroys far more lives than the jungle has ever done, and with less good cause. Many may claim that aether is a miracle. But it is also a curse."

They had reached what appeared to be a final door, which was heavier than the others. Sister Bernadette placed her hand on an iron boss and muttered a small spell that caused the lock to turn.

This ward was longer and larger, set with high, barred windows, and partitioned into stable-like stalls. Each was occupied by a figure, and each figure was uniquely strange. They would have been called changelings, back in the Old World. That, or goblins or freaks or trolls, or any of several dozen other bad names. In earlier Ages, such creatures had even been displayed inside cages in city squares as warning to the common guildsfolk. Now, they were tended inside high-walled guild asylums, and it was accepted that, no matter how horrible the transformation was that over-exposure to aether had inflicted on them, they were mere casualties of industry, and not personally to blame.

Would Clemency Arbuthnot be able to recognise her brother, Dampier wondered, and would he, or the thing he'd become, be able to recognise her? And, even if such a reunion were possible, what would be the point? Some of the figures in this pantheon of half-made gods sprouted gaudy feathers from suppurating wounds. Others were engulfed in intricate growths of stone. Goggle eyes peered from bony crowns of head-dress. Thickened lips and tongues in lurid colours lolled from the pelts of strange animals, or jagged encrustations of seashell, obsidian and jade.

"How long can they survive like this?"

Clemency Arbuthnot had to shout over of the growing clamour of screams, howls and ratcheting cries that filled the ward. Dampier didn't catch Sister Bernadette's reply, and neither did he understand why these sad instances of humanity were now lumbering out from their pens with arms or other appendages outstretched.

"I don't know what happened in there," Sister Bernadette said when she'd extracted them and re-locked the door. "We always think of our mission house as a place of peace and tranquillity, even for the most unfortunate of our patients."

Clemency Arbuthnot nodded. "I'm sure it is."

"And I do hope you find your brother in good health. Although there is one last place here I think you should visit..."

Clouds had thickened and the palm trees were flapping as Dampier and Clemency Arbuthnot walked the gravel paths that lay between neat lines of white wooden crosses in the mission house graveyard. Some were annotated with names, dates, the details of a guild, trade or nationality. Many were blank.

6

"It's almost as if he was never here..."

They were in Clemency Arbuthnot's room at the Casa del Conde late the following afternoon. Outside it was raining hard, battering the window and turning Verarica's main street into a gleaming black river. Dampier was leaning against of the jamb of the open door and she sat on the sagging bed as drips pinged into buckets or patted the floor. They'd tried the Calahorra & Calante Factors today, where jungle-rotted men waved maps or clutched lumps of stone, harrying weary Company agents who tended scales and aethometers inside spittle-flecked glass-fronted kiosks. That, and the several other local establishments which chose to call themselves hotels with even more liberty than the Casa del Conde. Not a single sighting of Benedict Arbuthnot. Dampier might have strained to believe the man was real had he not known for sure.

"So how does this work? I mean, if you come with me upriver into the jungle?"

He shrugged. "Some people pay in advance. Others offer a cut of whatever they're hoping to find. A fair few times, I end up with nothing at all."

"I can't offer you a cut of my dear brother."

He shrugged again.

"How can I trust you?"

"You can't. Any more than I can trust you."

"There is that, I suppose. And I'll admit that you have been helpful, Mr Dampier, despite my having got nowhere. You haven't robbed or assaulted me yet, either, which is also to your credit, I suppose. So I'll tell you why my brother came to New Spain. And after that, and if this *does* work out, and it turns out that Ben is safe... Well, money—as much as you could ever want—probably won't be an issue. Perhaps you could be so kind, though, as to close the door first?"

As lightning flashed and thunder shook the walls, Clemency Arbuthnot told Dampier of how the Arbuthnot family had once possessed great wealth and influence, with connections with all the great guilds, and a country estate in Lincolnshire, and a townhouse along Wagstaffe Mall. But things had declined, and their mother had died young, and their father had been a chronic alcoholic, and a habitual chancer.

"Not that I'm saying we had a *bad* childhood..." She smiled, gazing down at her laced boots. "We were a team—Ben and Clem, Clem and Ben—and we used to play this game. We'd dress up like old-fashioned explorers in hats and capes, and sneak out into some nearby park, and deliberately aim to get ourselves totally lost. It was fun. Our only worry was was that we'd be found and hauled back to whatever currently passed as home.

"We also loved discovering stories about imaginary places. It was Avalon, and it was Einfell, and then it was Camelot and the Knights of King Arthur, and then came all the tales of Araby—I know, of course, that Araby exists—and the Kingdom of Prester John. I suppose we liked to go exploring even when we were prevented from going out. And of course, we learned about Eldorado, the city of gold in these far-off lands of New Spain which the Conquistadors sought but never found. That, and Lamagica, the final place of all magic to which the last of the Mayan priests retreated, then sealed off with mighty spells..."

Dampier said nothing. What was there to say about a word that was already on the lips of half the madmen in Verarica?

"Then Ben was sent off to school, or rather several schools, seeing as the fees were rarely paid, and he studied hard to become a lower master of the Galvanic Guild. It's not a guild most people have heard of, but their work in manipulating currents of electricity is vital to commerce and industry. The switchgear on steam engines and weathertops, for instance. He used to say that if it hadn't been for aether, electricity might have become the engine which drove our modern Age. Anyway, he was proud of what he'd achieved.

"But then our father died, and we discovered he was bankrupt. Which was bad enough. But it also turned out that, because of the clever way he'd shifted his debts, Ben and I were both bankrupt as well. Did you know, Mr Dampier, that bankrupts are automatically expelled from their guild?"

Dampier nodded. In truth, this particular fact was commonly known in Verarica, it being the kind of place where the tellers of such tales often ended up.

"So, you might say Ben and I were in a difficult spot, and we certainly didn't expect the few oddments our father left us in a suitcase to offer any kind of escape. But some things... Well, maybe some things *are* destined...

"Of course," she continued, "they were mostly relics of a wasted existence. A few half-smoked cigars and worthless betting slips, along with some calling cards in a variety of names, all of which turned out to be false. Not much, really, to show for a whole life. But there was this one item... Well, I suppose I might as well show it to you now."

She reached into her many-pocketed canvas bag, took out a smallish but heavy-seeming wooden box and set it on the counterpane, then whispered a small, private spell which caused the catch to release. The box was lined with a grey metal—lead, Dampier presumed—and contained an intricately carved piece of stone. It was about six inches long, and shaped almost like a wedge of cheese.

"You see…?" She held it carefully by the tips of her fingers. "These serpentine curves, these wings and feathers, and what looks like half a human skull, immediately reminded us of the illustrations we'd seen of Mayan carvings. Although, and seeing as it had belonged to our father, we imagined it was probably a fake. But one of our ancestors had been a privateer. You know what that is?"

"A kind of state-authorised pirate, with letters of marque, back in the days when the English fought the Spanish, and wanted a share of the New World."

"Well done, Mr Dampier—that's exactly right. Of course, this was before Joshua Wagstaffe discovered aether, so it was all about jewels, silver and gold, but by all accounts Oswyn Arbuthnot was successful, so it seemed possible that this stone really had been looted from the hold of some Spanish galleon, then passed down as a family relic until it finally reached Ben and me. If it was real, we thought we could sell it for a few guineas to some guild museum. And there was even a chance it might contain enough aether to be worth having it assayed… Anyway, that was what we were hoping. But look…"

She produced something else from her bag. "You know what this is?"

An aethometer, and a good one at that. Far better and more accurate than the gimcrack knock-offs sold at the supply stores here in Verarica, or even those used by the Company factors. Jewelled cogs, a steel-sprung mount, and a graded and adjustable dial set within diamond-cut glass. A small marvel of aethered engineering in its own right. Not the sort of device, in fact, to be owned by someone who had no money.

"Frankly, at first we thought the readings were faulty. You see what I mean?"

She touched a brass toggle, and the device leapt into life; *leapt* being the operative word.

"You see? There's enough aether in this one piece of stone to empower the spells to drive a whole British factory for years. Now watch..." She bought the aethometer close to the stone, and something extraordinary occurred.

"It's called ghosting," she said. "The effect, I mean. The calibrating spell within the aethometer actually conjures the spell it's measuring into a kind of half-life."

The fragment had gained a translucent sheen of colour, and a spectral vision of the much larger circle of stone of which it was clearly only a fragment now filled half the room. An intricately decorated wheel, and the detail, the workmanship, the sheer *clarity*, was extraordinary. There was gold leaf, and there was silver, along with porphyry, coral, turquoise, emerald, onyx and jade.

"An astounding example, as I think you'll agree, Mr Dampier, of Mayan magic and Mayan craft. Not, of course, that the Mayans knew about aether. But, like many other so-called primitive civilisations, they were certainly aware of the special power of certain sacred locations. Think of the rich seams which have been exploited at Stonehenge, Giza, Chatres in this modern Age..."

Far more than the rain streaming across the window, the shapes and colours made a strange play of watery pinks and darker reds, almost like dripping blood, across Clemency Arbuthnot's clothing, face and hands.

"Ben and I thought at first that it was part of a calendar stone. I'm sure you know how obsessed the Mayans were with the cycles of the years. But, and even allowing for its obvious power and beauty, there are differences in its execution that led us—well, Ben, really—to conclude that it might be something else. You see this line of turquoise here on the outer circle of the wheel, the way it meets and follows the jade line that's next in from the rim? Does it remind you of anything?"

"It looks like..." He made himself hesitate. "Like this stretch of coast."

"Well done again. And this isn't some vague resemblance either. Ben spent a great deal of time comparing these lines with modern surveys, and the match is remarkable. In other words, it's a map.

"You can follow the curve of the river as it winds in toward the centre of the wheel—you can even see where it breaks around an island here—and these carvings picked out in silver are the Sierra Madres, and this rendered here in red coral is desert, while this wide band of jade is obviously the jungle. All of it leading on and in, circle after circle toward the centre, the hub, the heart of the wheel..."

It was a vortex; a hissing plughole. It made Dampier's head hurt.

"Hard to look at, isn't it? It seems to be moving in some way that's contrary to our normal sense of up, sideways or down. And, as those readings tell us, it really isn't safe for us to be exposed to it for too long. In fact, it may even be the reason for us Arbuthnots' slow decline."

She drew the artefact away from the aethometer, placed it back in its lead-lined box, then turned the aethometer off. The sound of the rain and the shabby circumstances of the hotel room washed back in.

"This is what your brother went in search of."

"Who wouldn't? We'd known all about Lamagica, the last place where the Mayans retreated, and guarded with incredible spells, since we were children. Ben came here with all his ideas and drawings, but I had the salient details privately transcribed onto a map before I came. Here, let me show you..."

Dampier watched as she traced her brother's planned journey across an annotated and contoured sheet of waxed paper. Lamagica; it was enough to stir anyone's blood. But he couldn't help wondering how it was that the aethometer's reading had remained so high even after she'd placed the artefact back inside its lead-lined box.

7

The Tokotahn ferry huffed across a wide expanse of cloud-hung blue next morning. Egrets stood one-legged on mudbanks. Fisherboats slipped amid the mangrove shallows. Broad, dirty steam-tugs hooted as they drifted by, low in the water with another load of aether-rich stone. Logs or crocodiles rippled and rose.

The ferry was primarily driven via its side wheels, at least since the spells cast into its weathertop had weakened to a silvery residue of engine ice across its bronze dome. What winds its captain could now summon were barely enough to cool the passengers sitting under tarpaulins strung across its deck, let alone fill its remaining sail.

There were far fewer passengers, prospectors especially, on board than there'd have been ten, or maybe even just two or three, years before. The world's attention had shifted: there was talk of fresh aether beds beneath the temples in the high mountains of India, and of gold up in Alyaska, and of mineral oil on the Mexica plains. Almost as much as Lamagica, this whole province subsisted mainly on hope.

Clemency Arbuthnot sat beside Dampier on a bench between a woman with two chickens and a man with a goat, looking a whole lot cooler than he felt. Her clothing, that broad white hat, the loose-fitting cotton blouse and green linen skirt, were clearly made for these conditions in ways that his own ragged getup—workman's pants and boots, a sweated-through shirt of no particular colour—wasn't. Maybe a little aether infused into the threads; some canny spell that took care of the moisture and the heat…? That, and he'd noticed the pearly butt of a pistol briefly protrude from a pocket of her brown canvas bag as she shifted her laced boots up onto the rail. One way or another, Clemency Arbuthnot wasn't a particularly good match for the person she claimed to be.

"So Mr Dampier…" she said, gazing at the passing scene. "Your first name is Ed, right? And I'm pretty sure that Ed means Edward rather than Edmundo or Eduardo."

"How did you find that out?"

"Call it due diligence. That, and you tend to find board in Verarica's houses of ill repute when you're in town."

He felt a reddening prickle across his face, and was grateful she was still looking out. "That isn't for the reason you think."

"And what other reason might there be?"

"It's just… It's just I find whores more honest company than most other folk."

"More so than the Grey Sisters?"

"There's less difference than you might think."

"Then there's your accent, or at least what's left of it. You're originally from London, aren't you? And I'm guessing south rather than north of the river."

"You must know the place pretty well."

"Didn't I tell you Ben and I liked to explore? So tell me a bit about yourself, Mr Edward Dampier. Where exactly did you grow up?"

"Round about World's End," he said, "if that's any of your business."

"Ah, yes!"

"You know it?"

"Who doesn't? Although I have to say, its reputation is mixed."

World's End being the loop of land beside a bend in the Thames where a great exhibition had been held at the formal dissolution of the last Age of Industry, centred around a vast glass edifice filled with all the latest wonders of the modern world. Anyone who was anyone had come to witness it, along with millions of the common guilds, and it had remained open as an attraction long into this new Age, although its reputation had dwindled. From being somewhere to be noticed, World's End became somewhere where it was better not to be seen, and Dampier doubted if it had improved much since he'd left.

"Were they already heaping that sandy, glassy stuff there—you know, the rainbow dregs of worn-out spells?"

"Engine ice? Yes."

"I thought it gave the place a kind of tawdry mystery. A little bit like you, in fact, Mr Dampier."

Now and then they passed quarries and loading platforms along the banks, some still rumbling up rockdust and pushing out grey-white fans of slurry, others eerily silent as they gave themselves back to the jungle. They also passed the Isla San Amaro, once a leper colony, and which the image which Clemency had summoned from the artefact had shown in as much clarity as any modern survey. Meaning they were already within its second circle, moving on and inward toward whatever lay at its heart.

With the settling dusk they reached the town of Tokotahn, which was as far into the jungle as the ferry went. Disembarking here was a lesser version of arriving at Verarica, at least if you happened to look European, with kids, pigs, guides and map-sellers milling around the creaking wharf. The buildings along the unmetalled road were low and palm-roofed, with pens for the animals and open sides.

"You'd think *someone* would remember Ben in a flyspeck place like this," Clemency Arbuthnot said, using a piece of flatbread to pick up bits of so-called chicken from a dented plate. They were sitting under a palm awning. Rustling, hooting darkness lay beyond the yellow sphere of a lantern. The air was a moist fug.

"White people tend to look the same to the natives. And two years is a long time."

"Why on earth do you do this to the food here?" She pushed at another lump. "You must all have insides made of stone. And to think I said the Casa del Conde was a sorry excuse for a hotel!"

Dampier studied his own plate. He certainly was well used to eating this stuff, even if it was probably iguana. But he hadn't felt hungry all day. "Did your brother expect you to follow him?"

She shook her head. "He expected to succeed. And if he didn't—well, that was why he left the artefact back with me in England. If the worst came to the worst, I could sell it for the raw aether it contained."

"But you're here anyway."

"Your powers of observation are extraordinary, Mr Dampier. I can see why you've been such a notable success as a guide."

"And you're not worried?"

"Not worried by what?"

"By what lies out there. The jungle, the pumas and the crocs and the insects and the snakes… And whatever is really signified by that piece of stone…" He gazed down, feeling a rise of sweat as if he'd eaten something far worse than what was on his plate.

"I'm not afraid, Mr Dampier, and I'm not worried. And if you are, you might as well tell me right now so that I can employ someone else."

Later, after checking for scorpions in the lean-to shack where he was supposed to be sleeping, Dampier extinguished the lantern and sat on the edge of his hammock and worked his fingers into the bottom of his knapsack. Feeling a slide of silver, he lifted out a broken chain and locket, opened the catch, and made the small effort of will required to conjure up the image it contained. Although she wore an evening dress and her hair was made up and her shoulders were bare, Clemency

Arbuthnot looked very much as she did now. The same knowing green eyes. The same mocking edge to her smile. He studied it awhile, just as she seemed to study him, then shivered, and pushed the locket into a pocket in his pants, and lay down.

But sleep wouldn't come. The things she'd said about World's End; as if she knew him, and knew the place. A strange neighbourhood to call home, admittedly, but that was what it had been for him, and he'd been happy there, climbing the crystal dunes which piled around the half-ruined edifices, making the engine ice into snowballs hard enough to throw through the remaining windows by muttering the small binding spell Ma had taught him. Sometimes, in winter, it even actually snowed. Then back, knees gritted, toward that sign above a doorway, that spelled out LAMAGICA in fizzing, glowing red, although he'd known even then that this was a kind of joke.

Inside and upstairs was a large ballroom with cobwebbed chandeliers and a peeling ceiling painted to look like the sky, and walls that had once been part of a great diorama of all the world's territories, from burning deserts and steaming jungles to the icy fastnesses of the far north and south, which had once been so cleverly magicked that you could almost walk into them, and even now gave a stuttering sense of depth and movement. And over there was the bar, from which only the johns—the paying customers—were ever allowed to drink. And this, right in the far corner, was probably his favourite thing of all, a great big wardrobe of a machine called an orchestron, with turning brass plates, that played music all on its own.

Up another floor was a long corridor with more shifting dioramas, although it was curtained off into individual spaces that were known as the *working bedrooms,* and up above there was where he and Ma—and Grace, and Janelle, and Polly whose business name was Mistress Grind, and fair few other girls who came and went—lived.

Warm memories of their hugs and laughter, and their powdery, fleshy, lavendery smells. Scooped up and tickled, or put down and offered cocoa, or maybe a quick game of draughts or cards. At least, until the night arrived and he was expected to keep himself to himself. Not that he didn't creep down to watch the men arriving in top hats and evening suits, often talking too loud and uneasy in their stride. For this was Lamagica, ha, ha, and this was *work*. The orchestron playing fit to bust, and glimpses of gaudy feather boas, silks, furs and jewels, along with other things he reckoned he probably shouldn't be seeing at all.

Then came the long, slow, mornings, with the faceted dunes and fractured glass of World's End glinting as if in endless sunrise. Ma cooking eggy bread in her long blue gown and then stretching and smiling and saying it would do them both good to get some fresh air. Promenading World's End arm in arm in their best clothes, and Ma looking beautiful, and him feeling like her beau. It was mostly ruins, of course, but that didn't matter, for this was their home.

Sometimes, the place would give hints of its former glories as the light shifted through the afternoons, and the ghosts of long-dead guildsmen and their families, shadows within shadows, would drift by. Then back toward their doorway with its fizzing red sign, and maybe there'd be time to get the orchestron going, and they'd turn awhile together under the fogged chandeliers, and dance amid fluttering forests, until full night fell and it was time again for work.

8

THEY DID THE necessary trading next morning, stocking up on supplies and goods. Dampier bargained, and, for all her continued insistence that she was penniless, Clemency Arbuthnot produced the money from her brown canvas bag without complaint.

The plan was to head upriver for about fifty miles before turning east and inland into the jungle, basically following the same route that Benedict Arbuthnot had followed and she'd plotted out on her map, and they set off early in the afternoon on a well-provisioned flat-bottomed raft.

He sat at the bow with the paddle, and she was at the stern steering the rudimentary rudder by two ropes, although they'd agreed to take turns, and call out immediately if they saw anything amiss. For all his doubts about the meaning and purpose of this journey, he felt a slow unwinding of some of the knots in his thoughts. The mangroves knelt their boughs toward the slick brown water as if in prayer. The only sound was the drone of insects, the splash of the paddle and the occasional leap of a fish. The jungle always brought this to him; a sense of change and timelessness combined.

"So tell me, Mr Dampier...I'm curious as to why you came to New Spain."

He used the flat of the paddle to ease them around a half-submerged log, thinking of ignoring the question. But he knew the weighing, judging way she'd be looking at him without needing to turn around.

He began by telling her how you could say that everyone who came here was obviously in pursuit of the same thing, which was money. But it was never that simple in his experience. Men—and it was mostly men, Clemency Arbuthnot's presence excepting—might think they wanted to make themselves rich, but it was usually just the Company that got even richer. Others sought fame, or maybe notoriety, and planned on writing books, or staging shows, or giving lecture-tours. Others still were as much seeking to escape whatever lay behind them as to find anything ahead. That, or they'd been unlucky in love, or were actively pursuing death. Dampier, he'd seen men who'd made a good strike of aether and even got a workable deal, and had returned to the Old World with enough money for several lifetimes of luxury, but had then come back looking for more.

"And which one of those is you?"

He shrugged and shivered, still wielding the paddle and not looking back. "Guess I'm a bit of them all."

"And there's one reason you haven't mentioned, Mr Dampier. Or perhaps it's all of them, bound up into one."

"What's that?"

"Lamagica, of course."

9

They changed roles in the raft after mooring at a sandbank around noon and eating some of their supplies of jerky and dried fruit, although in Dampier's case that wasn't very much. The lay of the map against the intertwining of water and land grew less clear after that, as did his recollection of the way he'd found before, but that was to be expected; things around the river basin never stayed much the same from one season to the next. Every now and then, they raised a desultory conversation, but mostly they remained silent as the water slipped by and Clemency Arbuthnot paddled the raft.

As sky and river began to redden, and after checking for crocs, they moored again at a patch of beach, and he found some dryish wood to make a fire, even though she queried its need; the truth being that he was feeling oddly cold. Was the malaria returning just when he least needed it, and most needed his wits? As with so many other things about this journey, he simply didn't know.

"What did you do back in the Old World after your brother left?" he ventured after they'd set the hammocks and full night had fallen, affecting as little curiosity as he could.

"Can't you guess?" She was sitting a little further back from the dance of flames. Huge shadows threw across the trees from her broad-hatted silhouette.

He shook his head.

"I found work, Mr Dampier. Believe it or not, there's a market for young women of my kind of accent and deportment."

She sat in silence for a while, as if still expecting him to guess. Which, of course, he had, although he doubted if it could be true.

"I was a London shop-girl in a square just off the Oxford Road. The kind of place where the smart set of the highest guilds expect to be served by someone with manners similar to their own. A gentlemen's tailors, if you're interested. How else do you think I can afford these clothes?"

Cradled in his hammock, stars splintering through the tangled branches above and the night-sounds of the jungle playing around him, Dampier considered the things Clemency Arbuthnot had said, and the knowledge that he'd camped at this very spot with her brother two years before.

She was right, of course. Lamagica was the distillation of everything that was possible and impossible, just like aether itself. It had certainly once drawn him to New Spain. If only he could properly recollect what had happened out here on his previous journey... But his mind slipped like the gears of an unmagicked engine, and settled on another Lamagica; a flickering red sign above a doorway, leaking fizzing drops onto the step below. Ma cooking eggy bread as usual in her long blue gown, and sometimes she was happy but more often now she was sad, and they hardly went out together, or danced to the orchestron, any more.

But this was how things were, and this was the way the years slid by. The real Lamagica being somewhere far off and dangerous and possibly not even real, and not this London whorehouse set amid the ruins of another Age, and now he finally got the joke. And Gracie left, and someone made an honest woman out of Polly, and then Janelle did something bad to herself, and the few other girls went but never came back, and the orchestron fell out of tune, and sounded less like music than dropped glass. But they stayed on, he and Ma, because where else was there to go?

The eggy bread tasted less good now. And Ma screamed as the pan splatted fat and he had to help her lie down, glimpsing a landscape of sores and craters like a reddened moon beneath her long blue gown. This not being the life she'd wanted for them, no, no. But they needed money, and she needed customers, clients, johns—to live, but also to pay the landlord, who was not the sort of person you crossed. So what I want you to do, Edward, is to be my soldier, my sentinel, my envoy, my messenger, my guide, my guard. And here's the money and this is what you should ask for and this is where you should go, and you know the spell, or whatever's left of it, that opens our front door, and now you must leave. So off he went to a dark road beyond the homely glitter of World's End, where a man with unmatched socks laughed as he gave him the tin of cheaply magicked ointment, because wasn't he a bit young to have the pox? Funny, really, how people talked about things that were not funny at all. Heading back, he noticed that the red-lit sign had lost the glow out of most of its letters and now merely spelled out MA. Then up the stairs with the piano playing like whooping bird calls, and the ceiling must have fallen in, because light was burning his eyes.

"Mr Dampier... Mr Dampier..." a voice was saying. "You really must wake up."

10

They took turns in paddling as before, picking through a confusion of muddy inlets and dead ends more by hunch than by compass work or map, along with whatever Dampier could admit to knowing of the way ahead. Once, he called forward to ask why she didn't consult her aethometer, which was what most prospectors did, although she laughed in reply. The whole point of Lamagica's existence being that its magic was hidden, so what would be the point? As they steered again into a broader stretch of water and the sun beat down on the water like a struck gong, he recollected how Benedict Arbuthnot had said much the same thing.

Not that the man, despite the clear physical similarity with his sister, was much like her in other ways. He remembered sitting with him at the same table of the Casa del Conde, and how he'd been as full of dreams, suppositions and sheaves of wild drawings as she, with her printed and waxed map, had been clear-headed and blunt. Not so much a man coming here to make their fortune as someone deliberately fleeing into the unknown. Usually, Dampier made a point of offering his services only to those who were properly prepared, or those who had no idea of what they were doing at all. Somehow Benedict Arbuthnot had been a combination of both.

But he'd known a great deal about the Mayans, that was for sure. In fact, he'd spoken of little else. How, if there really was a Lamagica, which he didn't choose to doubt, the prospectors and theorisers had gotten it all wrong. It wasn't some temple or city hidden deep in the jungle. Neither did it lack any proper location, or float amid the clouds. It was simpler than that, and should have been obvious to anyone who knew how the Mayans lived.

The most sacred of all Mayan places being the many sinkholes, cenotes, which dotted the jungle where the harder rock which had formed the mountains gave way to limestone and the rivers ran underground. Every major Mayan site lay close to one, where procession was made, and sacrifices given, and guidance sought. But—and this again was obvious—all the cenotes joined to form one vast, hidden network. So this was where the last of the Mayans had retreated and sealed themselves away from the war and disease the Conquistadors had brought.

"Wouldn't it be wise," Dampier said as they paused and moored in the lee of a low white cliff at noon. "To take another look at that piece of stone. I mean…" He shrugged and picked at a fingernail that somehow, and like a piece of rotten cladding, peeled right off. "Now we're getting closer to wherever we're supposed to be going, it might offer up something more."

"That's not a bad idea. Now, let me see…" She rummaged into her brown canvas bag, spoke the spell which opened the lead-lined box and took out the artefact, which was clearly made of the same rock as the cliff beside them, and now looked grey and small. "Odd, isn't it, that something so old and unimpressive should amount to so much. At least, that was what Ben thought. You hold it, Mr Dampier."

He took the offered triangle of rock. For a moment, it felt light. Then it seemed to dig into his flesh with surprising, burning weight; no wonder she kept it wrapped up in spells and lead… Shapes, colours, were welling up, not as if to make some ornate stone wheel, but filling his entire sight.

The leaves and vines dangling above them were shards of jade; the cliff itself was polished ivory or bone. And the river was amber, flashing with a scatter of diamonds, and when he looked back down at the artefact, he saw that it was dripping with rubies, each descending slowly to scatter on a beach of finest glass.

"Mr Dampier! Mr Dampier…!"

The shadow of Clemency Arbuthnot reached and took it back from him, and as his vision contracted he saw her wipe some redness off with a scrap of cloth before placing it back inside its lead-lined box. Looking down at his hands, he realised that the keystone hadn't been dripping rubies, but his own blood.

"Here—bind yourself up with this. If we didn't know that this thing was getting more powerful before, we do now."

Dazedly, he wrapped the offered handkerchief around the cut in his right palm. It hurt like hell, and gave her an easy excuse to take next turn with the paddle at the prow.

Gripping the rudder rope with his left hand as low limestone cliffs grew closer on both sides, he bit absently at another loose nail and—what the hell was wrong with him?—the thing also peeled right off.

Spitting it out into the current, he told himself to focus, concentrate on what he really remembered; what he actually knew…

Benedict Arbuthnot, for instance, sitting at the prow of a raft as they worked midriver against the quickening pull, just as his sister was doing now. The same features, maybe, at least the same green eyes, but he'd seemed younger in a way that had little to do with age, and the grizzle of reddish fuzz that had grown across his cheeks by this point in their journey—you could hardly call it a beard—had made him look younger still. And all that talk! And the notes, pages of them, he was still scribbling out.

He'd shared, enumerated, the Mayan obsession with calendars. Not one way of counting the days, it seemed, but several, interlocking and turning just like the stones upon which they were carved. In many ways, he said, his high voice echoing from bank to bank, they were a far more advanced civilisation than our own.

Yes, the Mayans fought wars, had armies, Mr Dampier, but their conflicts were slight and ceremonial compared to the blood and slaughter of European battlefields, and started and ended at previously agreed times. Which, aside from their steel weapons and horses, was why the Conquistadors defeated them so easily; they simply carried on fighting and killing until there was nothing left to kill.

The Spaniards, they had it wrong about so many things to do with the Mayans. Obviously, the varieties of snake deity they worshipped weren't incarnations of the Christian Devil, although that was why the Franciscan monks had their temples ransacked and their codices burned. Neither were the Spaniards right to be horrified by their rites of human sacrifice. The crucial thing to *know*, the crucial thing to *understand*, Mr Dampier, was that to give yourself up to the gods was the greatest imaginable honour.

That ball game they played? Those stone hoops in walled courtyards? That was part sport, but it was part ritual as well. And it was the captain of the *winning* team, the one who'd fought hardest and most skilfully, who knelt before the priests in all their jewelled and feathered finery, and pleaded himself unworthy.

But, if he was lucky, if he was privileged, he might be accepted as an offering to the gods. Then he was stripped and shaved and anointed, and placed for a whole day—or perhaps two or three; such things depended on the turning of the stars—in a sweatlodge, to pray without food or water until he was finally brought forth amid great rejoicing, and given the most precious medicines, magics and herbs to help him through the journey ahead.

Can you imagine, Mr Dampier, how such a moment must have felt? To be borne up toward the steps of a great pyramid such as the many we Europeans have razed to the ground? And then to ascend slowly, step by trembling step, with the sacred power roaring through your blood? Brutality and godlessness are surely the last words for such a ceremony. There was barely even any pain. As a final mercy, once you had ascended to that high place between the sky and the land, you were stretched across a special stone and your spine was snapped in one quick pull, so there was nothing left to feel but joy as the high priest wielded the obsidian blade and your pulsing heart was lifted toward the sun.

Dampier blinked hard. His hand still hurt, and everything seemed too bright. Even the curl of Clemency Arbuthnot's hair which had fallen loose recalled the whorls of Mayan decoration, and the echo of her brother's voice lingered in his head. For once a sacrifice had been made, it seemed, be it either human or animal, and after the heart had been offered up to Kinich Ahan, the god of the daytime sun, and it was taken in procession to be given to the waters of the sacred cenote, it was common for the priests to delicately remove the skin of the offered body, and don it as a kind of garb…

"Quick—Mr Dampier!"

The rudder rope tore painfully at his right palm as a sudden swirl threatened to twist them round. The gorge was narrowing, and the shadows were dark, and the sun sunk so quickly beneath the over-reaching trees that they scarcely had time to find a place to moor.

What strange and over-complicated beings we humans are, Dampier told himself as he set a fire—this time, Clemency Arbuthnot didn't question its need—and went about rigging the hammocks amid the dangling roots and doing all the simple, basic, necessary things, albeit favouring his left hand, that any person had to do. The rest—out here in the simplicity of the jungle, this had struck him before—didn't matter that much.

So why was that last journey he'd undertaken with Benedict Arbuthnot so unclear? Why was he remembering things only as they recurred? He guessed that was what he'd come back to find out, but it still made no sense. All he did know for sure was that two years earlier the river's widening flow had borne him back toward Tokotahn, and then on to Verarica, alone. And yes, he'd lived, breathed, shat, slept, talked and drunk a fair amount of mescal in the time since. He'd even given Nettie Muller the money to pay off her debts so she could join the Grey Sisters and quit being a whore. But he hadn't worked or done anything else remotely useful. At least, if you discounted studying the face in that broken-chained locket, and waiting for Clemency Arbuthnot to arrive.

11

He was walking uphill, and the going wasn't good. Every step he took, he slid back at least half as far, and the light was like a crystal held up to the sun. But this was nothing surprising, this was his home, and there the sign above the doorway, even though it had now entirely ceased to glow. He pushed his way in, climbed the stairs, sudden urgency in his breath, and shouting *Ma, Ma, Ma?!* Surely there had to be a reply, and surely she had to be on the mend, after all the cheaply aethered potions he'd bought from that man with the unmatched socks to make her well. He turned, spun around, and the walls of the ballroom spun with him, offering crazy glimpses of stark white mountains, deep forest dells. That, and other things—gaudy feather boas, silks, furs and jewels, melting puzzles of putrescing flesh and protruding bone—that he reckoned he probably shouldn't be seeing at all. But the place was dead and empty now, even the clattering orchestron was finally silent, and Ma and the smell of eggy bread were gone. So he turned and walked back out across World's End. Toward the river; toward the docks.

He could still hear the sound of a river, that snakelike hissing, but now instead of the chuff of engines, it was interrupted by the wild whoops, screeches and howls; the sounds of the jungle. Even before he opened his eyes, Dampier knew exactly where he was, which felt like far more of an achievement than it should. But something still seemed amiss. He moved his sore right hand down toward his belt, and felt for his gun. It was gone.

"What..." He staggered up and out of the hammock. Clemency Arbuthnot was sitting nearby on a weathered log. Beside her was his gun. She gripped her own, the one he'd glimpsed with the pearly handle, in her right hand.

"I thought I'd better take your firearm away from you, Mr Dampier. After all, you can hardly expect to be able to use it with that cut."

Other people had pointed guns at him over the years—some of them had even been women—but few had done so with such purpose. The hammer was cocked, and her finger was curled tightly around the trigger.

"You're going to shoot me?"

"That depends. All you have to do, Mr Dampier, is stop lying."

"About what?"

"Oh, come *on*." She laughed, although she wasn't smiling. "You're transparent as a tapeworm, and twice as low. Not, I suppose, that I immediately realised you were the last person to see my brother alive. But what kind of guide has a business that involves telling people they're wasting their time?"

"So why did you trust me?"

"I've told you often enough before—I don't. And you kept telling me Ben was dead. Not that you seemed to have found much profit in taking him out into the jungle and shooting him, although I know that's what some of your sort do. And I'd hardly credit you as the sort to know about privateers and letters of marque. Oh, and I looked through your rucksack the first chance I got. The moment I found the locket with my likeness that Ben took with him was the closest I've come to killing you—at least, until now. And I think you should see this..."

Her gun only wavered slightly as, one-handed, she took the expensive aethometer from out of her canvas bag and turned it on. The dial showed a low latency at first. Until she pointed it directly at Dampier, when it shot right up.

"You reek of aether, Mr Dampier. You didn't realise that, did you? Along, I'm guessing, with a great deal else. So why don't you just tell me everything you *do* know about what happened to my brother, and then I'll decide whether to shoot you or not. That, and where. Perhaps cleanly in the head, or perhaps low in the gut. Really it depends on if I decide you're told me the full, exact truth."

Dampier still felt surprised and dizzy, and asked if she'd let him sit down on that log. Which she did, after moving herself and his gun further up. Then he spoke, slowly at first, his head sunk between his shoulders, but then more quickly, and soon even finding himself wondering why he hadn't told her before. Although she probably wouldn't have believed him until now.

"So you're telling me you think my brother actually *found* Lamagica somewhere further upriver and into the jungle, and that he just walked right into it, and that you turned back, but you can't remember why or how?"

Dampier nodded, then spat out a wad of oddly blackish phlegm. "...And it wasn't even just Lamagica. As we got closer upriver he started saying it was the sum and substance of every lost land. You know—Albion, Camelot and Cockagine. That it was the place called Sierra de la Plata—the silver mountains—and El Dorado as well. That it was Einfell, to where Goldenwhite retreated when she was betrayed outside London by Owd Jack. That it was the Isle of the Blessed and the Spring of Eternal—"

"Thank you, Mr Dampier. I do believe you're starting to sound more than a little like my brother yourself. Ben, he took after my mother, and was always the dreamer. Whereas I, I suppose, am more like my father. Oh, I'm not saying I'm some spendthrift alcoholic, but I do have a cynical slant. Ben was clever, but he was never clever about anything that was simple or real. I believe that was why he chose the Galvanic Guild—what could be more ethereal that electricity, other that aether itself?—although I'm not sure if he'd have made a good common guildsman, with a toolbag and a workbook of spells. The pity is he never got the chance to find out. My father was declared bankrupt soon after Ben qualified—I've told you that already, haven't I?—but it was before he died.

"That artefact—the keystone—we didn't find it forgotten in the bottom of some family suitcase, either. Our father kept it as a paperweight on his desk throughout our childhood, and Ben had often wondered aloud about what it was. In fact, he'd already had it assayed and come up with all the stuff about Lamagica when he went to see our father for the last time. So perhaps it wasn't as much to remonstrate with him as with a proposal. I don't know precisely what happened, but an argument ensued, and Ben came to me in tears with the keystone still encrusted with our father's brains and blood.

"Clearly, he'd be arrested as soon as the body was discovered. I at least could prove I was working in that ghastly shop, but what possible defence did he have? So we sealed the keystone inside a lead-lined box with a spell for which only I knew, and he set off to take the first boat from Portsmouth and on to New Spain...

"And I waited. And, meanwhile, I served in that shop telling fat guildsmen how marvellous they looked. It was boring, demeaning work, but I began to realise there were better ways of making money through fluttering my eyes at rich idiots and lying through my teeth. Oh, it's still not what you *thought* I meant, Mr Dampier! The sad thing about whores being that they never realise you can make better money by keeping your clothes on. You could say I'm a trickster, if you have to call me anything at all. It's interesting work—enjoyable, if I'm honest, which of course I'm not—and the only people I leave poorer are those who deserve to be made so. But I still had no idea what had happened to my dear brother after that last letter from the Casa del Conde in Verarica. Eventually, I knew I had to confront whatever was inside that box.

"So perhaps I should have come to New Spain earlier, and perhaps I shouldn't have come at all. But here I am. And here you are..." She picked up Dampier's gun from the log and turned it slowly around. "Seeing as you haven't tried to kill me yet, you might as well have this back, I suppose. That, and it probably still makes sense for us to carry on together, seeing as you claim to have at least some idea of where we're going. Although I have to say, Mr Dampier, you don't look at all well..."

12

THE FLOW OF the river was so strong the raft almost shot away from them as they eased it out into the current, and Dampier ripped some of the underflesh off his sore right hand as he grabbed the flailing rope.

It didn't get much better after that. The gorge was still narrowing, throwing up spumes and fogs which the filtering daylight transformed into scintillating rainbows or pits of gloom. Swapping roles was difficult, with fewer backwashes where they could reach and hold onto a dangling bough or root, and with every push of the paddle Dampier's right hand gave another stab of pain. They could scarcely hear each other's voices, either, over the wet roar.

Dampier wondered if this was how it had ended as he struggled between holding the rudder and wielding a bucket to bail out the water washing over the gunwale. Had Benedict Arbuthnot simply fallen in and drowned, while he'd somehow managed to survive? But he could still hear the man's voice raised over the bellowing brown rush, see his eager back bent to the paddle at the half-misted prow.

The cliffs were higher now, walls of wet limestone that convoluted into elaborate pillars, pinnacles, whorls and scrolls. The day would have been exhausting even feeling better than he did, and the nails were now shedding from his left hand as well, and the stickiness in his boots told him that his feet were probably bleeding.

If this wasn't malaria, maybe it was scurvy? Like the problem of where they were and what they were supposed to be doing here, whatever was left of Dampier's instincts as a guide were screaming that they should turn back right now. But he'd come this way before, hadn't he? They had to go on.

They managed a break of sorts at about midday by looping a rope around a larger rock that stuck out from the middle of the flow.

"You're sure this is the way you came with Ben?" Clemency Arbuthnot shouted. Even she was starting to look bedraggled. Her clothes were soaked and her hat drooped.

All he could do was nod.

Soon, it seemed more and more probable that the river itself would soon force them back. The narrowing glimpses of sky were starting to close over entirely, forcing them to navigate through torrenting darkness toward the next show of light. But then, just as even Dampier was starting to doubt if he and Benedict Arbuthnot had ever gotten this far, a sudden, sideways surge almost threw them into a much bigger space where the cliffs fell away and the cloudless evening sky was mirrored with dizzying exactitude in the quiet water of a wide, still lake.

"Where do we go now?" Clemency Arbuthnot's voice echoed harshly—*now now now now...*—against the cliffs behind.

"The way's over there." Dampier pointed with new certainty toward a small stretch of shore, and the sky shivered against the raft's prow as they paddled across, moored and climbed out. It just another stretch of jungle. No stones, no ruins, no towering pyramids, pillars or temples. There was nothing here but trees, snagging vines, giant ferns, immense deadfalls.

"You—Ben—really came this way?"

"Yes..." He coughed and spat out some more dark-looking gunk. "I'm sure."

"But there's nothing *here*. No landmarks..." She climbed around a huge crown of blackened and decaying roots, then dug into her bag and took out the aethometer. The only leap in the dial came when she pointed it directly at him.

It wasn't far now. Even though night was falling, he pushed on. Then, suddenly, the sky opened above a huge drop so close to his feet that he almost fell right in. As did Clemency Arbuthnot as she stumbled up behind.

"This is *it?* Really?" She peered down, then wavered back. There was nothing to see inside the mouth of the cenote but rising darkness. No bottom, or glint of water, or sign of light or life.

"Yes—I'm certain of it."

Slowly, carefully, they picked their way around the edge, occasionally loosening stones that stirred up near-endless echoes as they skittered down. A half-moon was rising above the mass of the jungle. It had a strange effect on the nearby vegetation, and the vines that straggled into the drop. They seemed silvered, varnished with a kind of other-worldly gloss. Then, inspecting his damaged hands and seeing rainbowed dust, Dampier laughed out loud.

"What *is* it?"

"It's just engine ice—the same stuff you get anywhere from a used-up spell..."

Finally, about halfway around the edge of the cenote, he pulled the bindings off his right hand and began to scrabble amid a pile of dead creepers. For a long moment, he encountered only dry leaves and dirt. But then he glimpsed something more solid, and began to work much more slowly and carefully. After a while, Clemency Arbuthnot gave an impatient sigh and leaned over to help, but then she gasped, and he glimpsed the brief, bright leap of her aethometer.

"Get back, Mr Dampier! That thing isn't safe. The readings are sky high—"

"You forget—I've been here before. Whatever's happened to me, it's happened already."

And there it was, the entire stone circle, fully revealed but for their one missing piece. It looked rather beautiful, even if the carving was an undecorated grey. He took a swatch of leaves to it now, reverently brushing away the last of the debris much as a priest might with a holy relic, which was exactly what it was. Other things were much clearer to him now, too, weary and ill though he felt.

"It's just over there—the place Ben entered the cenote. Look..." He pointed, and it was true; there was the suggestion of a series of steps circling down and out of the moonlight, although they were so worn and irregular it was impossible to tell whether they were the work of man, nature, or of some other force.

Warily, Clemency Arbuthnot nodded. She was holding the aethometer close to her chest as if it might offer some protection. "But... How...? It's still just a big hole in the ground."

Dampier smiled. "That's easy. I just had to hold open the door to let your brother go through. Watch..."

Slowly, and as if in supplication, he knelt down and laid the splayed fingers of both hands across the stone, and spoke a spell of a lost language, and felt the power of it pour into him. It was like being ridden by a storm, and struck by fire, ice and lightning, all at once. Yet he could see that she saw it as well; that all of this was real and true. The wheel was the world, and the world was turning, and both were illuminated, fused, glorified. But the wheel was also a calendar—that is, if calendars made the years instead of merely echoing them—and the cenote was at the heart of everything; a swirl of wyrelight that rose up from the depths in a blaze of voices that sang of something stranger than mere life or death, and further away than the stars, yet was somehow endlessly and irrevocably *here.*

It was a firestorm of living magic such as the world had never glimpsed or imagined in all the pomp of its Ages of Industry, and it was beautiful, but it was terrible as well. Benedict Arbuthnot, Dampier thought as he pulled his hands away and the grey, ordinary moonlight crashed down around them, had been a very brave man indeed to have walked into that.

"So that's… That's where Ben went?"

Dampier's skin still crawled, and his head was still ringing, although he noticed that the dial of the aethometer Clemency Arbuthnot was clutching had shattered. Then, remembering something, he worked his numb fingers into a pocket, and held it out.

"Your brother broke the chain and said that I should keep this until I found you."

She took the locket from him. "But this place… If it was ever found… If it was used, mined—exploited…"

"That's what can never be allowed to happen. And that's why we had to bring back the keystone. Even the Conquistador who removed it in the times before aether must have realised its power. Perhaps they wanted to keep it, or maybe destroy it. Perhaps it destroyed them."

"What does it do?"

"What does any key do? It unlocks things—or locks them. Here, I'll show you."

She reached into her brown canvas bag, took out the box and muttered the spell that opened it, then fumblingly held the keystone out. Taking it, Dampier knelt again, inserting it into the space in the centre of the stone, half-expecting to be swept up in another storm of aether as he did so, but there was merely a sharp *click*, and the wheel briefly glowed with colour, then settled and faded with a dull grinding, and all that was left was an ancient sinkhole, and a rather unremarkable Mayan relic.

"Well…" She sniffed. Sighed. "…now I know."

"I guess you do." Although he reckoned whatever story of their journey got back to Verarica would settle easily amid all the other wild tales of Lamagica that infested the place. Which was probably for the best.

"Wherever Ben is, I know it was what he was looking for even when we used to creep out as children. And I also know there's no chance of him ever coming back, which I think he wanted as well. So I suppose I have to leave him here…"

"What about you? Do you plan to head back to London and resume your…career there?"

"I don't think so, no. I've seen enough of the New World to realise the old one's nothing special. I might head up to New Amsterdam, or maybe Boston. Or perhaps down to Quinto."

"I reckon you stand as good a chance as any to do alright."

"If that's a compliment, Mr Dampier, I'll take it. And I don't need this." She tossed the aethometer into some nearby bushes. "Or this…" She held the broken-chained locket over the edge of the cenote. It fell, flashing, then was gone. "Although I'll keep my memories of Ben here." She patted her chest. "But this isn't a time for farewells, Mr Dampier—we really must get back to the raft. At least downsteam'll be quicker and easier. And, frankly, you need serious medical attention."

He shook his head. "Oh, I'll be fine."

"This isn't some joke! After what you've been exposed to, the level of aether… Didn't you see in that ward in the mission house—"

"Yes, I did see, plain as day. Which is why I'm not going back."

"But you can't just… Stay out here in the jungle."

"Why not?" He shrugged and shivered; truth was, he somehow felt pretty terrible and not too bad at the same time.

She stood for a long moment, her face in shade from the moonlight, but her eyes as green and clear and knowing as he'd ever seen them. "If that's what you really want."

"I do. And I'm glad to have been of some service."

"That you have, Mr Dampier."

Clemency Arbuthnot held out a hand. Very briefly, yet noticing how warm and smooth and living her flesh felt, he took it. Then she turned and headed off in the direction they'd come without looking back. Dampier remained standing a while beside the lip of the cenote, picking absently at a last fingernail, until another shiver took hold, and he noticed how strange the colour and texture of his skin had become, even allowing for the effects of the moon.

He began to push his way deeper into the jungle. It was difficult work, climbing, crawling, with frequent stops to cough up more of the black fluid which seemed to be filling his lungs. But the moon was still very bright, and the engine ice he'd noticed earlier appeared be growing rather than diminishing. It formed giant fans and ferns, enormous growths of shimmering crystal. Soon, he was sliding over the stuff, and climbing, sinking, falling. But then he got his bearings, and heard warm laughter and music, and saw a familiar doorway ahead, with the single word LAMAGICA picked out above in glowing red letters. Smiling, he spoke the spell that opened it, and went through.

Razor Pig | *Richard Kadrey*

The morning David O'Meara took a leave of absence from the junior college where he was head security guard, he loaded his Chevy Suburban with maps, protein bars, and a recent birthday photo of his daughter. He'd taken the picture out of the frame the day after Lucy disappeared and laid it in a drawer. Putting it in his pocket was the first time he'd seen her face in a week. He knew there might be trouble when he tracked her down, so he packed a Glock 9mm pistol in a holster that fit at the small of his back. That way, the gun would be hidden under his untucked shirt. No need to show the thing if he didn't have to. Besides, when he found Lucy, he didn't want her first sight of him to be packing heat. That, he knew, wouldn't help the situation at all.

O'Meara drove north from San Marcos, Texas, north on I-35 toward Austin. He knew the road well. It was where, many years earlier, his secret, second heart had truly begun to grow. Following the route on the dusty map, he turned off onto Highway 21 and sped through Uhland, heading north to Mustang Ridge. The carnival seemed to be sticking to the smaller towns along the narrow highways that snaked through that region of Texas.

He'd been rigid with tension ever since Lucy disappeared, unable to sleep or eat. A tap on the radio button in the Suburban brought up his favorite broadcast, an old-fashioned local San Marcos AM news and call-in show. Today, though, something was off. The host did his usual rants, going attack dog on "liberal gay humanists" while mixing in homespun redneck wisdom. But O'Meara found himself strangely bored. He listened to the call-in portion of the show, hoping for a UFO weirdo or conspiracy nut who'd go on and on about how the government was controlled by lizard people. No such luck. It was just the same tired Mexicans, Jews, and lesbians infiltrating the schools. After a few minutes, he turned the damn thing off.

Reaching into the plastic bag on the passenger seat, he pulled out a protein bar and tore it open with his teeth. It was a bad idea. The thing tasted like sugar on switchgrass, or at least his sleepless brain made it seem that way. O'Meara rolled down the window, spit out what was in his mouth and tossed the rest of the bar with it.

As the window rolled back up he wondered what Lucy was doing at that exact moment. His mind hopped from images of her laughing with friends to ones of her tied up in the back of a van, helpless and abused. He'd seen what that could do to people.

O'Meara had had more than his share of strange encounters along this stretch of road. There was one before Uhland and two more on the empty stretch of road out of town. It bothered him when he couldn't remember who'd been first, the trucker or the Target cashier? The third was definitely the hippie boy heading to Dallas for a music festival. There had been enough of those brief, intense encounters by now that O'Meara was sometimes tempted to write them down. However, aside from it being dangerously foolish, it felt like cheating. Like he'd be diluting the experience. And if he did that, would he ever see the moon again?

He shook his head to clear it. None of that was important now. Bringing Lucy home safe and sound was all that mattered.

The day after his daughter disappeared, O'Meara called the police. Two uniformed officers arrived and asked a lot of stupid questions. Did Lucy take drugs? Did she have boyfriends? Had she and O'Meara been fighting? He practically had to drag them into her bedroom. They didn't even search it. After a half hour of pointless chatter, he knew they weren't going to be any help. When they asked for a photo, he didn't want to waste the birthday picture on them, so he tore a shot of her from her school yearbook. The officers said they'd do what they could, which O'Meara knew from experience meant they'd decided Lucy was a teenage deadbeat and unless she tried to rob a bank, they wouldn't do a damn thing.

After they left O'Meara, who'd barely been in Lucy's room since she disappeared, went to the small desk by the closet. The laptop was gone, which probably meant she wasn't planning on coming home anytime soon. He went through the papers on top of the desk and looked in and under every drawer. There was nothing but school work, print-outs of photos with friends, and one of the silly Tarot decks she collected. He went through her closet and looked under the bed. More nothing. It was when he stripped the sheets off the mattress that he found it: a dusty leaflet from a traveling carnival that had recently been on the outskirts of San Marcos. The front of the leaflet had pictures of clowns, a sword swallower, and acrobats. On the back was a map of Highway 21 with the names of several towns highlighted. Across the bottom of the sheet was a handwritten phone number.

O'Meara almost dropped his phone, pulling it from his pocket. He quickly punched in the number and waited. It rang several times, and went to voicemail. When he tried to leave a message, the recorded voice said the mailbox was full. O'Meara thumbed off the phone and sat down on Lucy's bed, staring at the map on the back of the leaflet.

A moment later, his phone rang. Hoping it was the police, he said hello. There was a few seconds of silence before a deep male voice said, "Who is this?"

"Hello?" he said. "Is this the police?"

There was another stretch of silence, then he heard an intake of breath and, "Friend, how wrong can one man be?"

O'Meara looked at the phone. The number displayed was the same one on the leaflet. He put the phone back to his ear and said, "Is Lucy there? I'm her father. I want to talk to her."

It took him a moment to understand what he was listening to. The sounds were low and staccato. It was a laugh, he decided, but punctuated with grunting sounds like a hog might make.

"Who is this?" shouted O'Meara. "I've already called the cops. Hell, I am a cop."

"That's not what I hear," said the voice. "You're just a girls' school rent-a-pig. Not much more than a janitor with a badge."

"Let me talk to Lucy. Please."

"There's no one here by the name."

O'Meara knew the man was lying because the moment he said it he burst out with his pig grunt laugh. "I'll find you," he said.

"Don't call here again," said the man and the line went dead. O'Meara hit the button to dial the number back, but the call went straight to voicemail. He hung up and sat unmoving, playing the conversation over in his head. From outside came the sound of cars and dogs. A plane flying overhead. In a few minutes he took the leaflet downstairs and got out a map of Texas.

When O'Meara reached Mustang Ridge, he found the fairgrounds, but the carnival had already moved on. He got back on the highway and continued to the next stop on the leaflet—Garfield. A few miles outside of town, O'Meara spotted a large sign for the carnival in an orange grove along the highway. He spotted someone sitting on a tractor along the edge of the orchard, so he pulled the Suburban onto the highway shoulder and walked across the road.

"Hello!" he shouted as he ran to the orchard fence. An old man in a plaid shirt and well-worn Carhartt pants looked up from his phone and came to the fence. "Can I help you?" he said.

O'Meara pointed to the sign. "The carnival. Was it here? Did you see it?"

The old man squinted. "Who are you?"

"I'm David O'Meara," he said, and put out his hand. They shook, though the old man looked at him warily. "I was wondering about the carnival. I think my daughter might have left with it."

"I'm Clemson," said the old man. "And I'm sorry for your loss."

"Did you see it?"

"The carnival? Sure. They gave me a handful of free tickets for putting up the sign. But I only went once and didn't stay all that long."

"Why? Did something happen?"

Clemson kicked at a dirt clod. "Nothing happened. It's just that I found the place a bit unsavory. There were lady acrobats, but they had tattoos all over. The clowns looked like something you'd see in an old horror movie on TV. There were games in the midway, only I think they were all rigged. But I didn't leave on account of any of that."

O'Meara took out Lucy's photo and handed it to Clemson. "Did you see her, by any chance?"

The old man pulled at his ear as he looked at the photo. "Maybe. It could be her. There was a young gal telling fortunes. Might be the one in the photo."

O'Meara flushed in the heat and excitement of the moment. He thought about Lucy's Tarot decks. She'd left the one behind, but he knew she had others. He said, "I take it you didn't get your fortune told."

Clemson made a face. "'Course not. I'm not an idiot. I don't believe in that nonsense."

A part of O'Meara wanted to get in his car and floor it for Garfield, but another part of him wanted to know as much as he could before he tracked the carnival down. "You said you left the carnival early. Why?"

"Are you a cop?" said Clemson. "'Cause whatever that carnival was up to, all I did was let them put a sign up."

"Ex-cop," said O'Meara. "I just want to find my daughter and to know what she's gotten herself into."

"Oh. Well, if she's with that bunch, who knows?"

"You still didn't say why you left early."

Clemson glanced at his phone. "Really, it was the whole place. It just felt wrong. Sordid. But, I guess if there's one thing that drove me off, it was the metal man."

"Tell me about him."

"I thought he was just one of those sword swallower acts. I'd seen them before and I never knew how a man could do that. But this man was different. He didn't swallow the swords. He ate them."

A car sped by and someone threw a couple of beer cans onto the side of the road.

"What do you mean he ate them?"

"Just that," said Clemson. "Put one in his mouth like a regular swallower act, then yanked it out and bit it in half. He swallowed the pointy end and chewed up the rest. Did the same thing with some knives too. I never saw anything like it and I never want to again. There's something *wrong* with that man."

O'Meara looked back toward the Suburban. Maybe he'd been wasting his time with an old coot who got spooked by a carny magic act. Still, he might have seen Lucy and that was worth something. "If the carnival is gone and you thought it was so bad, why do you leave the sign up?"

Clemson shook his head. "I thought about taking it down, but touching it gives me the willies. I figure I'll just let it fall apart on its own and burn the pieces."

O'Meara looked back at the sign as a cloud passed overhead. For the briefest second, the letters seemed to squirm, like earthworms on the ground after a rain. He blinked and the sign was back to its original form.

"See what I mean?" said Clemson.

"See what? It was a trick of the light."

"Believe what you want." The old man nodded at his tractor. "I got to get back to work now."

"Of course," said O'Meara. "Thank you very much for your time."

When he'd climbed on the tractor Clemson shouted, "Find your daughter and don't take no for an answer. If she's with those people, get her away from there."

As he slipped the photo into his pocket, O'Meara shouted back, "I can't kidnap her."

Clemson started the tractor's engine and said, "Then I'm sorry for you both." As he drove into the orchard, O'Meara went back to the Suburban and started again for Garfield.

But he'd missed the carnival there too.

As he drove, Lucy's face drifted through his mind like a time lapse photo on TV. Lucy from when she was an infant, morphing to a toddler, then a schoolgirl, then graduation and preparation for college. She hadn't wanted to go to the one where he ran security which, he supposed, was to be expected. But the school where she got a scholarship was all the way in New York. They'd fought about her going and, after a while, they fought about her staying. It felt like toward the end fighting was all that was left to them. At night he thought about her as a little girl, pulling her into his lap and telling her stories. Winnie the Pooh. The Cat in the Hat. What life would be like when they finally lived on the moon. His wife's disappearance had hit them both hard, especially Lucy, but the stories seemed to help.

An image of the squirming letters on the sign pushed its way into his thoughts for a few seconds.

Nothing, O'Meara thought, *in this world is right. Sometimes it seems like all that's left for a man is confusion and anger.*

He stopped for gas on the outskirts of the town of Manor. There wasn't any real need to fill up yet, but he wanted to walk around for a minute and, even though he swore he'd quit, have a smoke.

The gas station was the kind for long distance drivers and truckers, with a large grocery section attached. The sun was starting to go down, but there were no other vehicles in the parking lot other than a battered white and blue Camaro by the employees' entrance. O'Meara started the gas pumping and went inside to walk the aisles while the van filled.

A bored-looking young man sat behind the counter reading a motorcycle magazine. The interior of the grocery was cool and pleasant, but one of the overhead lights near the rear of the place winked and buzzed. The intermittent shadows almost looked like there was someone back there tailing him, but when he looked the aisles were empty.

At the counter, O'Meara set down a package of little chocolate donuts and a Coke. Before the kid rang him up, he also asked for a pack of American Spirits. As he got out his wallet to pay, he noticed a flyer for the carnival taped to the back of the glass door.

The bored young man told him how much he owed and O'Meara handed him the cash. He said, "The carnival over there. Did you go?"

The young man didn't look up as he counted the change from the till. "Sure did," he said. "Best night of my life."

O'Meara put the change in his pocket. "Really? Someone else told me that he hated it."

Grinning, the young man said, "Not me. It was like an Iron Maiden video in there. Fire. Monsters. Clowns that make Juggalos look like little bitches. This teacup ride that shook like it was going to fly apart. And the best part? Pussy. Lots of pussy."

O'Meara looked at him.

A nervous expression spread across the young man's face. "I'm sorry. That was disrespectful language to use."

It sure as hell was, O'Meara thought. But he wasn't going to let this idiot kid off that easily. "Tell me more about them," he said. "The girls."

"Yeah?" said the young man and he relaxed. He leaned closer to O'Meara and spoke quietly. "There were girls everywhere. Girls with the shows. And they'd do anything. I mean anything. And for free. You didn't have to buy them anything or give them weed. Not that I carry weed with me." He looked nervous again.

"That's good, son," said O'Meara. He quickly flashed his security guard badge. If you looked for more than a second it was obvious that it wasn't a police badge, but the kid behind the counter didn't strike him as bright enough to ask to examine it. "Keep talking. Don't skimp on the details. I'm not shy."

Smiling lopsidedly, the young man continued, "Sure. I partied all night with those girls."

"Did you see anything or did anything unusual happen while you were partying?"

"There was one thing. These three girls and me were starting to get it on and when one got my pants off another got real excited and—I swear to god—bit my leg."

"Bit? What do you mean bit?"

"I mean the stupid slut *bit* me. Took a little chunk out of my thigh."

Maybe the kid was too high or too dumb to take seriously, thought O'Meara. He wondered if he would show him the leg wound if he asked. The buzzing light in the back of the store was giving him a headache. Maybe it was time to come at it from a different angle. "Did you go to a doctor?" he said.

"No," the kid said. "One of the other girls started blowing me and I forgot all about it."

O'Meara put his hands on the counter and looked the kid in the eyes. "Did it occur to you that the girl who bit you might have been sick? That any of the girls could have been sick?"

The young man went a little pale. "No sir. I just put some Bactine and gauze on it."

"Go see a doctor tomorrow. Get a blood test."

"If you think I should."

"I do." O'Meara put Lucy's photo on the counter and opened the American Spirits. "While you were at the carnival, did you see this girl?"

The kid stabbed the shot with a finger. "Fuck yeah. She's the one who bit me."

O'Meara quickly picked up the picture and held it in front of the kid's face. "Look again. Be careful how you answer. *Is this the girl you saw?*"

After blinking a couple of times, the kid seem to deflate a little. "I mean it was dark and I was kind of messed up by then. I can't be a hundred percent sure."

He put the photo down and said, "But it's possible."

"Yes sir."

O'Meara thought it over. The idiot kid had been high and getting all kinds of attention from pretty girls. Probably a group of pros working the carny circuit with the show. Instead of asking if the kid got bitten, he should find out if he still had his wallet after the party.

When O'Meara looked again, the kid was staring at the photo. "You have something else to say?"

The kid nodded. "The more I look the more it seems right. It was her. The whore bit me like a damn vampire."

It took all of O'Meara's self-control not to pull the kid over the counter and beat him bloody right then and there. His hand even twitched to where he kept the riot baton on his work belt. Instead of hitting the kid, he put away Lucy's photo and said, "Bag up my shit."

Outside, O'Meara took a few deep breaths and held the still hot, humid evening air in his lungs. He set the bag in the van and unhooked from the gas pump. His temper told him to go back inside and settle things, but he knew the time wasn't right. Too many lights. Too many cameras. Anyway, he knew where the kid worked and what his car looked like. He could settle up later. Still. He thought about the tools in his suitcase and everything he could do with them. Everything he *would* do. Once he found Lucy, he'd come back, take the boy's soul and give it to Mr. Umbra. Then they'd walk the pale light path to the moon. The thought calmed him and he could breathe again.

Driving onto the freeway he thought, *Lucy, where are you and what have you gotten yourself into? Is it drugs? Is it money? I'll fix it for you. Eat all their souls and spit them out on the moon path. But before then, I'll have my fun with them first.*

He lit one of the cigarettes.

Sure as hell, I'm going to get some enjoyment out of this madness.

LATER, O'MEARA STOPPED at a highway cafe for dinner. His eyes were weary from the road and the donuts he'd bought earlier were inedible. He knew he needed food if he wanted to keep going. There were two empty stools at the far end of the counter. A highway patrol officer sat on the third stool quietly eating a burger. O'Meara took the last stool and ordered a cheeseburger, fries, and a strawberry milkshake. After the waitress left, he looked at his watch. It was later than he thought. His eyes burned and the headache he'd picked up at the gas station light refused to let go. He touched his napkin into the ice water the waitress had left and rubbed its coolness across his forehead, hoping that would help.

Someone said, "Are you all right?"

O'Meara turned and saw the highway patrolman looking in his direction. He nodded to the man. "I'm okay. Just can't seem to shake this headache."

The officer took a small tin from his breast pocket and held it out. It was aspirin. O'Meara took three and dry swallowed before handing the tin back to the officer. "Is aspirin regular issue for the highway patrol these days?"

The officer smiled faintly. "No, but I always have some handy. It helps keeps the drunks with hangovers quiet."

"Thank you for the pills."

"Thank you for not being drunk."

O'Meara laughed a little at that. The trip was so surreal that he'd felt a little drunk for a good part of the day. He knew he wasn't going to last much longer. "Are there any decent motels around here?" he said.

The officer thought for a minute. "On the highway? There's the Rancho Grande. Lot of truckers stay there. It's not much, but it's clean."

"Thank you." It was such a relief to talk to a sane man. "I'm David O'Meara."

The patrolman wiped his hand on his napkin and they shook. "Mal Jackson," he said. "You just passing through or are you staying a while, because there's nicer places than the Rancho Grande in town."

O'Meara shook his head. "I'm just passing through. Trying to catch up with a carnival that passed through here."

Jackson rolled his eyes. "That place. What a bunch of freaks. I can't say that anyone around here misses them."

He'd been wondering why the carnival moved from town to town so quickly. Maybe that was the reason. They pissed off people everywhere they went. "Did you have trouble with them? Any kids from around here get mixed up with the place?"

Leaning an elbow on the counter, Jackson said, "Are you on the job?"

He knew what the question meant and hearing it ruined the good mood he was working on since sitting down. "No," O'Meara said. "I was on the force for two years, but no more. I'm just a college security guard these days."

"There's no shame in that," said Jackson. "Why did you leave?"

O'Meara thought about his answer carefully. Lying was easy with most people, but this was a law enforcement officer. A seasoned one, too, by his look. He had to say it just right. "I couldn't take the politics. Crooked promotions. Who got assigned where for how long depending on who laughed at the brass's jokes. I don't mean to sound bitter, but I joined up to take care of people, not kiss ass." What O'Meara didn't say was how grateful he was for all he learned during those two years. He couldn't do his work without that knowledge. Moving quickly and randomly. Never taking the same kind of person twice in a row. And always taking them in different ways so it was hard for the authorities to zero in on a pattern. His secret heart wouldn't be nearly as dark as it was if he hadn't been careful all these years.

Jackson leaned across the stool that separated them and whispered, "I know what you mean. It's no different out here. I mean, my station is better than most, but we have the same problems. Maybe everywhere people like you and me work are like that if you dig deep enough."

"Thank you for saying that. Sometimes I'm ashamed for not sticking it out," said O'Meara, another careful lie.

Jackson moved upright again and took a bite of his burger. After he swallowed he said, "You know, we arrested one of those carnies. Aaron something."

"Do you still have him?" said O'Meara.

"That," said Jackson. "No, we don't. Someone fucked up somewhere, somehow. I blame all the cutbacks the state's been doing. These days, we barely have enough people to file the paperwork."

"So, where is he?"

"God knows."

"You mean he escaped?"

"It baffles the hell out of me," said Jackson. "He wasn't that bright. He must have had help. Maybe someone on the inside."

"What did you arrest him for?"

Jackson wiped his mouth again, pushed the remains of his food away, and turned to face O'Meara. "The crazy son of a bitch killed and skinned a full-grown bull. No easy feat, as I'm sure you can imagine. Slit its throat from ear to ear. Ate pieces of the raw flesh. We found him in the morning wearing the bull's skin and horns. He was praying and crying before some kind of altar he'd set up in the woods. There were dolls all stuck through with nails, razors, and old saw blades."

Hearing that the carny had eaten the bull's flesh made O'Meara think of what the gas station kid said about being bitten. But it felt too early to pursue that. Instead, he said, "Did he say why he did it?"

Jackson signaled for his check. "He talked about the iron man."

That made O'Meara stop for a minute. "Like the guy in the movies?"

"That's what we thought at first too but, no, this is someone else. According to Aaron, someone a lot scarier."

First Clemson's metal man and now an iron man, O'Meara thought. And a flesh-eating lunatic. *My god, Lucy. Who have you fallen in with?*

"I wish I'd been the one to find him," said O'Meara. "I'd love to have questioned him."

Jackson said, "I can do the next best thing. I have a friend of his locked up right now. Want to talk to him?"

"You would do that?"

Jackson laid out the money for his dinner. The waitress took it and he said, "A favor. Cop to cop."

O'Meara smiled at him and said, "Thank you so much."

"Have Cindy box up your food and I'll meet you outside. You can follow me to the station."

"I'll be right out."

He signaled for the waitress to put his food in a to-go container and paid quickly. Whether it was the aspirins or the offer to talk to the prisoner, O'Meara's headache had vanished. When he got in the van, Jackson blinked his lights and they slid out onto the highway.

On another night, in another place, he thought that Jackson's soul might have been an interesting one to take. He'd taken a police woman once, but that was a long time ago and in another state. It might just be time to take a male officer's soul. Would it feel or taste different? Once he got Lucy home and dealt with the idiot at the gas station, it might be time to go hunting for someone in a uniform.

The highway patrol station was just a few miles up the road.

The place was larger than O'Meara had expected, but it was largely empty. A dozen desks sat vacant, the computer monitors dark. A woman in a patrol uniform waved to Jackson from across the office and he raised his hat to her.

"Is it always this empty?" said O'Meara.

"Not always," Jackson said. "Like I mentioned, we're understaffed, but it's also shift change. Most of the new crew isn't here yet. A good time to go in the back. Follow me."

They went around the desks and down a corridor past offices, many of which were dark. Jackson nodded to a few more co-workers and then they were in the back area with the cells. The familiar smell hit O'Meara even before Jackson had opened the door. Sweat, shit, and bleach. *Jailhouse perfume*, he thought.

Like the office, the cells were mostly unoccupied. The few prisoners O'Meara saw looked mostly like drunks sleeping one off, though down the row were a couple of large men with black eyes and split lips. *Bar brawlers. The bums look the same everywhere you go.*

They went to the last cell in the row. A man lay on a cot inside, but he wasn't asleep. "Get up, Flint," said Jackson firmly. O'Meara liked that the jailbird did what he was told. Jackson continued, "This is Mr. O'Meara. He wants to talk to you about Aaron."

"Why should I?" said Flint. His eyes were on O'Meara. "He don't look like a cop."

"You should do it because I asked you nicely," said Jackson. Flint's eyes moved back to him.

"You didn't really ask me at all."

"All right, then pretty please with sugar on top and I'll see you get an extra cup of coffee in the morning."

"Milk too?"

"Would you like me to stir it for you?"

Flint grinned, showing crooked yellow teeth. "That won't be necessary, sir," he said. He moved forward and leaned his whole body against the bars so his face was framed in dull metal. "Well, what is it you want to know?"

"Everything about Aaron and the carnival," said O'Meara.

Flint shrugged. "What's there to say? I don't know nothing about stuff he did to some cow."

"Bull," said Jackson.

"Could be a goddamn moose for all I care."

"I don't care about any of that," said O'Meara. "Tell me about the iron man."

The prisoner grunted. "Aaron was a crazy fucker. Always has been, since we were kids."

"What did he say?"

"He told me god lives at the carnival," said Flint. "The iron man. He said the guy was *the* God or *a* god. Some shit like that."

"Is that why he left the carnival?"

Flint made a face. "Hell no. He loved the guy. But he hated the place. Said he was scared all the time. Look, all that happened was that he got high and the carnival left without him. He said he tried to go home, but changed his mind. Only it was too late. The carnival didn't want him anymore."

"I see." O'Meara thought for a moment.

"Does any of that make sense to you?" said Jackson.

O'Meara saw the letters squirm on the farmer's sign. "I don't know."

"That carnival was spooky as fuck and the chicks were worse," Flint said. "If you're looking for it, you're dumber than Aaron. At least he had the brains to run the other way."

"How did he get out of here?" said Jackson.

Flint made a comical, imbecilic face and spoke in a childish voice. "Gosh, I don't rightly know, now do I, officer?"

"All right, calm down."

"Yes boss," said Flint in the same voice. He turned and spat into his cell. In his normal voice he said, "Are we done here?"

Jackson turned to O'Meara. "Are we?"

He shook his head and stepped closer to the bars. "The map on the leaflet said the next town on the spot was Weir. Did you see them here or up there?"

Flint laughed. "Oh, they're not on the map anymore, boss. Too many people in too many towns complained about them, so they had to change plans. That's why Aaron said he couldn't find them. They've gone commando. Wild in the country."

O'Meara felt a stab of cold inside. If the carnival really had left the map, how the hell was he going to find them? "Did your friend, Aaron, say where they were heading next?"

"Why do you care so much?" said Flint, frowning. "Why don't you go home and watch a fucking movie?"

"Be nice," said Jackson warily.

"Fuck this asshole. You offer me coffee. Okay. What's this shitheel got for me?"

"Listen to me," said O'Meara. "My daughter is missing. You said yourself that there were bad people in the carnival. Lucy might be with them."

Flint laughed hard and loud at that. "Oh man. Poor little Lucy hooked up with them? She must be one dumb bitch."

"That's it, Flint. No coffee for you," said Jackson.

O'Meara edged toward the prisoner. "You should watch your mouth."

In a split second, Flint had his hands around O'Meara's throat. He threw his body weight back from the cell door, slamming O'Meara's head into the bars. The next thing he knew, Flint had let go and was sliding to the floor. When his vision cleared, he saw Jackson with his riot baton in his hand.

"That's it, Flint. You fucked up." He pushed his way into the cell and cuffed both of Flint's hands to the bars. Jackson put a hand on O'Meara's shoulder. "You want to press charges?"

It took a moment for him to find his voice again. When he did, it came out raspy. O'Meara said, "Do you know where the carnival is now?"

Flint let his head loll back against the cell bars. "Of course. It's where Aaron went when they took him out of here."

"Who took him out?" said Jackson.

"I don't remember."

O'Meara said, "Where are they? What town?"

"Why, they're right up yonder in fuck youville."

Jackson tapped the baton against his hand and said to O'Meara, "What do you want to do here?"

For the first time, O'Meara was scared for himself. This man Flint—*this trash*—had hurt him and taken some of his power. But he needed to get moving if he was going to find Lucy. Trying to figure a way out of the situation, he said, "I don't think I can."

Flint laughed quietly to himself.

"You can't let a man like him off after doing that," said Jackson.

Torn, O'Meara said, "I just don't have time."

Jackson stepped out of the cell and handed O'Meara the riot baton. "Then take care of business now."

Flint's face flushed. "Wait a fucking minute, motherfucker."

O'Meara was frozen. This wasn't supposed to be how things worked. Jackson handing him power and a mere beating for the man on the floor, with no chance at all of finishing him and taking his soul. What would Mr. Umbra think? Still, the temptation to hurt Flint was deep and hot.

From behind him, Jackson said, "You're still a cop in your heart. A protector. You have a responsibility to the community."

Flint kicked at him awkwardly with one leg. "Get this fucker away from me," he yelled.

O'Meara said, "I don't know if I'm permitted to do this."

"I'm permitting you. That's enough in here."

"Can't you do it?"

"Then what would it mean? You're the one he attacked. If I did it wouldn't mean anything."

O'Meara felt the lunar light recede in his head. His secret heart itched like fire. He felt weak as he let the baton fall to his side. "All right. I'll press charges."

"Faggot," said Flint. "I'm going to call my lawyer and tell him about this. I'll be out of here tomorrow night and when I am? I'm going to find your little Lucy and fuck right up her juicy ass. Tell her Daddy sent me while I'm doing it."

It was too much. Without thinking, O'Meara slammed the riot baton down on Flint, over and over until his face and chest were bloody and he lay curled in a ball on the cell floor. Finally, Jackson grabbed O'Meara's arm and took the baton away.

"Tell me where she is," O'Meara shouted.

"Tell him," said Jackson. "Or round two will be mine."

Flint uncurled painfully and looked up at the men. "Up north. Town called Sundown," he said.

"Are you sure?" said Jackson.

"Yeah," said Flint and his head fell back.

Jackson looked at O'Meara. "You got some blood on you. Go clean up in the officer's wash room right outside the cell room. Get out here and find your daughter."

"What about him?"

"I'll put him in with one of those two toughs guys up front. If anyone asks I'll say they got into a fight."

"I can't thank you enough."

"Go. The new shift will be coming in by now."

From the floor, Flint yelled, "I hope Aaron's god cuts you down, fucker."

Shaken, O'Meara left the cell area and went straight the men's room. Indeed, when he looked in the mirror, there were streaks of blood across his face and on his hands. A few spots on his shirt too. He turned on a tap but stopped before putting his hands under the water. Blood dripped from his fingers into the bowl. Slowly, he put his index finger into his mouth and when he drew it out it was clean. The blood offering wasn't Flint's soul, but it was a small measure of his power. O'Meara closed his eyes and felt the lunar road open. His heart stopped itching. He washed his hands and face and left through a side exit.

When he got to the van, he took off his shirt and put on a new one from his bag. O'Meara drove away and didn't stop until he was ten miles from the patrol station. Pulling onto the side of the highway, he turned on the overhead light and took out his map. He looked north on every road he could find until he gave up. There wasn't a Sundown anywhere.

I need a new map. A bigger one. And I need to get somewhere I can study it.

O'Meara thought for a moment about going back to the highway patrol station, but he knew that he'd worn out his welcome. There was nothing to do but hope Flint had been telling the truth about the town being north. He pulled back onto the road, his stomach queasy.

SMOKE STARTED BILLOWING from under the Suburban's hood a few miles outside of Taylor. He had to call AAA and wait an hour for a tow truck to take him into town.

The tension and frustration were too much. Lucy was his priority, but he knew that if he didn't truly replenish his soul soon it would be too thin to save her when the time came. It couldn't be the tow truck driver. *I need him.* O'Meara knew the trick was to be patient. He'd had dry spells before. *Calm down,* he told himself. *Patience is a virtue.*

But not for long.

THE SERVICE STATION owner was a friendly, grease-stained man named Ray who told him as gently as he could, "I don't have the parts for some of these newer models on hand. I can get one in town, but the store is closed by now. I'm afraid I can't get you out of here until late morning or early afternoon tomorrow."

O'Meara wasn't angry when he got the news. Instead, a kind of weary numbness settled over him. He simply said, "I understand."

"The good news is that the Rodeside, a nice little motel, is right down the road. Just a five-minute walk. A block over is the Buzzard Nest, a cozy bar with decent food."

"I appreciate it," said O'Meara. "By the way, do you have any Texas maps? Ones that go all the north to the border?"

"Sure," said Ray. He handed one to O'Meara from a rack by the door. "On the house. Hardly anyone uses them anymore."

"Thank you."

O'Meara took his boxed meal from the diner, his shoulder bag, and a heavy suitcase and walked the short distance to the Rodeside. There was no one at the check-in counter when he went inside.

"Hello?" he called toward an inner office. "Is anyone there?"

"Hang on a minute," said a brusque voice. O'Meara could hear tinny conversation coming from inside. Quiet laughter and applause. It was the sound of a television. When the last of the laughter died away the manager—a frowning bearded man—came out of the office. He didn't look at O'Meara when he said, "Checking in?"

"Yes. Just for a night."

O'Meara raised his eyebrows a little when the manager told him the price. He obviously knew that a man carrying food and his bags was stranded and had no choice where to stay. O'Meara pulled out his credit card and slid it across the desk.

"We charge an extra day for key deposit."

"That's ridiculous."

The manager tapped a finger on the counter. "Folks lose them or drive off with them in their pocket. I have to pay to make new ones. Of course, you can always sleep in your car."

It was a cheat, but O'Meara knew he was stuck. There was no way he could do what he had to do curled up in the back of the Suburban.

"Well?" said the manger impatiently. He glanced back at the office. "Look, my show is on and I can't pause it like at home. Take it or leave it."

"Will I get the key deposit back when I return it?"

The sound of voices came from the office again. "Yes, yes, you'll get your money. Wait here while I run your card in the office." It was a good five minutes before the manager returned. O'Meara knew that he was watching the show again and wouldn't return until there was a commercial. He opened the box and ate a few French fries while he waited. His milkshake was warm by now, so he threw it away in a trashcan by the door.

When the manager returned he set a key to room seven and the credit card on the counter. "Thanks," said O'Meara, but the manager was back in the office again.

He went to his room, he ate his lukewarm burger while studying the maps he had spread over the bed. There was a Sundown City, but it was way over by New Mexico. *That can't be right.* He even checked the parts of southern Oklahoma at the very top of the map. Still nothing. He tossed out the lukewarm remains of his food. O'Meara felt tired and weak. Nothing since Lucy's disappearance felt right. Home was unreal and the road felt tenuous, with each stop giving him something, but also taking away some of his certainty and power. He felt lucky that he'd taken a speck of Flint's soul back at the highway patrol station, otherwise he wasn't sure what state he'd be in.

He finally gave up on both the map and the food and walked along the road to the Buzzard Nest.

Inside, it was dark and cool. There were perhaps a dozen people, spread out among the tables and chairs. A few of the seats at the bar had lights above them. O'Meara settled into one of those and ordered a Corona. The bartender, a woman in a sleeveless Pendleton shirt, held up a glass. When he shook his head, she brought him the bottle. He thanked her, took out the map and began looking it over again. He drank the whole bottle without seeing a Sundown anywhere. The bartender was talking to a young man in a dirty John Deere hat down the bar a few seats. When O'Meara held up his empty bottle she took it away and gave him a fresh one. After she set it down, she lingered for a moment.

"You've been staring at that since you got in. Don't you have GPS on your phone?" she said.

"I do," he said. "But I prefer physical things. Things I can touch with my hands."

"You've been touching that map all night. Is it helping?"

"Not a bit. Someone gave me the name of a town. I need to get there, but I just can't find it."

"What's it called?"

"Sundown."

She shook her head. "I haven't heard of that around here."

"I'm not surprised," said O'Meara.

The bartender called down to the man at the John Deere hat. "Hey Claude. You ever heard of a town around here called Sundown?"

Claude strolled down to where O'Meara sat and dropped down onto the next stool. "Sundown? Nothing like that around here."

The bartender looked back at O'Meara. "Sorry. Wish I could help."

"Thanks anyway." He gulped down half of his Corona and thought about ordering a third, but without much food in his stomach his head was already beginning to swim. "Maybe this whole thing was a mistake. I should check with the police back home."

The bartender gave him a sympathetic look. "You lost something, haven't you?"

"Indeed, I have."

"Wife or daughter?"

O'Meara thought about saying both, but it didn't feel like a moment to try and be clever. "Daughter," he said.

"I'm sorry. I'm Jillian, by the way."

"I'm David."

"Nice to meet you, David. Sorry we couldn't be more help."

"Get a room, you two," said Claude. They both looked at him. He beamed at them and said, "Jillie here is getting ahead of herself. She can't help you, but I bet I can."

"How?" said O'Meara.

"Give me that map."

O'Meara handed it to him and Claude opened it across the bar. "You're looking for Sundown, only there ain't one, right?"

"I think we established that," said Jillian.

"Not so fast. See over here? Puesta del Sol. That's Sundown in Spanish. Your friend was either dumb or fucking with you."

O'Meara shook his head. Of course Flint had both given him the answer he wanted, but in the worst way possible. "I'll be damned."

"Won't we all," said Claude.

Jillian frowned. "You sure your daughter is up there?"

"I hope so. Why?"

"There's a lot of shady stuff in that area."

"Like what?"

"The only witch trials in the Southwest, for one thing," said Claude. "Bunch of gringo missionaries came in and put some local Mexican gals on trial. The women got off, but a few days later some old coot found them strung up on a tree on his land."

"Stop it," said Jillian sharply. "That's just fairy tales and you know it. Any killings up there nowadays are 'cause of tweakers cooking meth."

"What about the kids?" said Claude.

O'Meara looked at Jillian. "What happened to the kids?"

She crossed her arms and said, "Some kids disappeared. But that isn't all that uncommon around here. There's no work and kids today don't exactly find Taylor exciting."

"So, they're just runaways?"

"Of course."

"You're the expert on that, right Jillie?" said Claude.

"Shut up."

He looked at O'Meara. "I heard that some of those runaways wound up dead," he said, adding air quotes around "runaways."

"Will you stop it?" snapped Jillian. "Next thing you'll be saying a witch in a gingerbread house ate them."

"Just telling you what I heard. What everyone with an open mind knows about."

Jillian inclined her head at the door. "You're drunk, Claude. Time for you to go."

He got to his feet slowly, but instead of moving for the door he moved closer to O'Meara. Leaning an elbow on the bar, he said, "If I didn't give you the name of that town you'd never know where to look for your little girl. Don't you think that kind of favor deserves some kind of reward?"

O'Meara pulled a wad of bills from his pocket, peeled off a twenty and gave it to Claude. "I appreciate your help."

"Any time," Claude said, tucking the bill into his breast pocket.

"'Night Claude," said Jillian. He blew her a kiss on the way out. When he was gone she said, "Don't let him get to you. He's an asshole, but it looks like he's right about that town."

"Let's hope so," said O'Meara. Jillian gave him a sympathetic smile. Despite his earlier dark mood, he found himself liking her. He wondered what her soul would taste like. "I understand that you serve food here?"

"Sure do," she said. "The grill is closed now, but we open for breakfast at nine."

"That sounds great. I'll be back then." O'Meara paid for his beer, adding on a hefty tip.

Holding up the cash, she said, "Thank you very much. See you in the morning."

"Good night."

O'Meara was slightly annoyed as he walked back to the motel. His head was swimming, but a couple of beers shouldn't have hit him that hard. It felt like there was something squirming around his head, something that wasn't him or Mr. Umbra. He tried to shake it off. Probably just tired and worn out from worry, he thought. Things would be better in the morning.

An unlit vacant lot sat between the bar and the motel. As he passed it, two men stepped from the darkness. One was Claude and the other was a bigger man O'Meara didn't recognize. "Howdy again," said Claude.

"Evening. Thanks again for the help earlier," O'Meara said.

O'Meara started to walk on by when Claude got in front of him. "It really is dangerous territory where you're headed. That info I gave you might save your daughter's life. Don't you think that's worth more than twenty dollars?"

"How much do you figure I owe you?"

Claude put a hand on his chin like he was thinking. O'Meara realized that he couldn't see the big man anymore. A fist slammed into the back of his head and he dropped down to his knees. Someone kicked him in his ribs and he fell onto his side, curled in a ball. After a few more kicks, he felt someone's hand pulling the cash from his pocket. Then nothing happened for a while. O'Meara blinked and it occurred to him that he might have passed out for a few minutes. When he looked around, he was alone in the vacant lot. He crawled painfully to his feet and stumbled the rest of the way to his motel room.

Inside, he slumped on the bed and probed his sides. It didn't feel like he had any broken ribs, but there was a throbbing knot at the back of his head. He looked at himself in the bathroom mirror. His shirt was torn and filthy. There were some bruises around his left eye and long scrapes on his right cheek. *Probably from when I fell.* Over all, he counted himself lucky. In the dark lot like that, and with two men working him over, he knew from experience that he could be a lot worse off. He wished he hadn't left his damn gun in the van.

He took off his shirt and splashed some water on his face, then lay down on the bed. Sleep came quickly, but it wasn't pleasant. In his dreams, Lucy was with him, but when he tried her hug her her face squirmed like the wormy letters on the farmer's sign. Something loomed behind her, black and pulsating. When he reached for her she wasn't there but far across a field, hung from a tree like the old witches. He looked into the sky and the moon seemed to drift away from him, growing smaller as it went. O'Meara knew that he'd disappointed Mr. Umbra. It felt like the whole day—Hell, everything in his life since Lucy left—had been about him losing power. He could see Mr. Umbra on the moon, tiny and mournful as he drifted away. The sadness that hit him came from deep inside. His fear was total and gut wrenching, like a child watching a parent turn their back on them.

O'Meara awoke suddenly with tears on his face. They stung where they touched his scraped cheek. He'd brought a towel with him from the bathroom and he used it to wipe his face. As he did it, the sadness and fear was replaced with the kind of anger that unnerved him. It was reckless. The kind where rash men did stupid things. He sat up and took deep breaths until he got control of himself.

Patience is a virtue, he thought, *until it's not.* He put on a new shirt, picked up his heavy suitcase and walked around the motel. From what he could see through the windows, most of the rooms were unoccupied. O'Meara tried five doors before he found one that wasn't locked. *Mr. Umbra hasn't left me. Not completely.* He opened the suitcase on the far side of the room and gazed down on his tools in the moonlight that filtered through the open windows. They glowed with a magical light all their own. After he pulled the curtains closed, he set a pair of heavy Kevlar gloves on the table. Then O'Meara called the office for the manager to come up and put on a set of brass knuckles.

Later in his room he took a long, hot shower. When he was completely clean, he toweled off and took a safety pin and bottle of India ink from the heavy suitcase. In the bathroom mirror, he darkened another black spot within the secret heart tattoo on his chest. There were dozens of other marks, filling over half of the heart. The sting of the needle was familiar and comforting. It brought back good memories. How Mr. Umbra had come to him as a child and encouraged his first fumbling attempts at the work. Later, as a teenager, he grew more confident and cleverer. Then, there were the sweet years on the force and now. All it took was the flash of a badge to make most people stand still. Even the ones who ran were no match. O'Meara kept himself in good shape and worked out regularly for just such occasions. It still made him sad that his wife had discovered his work. She was a lovely, funny woman and when he took her, her soul was as sweet as candy.

Afterwards, his sleep was deep and relaxing. Mr. Umbra was there in his dapper black and white striped suit, his white face shifting through the phases of the moon. He called O'Meara to him and they walked the lunar path to the edge of a crater, where they sat together. Mr. Umbra put a hand on O'Meara's leg and gently said, "I thought I'd lost you, David. You seemed to step off the path."

"It won't happen again," said O'Meara. "When I find Lucy, when I find who took her, I'll drag his soul up here and lay him at your feet."

Mr. Umbra looked wistful. "That sounds lovely. It made me so sad when I thought you were gone. Remember what I said about stepping off the path."

"That if I did I'd fall into the abyss. The filthy trough filled with swine."

"Good boy, David. You were always my favorite." Mr. Umbra put an arm around his shoulder. It was both cold and reassuring. "Because of the fine ending to your difficult day, you may spend the night with me here on the moon."

"Thank you, Mr. Umbra. Thank you."

"But I need more souls, and so do you. Keep up with the work and soon your heart will be full and you can stay here forever."

O'Meara was so grateful that he didn't have the words to respond. Instead, they went to the manor house Mr. Umbra was building with all the souls his children brought him. The walls moved gently as if in a breeze as the souls shifted in their suffering. "You have to find Lucy soon," Mr. Umbra said. "Take her back from her captors. Then your power will be fully restored."

With those words, O'Meara woke up again. He fumbled his phone off the nightstand and dialed the number he'd found on the carnival leaflet. The call went to voicemail, but instead of getting a message that the box was full he heard, "Go home. She isn't here." The line went dead.

He checked the clock. It was four a.m. Ray said it would be late morning or early afternoon before he could get the van fixed. There wouldn't be food at the Buzzard Nest until nine. For now, he had time to rest and let some of his strength return. He'd feel better and stronger in the morning, and then he'd find Lucy. Tomorrow would be great. Tomorrow would be perfect.

He made it to the bar at nine thirty and Jillian served him very good scrambled eggs, toast, and bacon. There were other servers in the bar during the breakfast rush, so she hovered over him as he ate.

"Nice face," she said. "Looks like you got hit by a bus last night."

O'Meara took a sip of coffee and said, "I got hit by something. Your friend Claude and a big man he had with him."

"Randall," said Jillian in disgust. "Did you call the cops?"

"I don't have time for that. The moment the van is ready, I have to hit the road. Besides, it's embarrassing for a man in law enforcement getting his money taken by a couple of morons. The last people I want to see me like this are the police."

"I can understand that," she said. Jillian laid her hands on the bar and leaned in closer. "You weren't the only one who got what for last night."

O'Meara looked up at her. "Someone else got hurt?"

She looked around to make sure none of the other customers were listening. "The motel manager. He got killed in one of his own rooms."

"Last night?"

Jillian nodded. "I heard they found him cut up and wrapped in barbed wire like a bug in a cocoon."

O'Meara put down his fork. "That's awful."

"And that's not the weirdest part. They found his head across the room watching TV with the sound off."

"I guess I got off easy then."

"Did you hear or see or hear anything strange last night?"

O'Meara shook his head. "After the beating, I took a shower and fell right asleep."

"From the look of you I'm not surprised," said Jillian. "So, Claude and Randall jumped you." She seemed to think for a minute. "Those boys get wild sometimes. Still, it's hard to see them doing something like what happened at the motel."

O'Meara said, "I agree. They seemed like just another couple of punks. I've seen a thousand of them."

"Still. It makes you wonder."

He shrugged. "I mean, who really knows what's in another person's heart?"

Jillian stood back up straight again. "Have you checked on your car yet?"

"Ray said it would be ready in a couple of hours."

"Why do you think your daughter ended up in Puesta del Sol?"

"A carnival. I think she might have left with them."

Jillian looked around the room. "Breakfast rush will be over by then and lunch won't have started yet," she said. "What do you think about taking a passenger with you?"

O'Meara sat back in his seat. "You?"

Jillian looked down at the counter. "You might have noticed Claude giving me a hard time last night."

"I did. He seemed to imply that you might have a missing child too."

She half-smiled. "He ain't a child anymore. Just a big, reckless bundle of trouble," she said. "Abel isn't a bad boy, you understand, but I think he might have taken up with some bad people."

"Carnival people?"

"I don't know. The carnival passed through here recently. He went off right after that. The cops are supposed to be looking for him, but you know how useless they can be." Jillian caught herself and looked at him. "No offence."

"None taken. That's why I'm on the road. I doubt the police give a damn about Lucy."

"So, what do you think? I can leave the crew to run the place for a day or two. Take me with you?" She added, "There's an extra order of bacon in it for you."

O'Meara thought about it. Having Jillian along would complicate things, but it would be interesting. He sensed that her soul might be something special, something bigger and richer than the paltry thing he took last night. He said, "If bacon is part of the deal, how can I say no?"

Jillian looked happy and bright.

Yes, she is something special.

"Great. You let me know the moment Ray gets done with your car. That'll give me time to set things up here."

"It sounds perfect," O'Meara said. He sipped his coffee and thought, *things are finally going my way.*

RAY GOT THE van working earlier than expected. When O'Meara told Jillian, she came straight from the bar and they set out for Puesta del Sol.

After a day's driving, when the setting sun was just hitting the tops of the trees, they found the carnival in a large field on the outskirts of town. Even from the parking lot, the place looked seedy and decrepit. Paint peeled from signs and the rides O'Meara could see beyond the fence looked like ones that were old when he was a boy.

He drove around for a while before finding a space for the van close to the carnival's entrance. "In case we have to get out of here fast,"

O'Meara said. He took his .9mm from the glove compartment and slipped it into the holster at the small of his back.

"Do you think we'll need that?" said Jillian.

"Better to have it and not need it than the other way around."

"Good point. Let's go."

O'Meara took out Lucy's picture and after Jillian reassured him that she'd keep an eye for her too they split up.

The carnival was as crazy as the idiot kid at the gas station said it was. Girls in tank tops and skinny jeans gave him the eye. *Definitely pros.* The clowns were right out of a child's nightmare. The concession stands were filthy and the only people who went near it didn't buy anything, but left money on the counter and went around back. He wondered if the stand was dealing meth or weed. He'd heard that coke was making a comeback in some towns but it would be too expensive for a cheap setup like this.

The carnival acts weren't any better than the rides or clowns. There were half-assed magicians doing kiddie party tricks, a mangy petting zoo, and dancing girls who looked like they'd faint if they didn't get a fix in the next ten minutes.

The only real excitement he heard was near a tent at the far side of the carnival. A chipped, hand-painted placard nearby read RAZOR PIG—THE IRON MAN. The image on the sign was of a great black hog holding huge swords over its head. He thought it was like an ad for some old-time drive-in theater horror movie. Something for fifties teens to Ooo and Aah over. However, even the absurdity of the sign couldn't dampen O'Meara's excitement.

The Iron Man.

He pushed his way through to the front of the crowd.

Though Razor Pig wasn't quite the monster he'd been promised, he was still an imposing figure. He had a thick nose ring hanging from his septum, like something you'd see on an old cartoon pig. His skin glistened. It didn't look like sweat, but more like some kind of blue-black oil. Probably to darken him so that he looked more like the black hog on the placard. O'Meara was also sure the man was on steroids. Every one of his muscles bulged, but not like a bodybuilder. More like the giant weightlifters he'd seen during the Olympics.

To O'Meara's surprise, Clemson, the farmer, hadn't exaggerated Razor Pig's act. He invited people from the audience to examine the array of swords, straight razors, and daggers he had on stage. Each one nodded in agreement that they were real. Of course, it was just a carny trick. Mind readers did it all the time, he thought. Plant some people in the audience to convince the rubes that the act was on the up and up. Still, however Razor Pig was doing it, the act was impressive. He chewed up straight razors like candy bars and swallowed small knives whole. Someone from the crowd held up a rusty Civil War sabre. Razor Pig bit the thing in half and started eating it.

Now I know it's fake. No carnival, not even one this shabby and degenerate, would let someone walk through the crowd with a real sword.

But like any good magic act, O'Meara could understand how someone predisposed to foolishness might buy what they were seeing. All he really knew at that moment was that he was going to talk to Razor Pig and that no one was going to stop him.

Half an hour later, he met Jillian by the gate. She hadn't found any sign of her son or Lucy. He told her about finding the Iron Man. However, they still walked by the fortune-telling booths because he remembered that Clemson had said one of the girls might have been Lucy. But she wasn't there and all of the women in the booths claimed not to know her. They hung around the booths for another thirty minutes, hoping someone might spell the current fortune tellers, but none of them budged. When the sun set and the lights came on, they headed back to the van to wait for the carnival to close.

O'Meara was still sore from the previous night's beating, and the knot on the back of his neck felt hot. He and Jillian bought big cups of beer and drank them in the Suburban.

"I'm sorry you haven't found your boy," O'Meara said.

Jillian took a sip of beer. "This whole thing might be a wild goose chase. I was just guessing about the carnival. You know Colleen, a friend of mine, her boy ran off and joined the Marines without telling her. I'd like to think that Abel ended up there rather than here. Unfortunately, this is more his speed."

"You know, when things thin out in there, you look again while I talk to Mr. Pig."

She shook her head. "No, I'll come with you for moral support. That way maybe one of us might get what we came for."

They finished their beers and smoked and chatted for another hour before the carnival closed. O'Meara found himself attracted to Jillian, more than he thought he could be after his wife. Of course, having to deal with Lucy at home, there was no way he could start up any kind of long-distance relationship. But there were other ways to keep Jillian close to him, and taste her in ways even more intimate than sex.

When the lights dimmed and the final patrons were ushered out of the carnival, they left the van. The entrance was just a row of turnstiles that someone had run a chain across. O'Meara stepped over it easily, then helped Jillian over. He checked the gun at his back one more time, pulled his shirt over it, and they went to Razor Pig's tent.

He was alone inside, still glistening with oil, smoking a cigarette. He looked up when O'Meara and Jillian came in.

"So, you're the famous Iron Man I've been hearing about," said Jillian.

He barely turned his head in their direction. "It's not my favorite name among the ones I've used, but it brings the crowds in. And now it's brought you. What do you want?"

"If you answered your phone and gave straight answers, we might not have to be here at all," said O'Meara.

"I don't like phones. I like face to face, and you still haven't told me what you want."

"My daughter."

Razor Pig dropped his cigarette and ground it out with his boot. When he came over, he loomed over them. O'Meara was happy that he'd brought his gun.

Razor Pig laughed. "We all want someone's daughter." He glanced at Jillian. "Or son. But there have been so many. You're going to have to be more specific."

O'Meara held up the photo. "Lucinda O'Meara."

Razor Pig grinned and pointed. "Lucy! Yes, she's here."

"I want to see her."

"And Abel Stone. Is he here?" said Jillian.

Razor Pig looked her up and down. "I know him too. Lovely children. Tasty, if you take my meaning."

"Stop talking and get them here," said O'Meara. The back of his neck was throbbing, and he was dizzy in the same unnerving way he was the night before. Maybe the heat, he thought. Maybe the beer.

"Sure," said Razor Pig. He dialed an ancient flip phone he took from his pocket. It was greasy with the oil he used on his body. "Are Lucy and Abel around? Good. Have them come to my tent. I have a surprise for them." He sat down on one of the sets of bleachers that took up half of the tent. "Sit down. Make yourselves comfortable. This might take a minute or two."

"No thanks. I'll stand," said Jillian.

"Me too," said O'Meara.

Razor Pig narrowed his eyes at him. "You sure about that, Hoss? You don't look so good. The heat getting to you? Be careful. You don't want to fall on your face and scare Lucy."

"I'm fine." But he wasn't. The inside of his head squirmed. Razor Pig stared.

A flap opened at the far end of the tent. A young woman and man came through. "Daddy?" said the young woman. "What are you doing here?"

"Abel," shouted Jillian, but he didn't go to her. He went over and sat down next to Razor Pig.

"What are *you* doing here, Lucy?" said O'Meara. "Who are these people? What hold do they have on you? If it's drugs or something, I'll get you any help you want."

Lucy hugged him warmly and said, "It's nothing. It's just that I've found a home here. This is where I belong. Abel too. We're finally happy."

Jillian took a few steps in Abel's direction, but when he cowered behind Razor Pig she stopped. "Is what she says true? You're here of your own free will and happy?" she said.

"Yes," said Abel, barely more than a whisper.

"You'll have to forgive him," said Razor Pig. "He's really taken to us. If you're here to take him home you're too late. He is home."

"It's true, Mama, I am," said Abel.

Razor Pig put a big hand on his head and tousled his hair. "You see, Mommy? He's with us now. If he was ever with you at all. Like dear

Lucy over there, they felt their lives were on hold. They were waiting for something. They were waiting for me."

Jillian frowned and her face turned red. "What have you done to them?" she shouted. "Is this some kind of cult? This man is a police officer. He'll drag your ass to jail."

Razor Pig laughed and stood, pulling Abel with him. "He tried that line on me already. But I know he's not a cop, just as I know that Abel is mine now."

Jillian rushed to her son, but Razor Pig got in front and shoved her to the ground. She scrambled back to her feet and ran back to O'Meara. "Give me the gun."

O'Meara put up a hand. "Hold on. We have to be smart."

Jillian was weeping now. "You have your Lucy. I want my boy."

"We'll get him."

She looked at Razor Pig. "He won't let him go."

"You're right," said the big man. "I won't."

"Wait a minute," said O'Meara. This wasn't how things were supposed to go. But it was too late. Jillian rammed her shoulder into his sore ribs, sending him to the ground. While he was there, she grabbed the pistol from his holster and fired six rounds into Razor Pig's chest.

When the bullets struck him, the big man grunted deep, like a hog. He staggered back a few steps, but didn't fall. Instead, he put his fingers into the red holes and slowly pulled, ripping apart the flesh of his chest. Jillian let out a short scream. His skin stretched, but when it broke open there was no blood, and inside his body there were no bones. Instead, he gleamed with decades of knives, razors, and sword blades. Razor Pig took a couple of deep breaths and spoke. "Abel. Go say hi to Mommy. Show her why you're really here."

"Abel?" said Jillian. She dropped the gun and held open her arms. The boy ran to her, but when he embraced her, she began to scream. Abel kept his face close to her and shook his head back and forth like a dog trying to kill a rat. Finally, he broke free with a mouthful of flesh from her throat.

Jillian fell to the dirty floor of the tent, gasping and gaping, coughing up blood. She kept a hand over the wound and never took her eyes off of Abel, even as he swallowed her flesh.

On his hands and knees, O'Meara finally knew where he really was. He'd been tricked off the lunar path and was in the trough with the swine now. There was only one way back to Mr. Umbra. Still, he had to ask the question.

"*Who are you?*"

Even with his body torn open, Razor Pig stood tall. He said, "I am Bereft. Void. The Devourer. I know you know my brother, Umbra. He brings people to one side of the moon and I to the other—the black side like a hole in the dark. The endless abyss. You think you've known power through him, but I am the real power. Ask me how I know."

"*How?*" said O'Meara.

"Because Umbra called you to him as a child. I, on the other hand, have led you here as an adult. A grown, whining animal." He crouched so that he was on O'Meara's level. "You want Lucy? Crawl to me now. Crawl like a pig."

O'Meara spotted the gun just a few feet away. There were still a couple of shots left in the magazine. He might be able to grab it if he leapt for it. Jillian had shot this beast in the chest. He would aim for the head. However, before he could crawl more than a couple of feet, Lucy pulled him upright.

"This isn't necessary," Lucy said to Razor Pig. "Let me talk to him."

She took him by the arm and pulled him down onto the bleachers. They sat there together for a minute and she held his hand. "I know all about Mr. Umbra, Daddy. I let you think I didn't, but I've known the whole time."

He looked at her. "How?"

"You told me about him when I was a little girl."

"No, I didn't."

"Yes. After Mom disappeared, you just pushed it from your mind. I know all about him and the souls on the moon."

"I don't remember any of it."

She set a cool hand on his cheek. It didn't sting the scrapes. "You said that I would meet him too. When it never happened, you told me it was all right. You knew him well enough for the both of us."

O'Meara looked down. "I'm sorry it never happened for you. He's wonderful. All light and peace and joy forever."

"You also said that one day you'd take us to the moon together. Like the way you took Mom?"

He shook his head, holding her hand tight. "No. Never that way. Not you."

She laid her forehead against his. "When I was little and you told me about Mr. Umbra, you drew a heart on my chest in ballpoint pen. You told me it was my secret heart and that it would link us forever. But don't you remember what happened?"

"No, baby. What?"

"It washed off." She laughed. "I'm heartless. Like Pig."

The big man stood behind Lucy. "You bring souls to the moon for your god. But I don't wait. I'm here and I eat every soul I touch. Every one that comes unto me."

O'Meara looked at Lucy. "You too?"

She cocked her head slightly. "Do you mean have I given up my soul to Pig or that I eat souls for him?"

"Both. Neither. I don't know." O'Meara's head pounded as his strength ebbed away. All his work for nothing. But Pig was so close.

Maybe I can still reach my gun.

He tried to lurch away from Lucy, but she held him tight. Without looking, she reached back into Pig's chest, grabbed a knife, and plunged it deep into her father's secret heart.

O'Meara fell back against the bleachers and looked up. He could just make out the moon through a gap in the top of the tent. As Lucy, Pig, and Abel began tearing into his flesh, others closed in hungrily around him. The pretty girls in tank tops. The fortune tellers, ticket takers, clowns, and the men who ran the concession stand. He barely felt his devouring. O'Meara understood that he'd moved into Razor Pig's domain, a realm beyond ordinary pain—for the moment. He looked up again to see Mr. Umbra turn his back on him. The lunar path began to fade until it was gone. Then there was nothing but the sounds of animal grunts and a cold and endless fall.

Skin Magic | *P. Djèjí Clark*

Makami stumbled, almost falling. The orange-colored cat he had nearly run over went still, the hair on its back raising. Its eyes reflected in the night, seeming to ask what bit of chance had caused their paths to cross in the sand-ridden backstreets of this small town, which only rats and shadows should have called home.

The answer came at the sound of heavy footsteps from somewhere far too near. Makami resumed his run, turning a corner while daring a glance back. The empty streets did not fool him; he was still being hunted. Who his pursuers were and their purpose in this mad chase was what baffled him.

He had noticed them earlier, like two jackals creeping after prey. They kept their distance, but their intent was too obvious. Makami had been a thief once—in fact, a rather good one. He had followed those he marked whole days, tracing their routines until he could predict their every move, waiting until they were most vulnerable and distracted to take his prize. It was done so seamlessly, most were not aware of the theft until he had long departed. Others however were not so artful—choosing to cudgel their victims senseless or leave a blade between their ribs, before seizing what they wanted.

Still, wrapped in torn and tattered clothing, Makami could find little to mark him as worthy prey. Unless these thieves were so desperate they now took to robbing paupers and beggars, these men hunted something more. But what? Had some merchant gotten wise to food he daily snatched at market? Unlikely. He could manage such simple sleight-of-hand in his sleep. Besides, the scraps were barely noticeable—certainly not enough to keep his belly from crying to him each night. No, these jackals were after more. He only wished he knew what.

The pain was sudden. One moment he was running, the next he was on his back. Bits of light danced before his eyes and he scrambled to get his bearings. Lifting a hand to his brow he felt something warm, trickling from where he knew a wide gash had opened upon his dark skin. Blood. Something had struck him as he rounded a corner, right across the face, with enough force to send him crashing down.

Dazed, a dark form took shape in front of him. It was a man—a very big man. His rounded head was cleanly bald, making it look as if his entire body were covered in one sheet of ebony. He gazed down with a scowl, pulling his spread out features closer. Bulbous and stocky, he had shoulders like an ox and meaty arms that Makami guessed were just as strong. In one hand he held a misshapen staff of wood crowned with a thick knot. Long dark cloth encircled his waist, covering his legs and coming to his ankles. His torso was left bare—save for two hide straps that crossed his chest. Up to three knives were tucked inside, their blades gleaming like sharp teeth. Little doubt about it, Makami thought grimly, this was definitely a jackal.

"Stay down," he growled, lifting his cudgel threateningly. His breath was labored and his massive chest heaved with considerable effort. "Should hit you again for putting us on such a chase." He looked up at the sound of approaching footsteps. "Over here! I have him!"

Still too dazed to turn around, Makami waited until the new arrivals came into his field of vision. Two more men. The jackal pack was complete. One was muscular, dressed much like his larger companion. He paced the small space, dull yellowish eyes threatening danger. The third man bent to his haunches, his dingy tunic parting just below the knees as he balanced his slight weight. He ran a hand across the triangular patch of hair atop his scalp, smooth brown forehead furrowing in thought. His bright inquisitive eyes remained fixed on Makami—as if trying to discern something. After a moment he broke into a grin, displaying perfect white teeth unnaturally large for his wiry frame.

"Now that wasn't so hard," he said. "Good thinking Ojo, leaving you out here ahead." He continued to grin at Makami, which seemed even brighter than the gold-hooped earrings he wore in each ear. "Didn't know there were three of us eh?"

Makami didn't answer. This was gloating, not a question. These men were decidedly not thieves. They all spoke trader's tongue, each tinged with differing accents. So they weren't locals either.

"Still say we should have waited," the big man grumbled. Makami noted something in his voice. Was it…worry? "We were warned—"

"Oh stop your old woman talk Ojo," the smaller man said impatiently, coming to his feet. "Doesn't look like much to me and we took him easy enough. We'll keep him locked tight for the next few days." A new light came into those bright eyes, reminding Makami of a ferret. "Or, maybe we might get more for him ourselves…"

Makami frowned. Get more for him? Were these men slavers?

"I don't know Matata," the big man said. Yes, there was definite worry there. "What do you think Jela?"

Their silent companion only shrugged, those yellow eyes trained on Makami. "Matters not to me." His accent was so thick it was obvious these lands were foreign to him. And for the first time Makami glimpsed his teeth—each of them filed to sharp points, giving his mouth the appearance of a shark. "Whichever one brings us the greater payment." He pulled one of the knives strapped to his chest, aiming a deeply curved blade directly at Makami. "You. Show it to me."

Makami stared up at the man perplexed. Show him? He shook his head, not understanding.

"I will not ask you again," the man warned, his voice betraying an edge as sharp as his cruel-looking blade. "Show me what lies beneath, what is on your chest—I want to see it myself."

The blood drained away from Makami's face at the man's words. How could these men know about what he had taken such great effort to conceal? And if they did, to ask such a thing, were they mad? Beads of sweat broke out across his skin as for the first time, he truly became frightened.

The man scowled deeply, displaying his sharpened teeth. With his free hand he delivered a blow, snapping Makami's head back and filling his mouth with fresh blood. Suddenly numerous hands were upon him. A blade flashed and there was the sound of cutting cloth. Summoning what strength was left in him Makami attempted to twist away from his attackers. But the big man was true to his earlier threat, rapping the back of his skull once with the cudgel. The blow crumpled him, leaving his head dizzy with new pain. Listless, he felt as the shirt that covered him was pulled and ripped until it lay at his waist in tatters. He was left on his knees, chest now bare as his captors stepped back to admire their handiwork.

"Oja!" the big man exclaimed in his native tongue. "Curse my eyes! Are they moving?"

Makami closed his eyes, not needing to look down at his chest to know what the man was talking about. They were markings, crimson lines and arcs etched into a circle upon his dark skin. And like always, they were moving—sliding across one another in a chaotic dance, spinning about a hollow center as if searching for order. He could feel them, whether awake or in slumber, always moving just beneath his skin. They had become a part of him—his own never-ending curse.

The muscular man, the one they called Jela, came forward, pointing the edge of his blade directly at the markings.

"No," Makami pleaded. "Please. Do not..."

"See here Jela," the smaller Matata laughed. "He thinks you will gut him like a goat."

The muscular man grunted. "He is worth more alive than dead. Only wanted to see what all this trouble was over." His dull yellowish eyes followed the crimson markings that continued their peculiar dance. Grabbing Makami by the chin, he lifted his head until their gazes met. "How did you come across such a thing?" he asked. "How do you make them move?" Getting no answer his tone became derisive. "Cease your trembling. We are not the ones you should fear."

Makami glared back at the man. Fear them? No, he did not fear these men—he feared for them.

Already the markings etched into his chest had begun to move faster. They burned now, the pain building quickly until it felt like hot irons seared his skin. The arcs and lines were coming together, placing themselves into a pattern like a puzzle. His captors stared at the markings, mesmerized by the display. He tried to speak to them, to warn them to run, but the agony that now consumed him stole his speech. As the markings finally settled and went silent, he knew it was already too late.

"What is this?" the muscular man whispered. He brought the tip of his blade to touch the new symbol that the markings had formed onto Makami's chest. The knife pushed through the pattern with ease.

What should have been human skin rippled as if it were water. The man quickly pulled his hand back, those yellowish eyes going wide. And then the nightmare began, again.

Makami felt the thick tentacle shoot from his chest, and watched as it wrapped itself around the man's neck. This part was always painful, and he screamed out now. More of the tentacle pushed out of him, a dull grey fleshy mass that reminded him of an octopus, only much larger. It squeezed tighter around the man's muscular neck, lifting him off the ground. Those yellowish eyes bulged as he dropped his knife, fingers clawing in vain at the coiling appendage while his legs kicked wildly. Behind him, his companions only stared in horror, backing away slowly—none daring to come to his aid. The doomed man let out a choked gasp of spittle and blood which was followed by an audible crack. His head fell to one side, hanging limply, looking like a swollen bit of rotten fruit. The rest of his body twitched in spasms as if celebrating its sudden and short-lived freedom, before going still.

Makami watched as a second tentacle emerged. Another quickly followed. And then another, until there were more than he could count. They pulled and heaved, making their way out of his chest in a constant stream, piling onto the ground before him. When the last of them flowed out of him he fell back, weakened and delirious with pain. As he lay there on his side, he gazed up at the nightmare he had given birth to.

The many tentacles were part of one being, a monstrosity that was only now rising to its full height, towering high above the remaining witnesses in the deserted alley. Nothing so immense should have been able to come out of his small body, but it had. Its many appendages writhed about, twisting and turning on themselves, burying away whatever lived within the horrid mass. The dead man in its clutches was pulled deep into its fleshy center, disappearing to whatever fate awaited him.

The smaller man, Matata, seemed to decide he had seen enough. Without a sound he turned, breaking into a run. As if sensing his movement a tentacle shot towards him, catching him by a leg. He cried out as he went down, his face hitting the ground hard. As he was pulled towards the writhing mass he tried to grab onto something, but only the dusty street gathered beneath his fingers. Between his bloodied and broken teeth he began to whimper, calling out a desperate prayer in an unfamiliar language to unfamiliar gods. Makami remained where he lay, listening to the man in pity. He himself had prayed enough in the past weeks for them all—and to no avail. Either the gods did not hear, or they did not listen. He watched as the hungry tentacles enveloped the small man, silencing his cries forever.

Only the big man was left. He stood there, his weapon dangling uselessly at his side. His eyes were wide, his mouth hanging open as he stared up at the great monstrosity before him in awe.

"Are you a god?" he whispered.

His answer came as the swarm of tentacles crashed down upon him, burying him within.

Makami shut his eyes, unwilling to watch any more. He knew he had nothing to fear. Moments from now, the nightmare he had unleashed would return, through the very way it had come. The pain would be so great he would black out. And the symbol on his chest would break apart, returning to the circle of crimson arcs and lines that would again begin their constant movement. That was the way it had happened before. And it was how it would happen again.

The fat man cursed in several mangled tongues as he lifted a long heavy stick, threatening to lash Makami with it. The two chins on his rounded face shook violently, as if joining in their owner's anger. Makami stepped back quickly, almost overturning a stand laden with earthen pots. He pulled what was left of his shredded clothing about his increasingly gaunt frame, lest it slip, revealing what he so desperately sought to hide. Turning away, he walked back into the bustling crowd of the open market who parted for him—their eyes lingering with disgust.

He must have looked a sight, barely clothed in filthy rags, the reddish dirt that passed for soil here caking his brown skin, and once well-coiffed bushy hair now matted into clumps. What he must have smelled like he dared not venture. That had been the sixth time he had been chased away, when all he asked for was work. He would do anything—haul goods, clean animals, even shovel offal—just so it earned him enough to leave this place. He had thought he would be safe in this drab town of mud-bricked buildings with dust-beaten roads, so small that foreigners more than often outnumbered locals. It was more a way station than a true settlement, a place for caravans and merchants to rest, water their animals and trade for supplies—before they ventured out into the open desert. He had expected to disappear in this isolated place, away from the large cities he had once called home. But the night past had shattered any such hopes.

He had stumbled from the alley earlier this morning, his chest throbbing in pain, and his head filled with the faces of the three men he had killed. Or the thing inside him had killed. *Is there a difference,* he condemned himself guiltily. More troubling, they had known about the markings, which seemed impossible. Those that saw the strange lines etched onto his chest never lived long enough to speak of them. Yet these men had known, and they hunted him—claiming they would receive payment for his capture. But who? What madmen would dare seek out such horror and death? He ran a hand across his chest absently, where beneath his torn shirt he could feel the markings gliding beneath his skin. He had no answers to these questions, but he had to keep moving, until he could not be found by friend or foe. It was better for him that way; it was better for everyone.

A familiar sound caught his ear, faint chanting and the beating of nearby drums. Curious he followed it, turning several corners until coming to an open clearing. There, in the center of a gathered crowd, atop a raised platform, several men pounded out powerful rhythms with their palms on ornately carved wooden drums. The instruments were slung across their bare chests, hanging at their sides where their palms could reach. Bright golden kilts embroidered with patterns hung from their waists to past their knees, offering a stark but fitting contrast to their dark bodies. Beside them were other men, these however covered in voluminous but equally brilliant colored cloth. They sat strumming and plucking their fingers across the strings of wooden instruments. But more captivating was the figure before them.

A woman stood in front of the drummers, dancing to beats with such ease and grace it seemed they had been created for no other purpose. Chest bare like the men that accompanied her, she wore only a girdle of beads and shells that covered her wide hips down to the top of her thighs. Muscles flexed and tensed across her coffee-colored frame as she swayed and shook, beads of sweat causing her oiled skin to glisten in the mid-morning sun. Her ornate hair was arranged in thick coils, held in place by rounded bits of gold. As she danced she sang loudly in some faraway tongue, calling to the drummers who responded back with their own chants. Small metal balls attached to her wrists and ankles rattled in accompaniment to her every move, blending into the music.

Makami watched entranced. The drums and dance reminded him of his own homeland, that he had left so long ago. No wonder they called to him. But even more so, the woman and her dance evoked other memories. *Kesse.*

He closed his eyes, swaying slightly as a rare bit of peace settled over him. Beautiful Kesse, whose rich laughter always tickled his ears. Kesse who would sing softly and dance for him in the morning as the sun crept into their room. How he loved to watch her hips sway, drinking in the way her ample backside jiggled as she glanced back and smiled brightly. How he loved to nuzzle his nose in her bushy hair, or trace his fingers across her mahogany skin as she slept beside him. Kesse, who had been his life, who was now forever gone. Dead.

The reality of that one word crashed in on him, banishing the fleeting moment of happiness. His eyes flew open, and he was struck with such deep anguish any other pain dulled in comparison. He would have cried, but there were no tears left to fall.

The drums suddenly hushed, and the dancing woman went into a still pose lifting her arms high. The gathered crowd erupted into cheers and applause, many throwing tiny sacks, most likely filled with gold dust or other valuables towards the entertainers. Armed men with swords and spears kept the delighted onlookers at bay, while smaller children rushed out to collect the tributes of praise from the ground. A tall man wrapped in rich cloth that barely hid his fat belly lifted a staff and cried out praise for his performers, urging the crowd to shower them with more gifts—to which they obliged.

"You have a fine ear."

It took a moment for Makami to realize the nearby voice was meant for him. He had become so accustomed to disgusted stares and curses, he did not expect conversation. A man walked towards him, a bright smile showing beneath a stark white beard that adorned his brown face. Hands clasped behind his back, his belly surged before him, as if trying to escape the white shirt beneath his long indigo robes. He came to stand before Makami, a gleam in his dark eyes.

"I was remarking on your ear for music," he said. Rather short and squat, he had to look up to meet Makami's gaze. "The way you swayed, your eyes closed, as if you could feel it more than the rest of us."

Makami didn't answer. He felt more than this old man could possibly know.

"Would you care to join me at my tent?" the strange figure asked. "I am returning for mid-morning meal. I have more than enough to spare."

Makami frowned now. This man was dressed well, not richly, but good enough to be a merchant or a trader. Why would he invite some filthy beggar from the streets to dine with him? He was suddenly gripped by fear, a hand clutching at his chest. Those men last night were to deliver him to someone. Could this be their paymaster? He stepped back slightly, eyes seeking a place to run. The old man must have noticed his alarm, for he lifted his hands in what was a common means of apology in these lands.

"The goddess burn my thick scalp," he admonished himself. "You must think me a rude old fool." He palmed his forehead before releasing it, nodding slightly. "Manhada, I am Master Dawan ag Amanani, of Kel Zinda. I offer you food and drink if you would have it, and do so in peace, under the sacred blessed goddess." He stopped and offered a smile. "Charity is favored by the goddess. And you look as more worthy company than these other men—whose tongues seem only gifted at haggling."

Makami took a pause to look the man over. The greeting was familiar to him—a ritual of the Amazi people, the desert-born—nomads who traversed the sands. Food and drink were offerings of peace, and were taken seriously, demanding that no harm would come to him under penalty of invoking the wrath of their gods. There was little safer oath he could ask for. As his stomach growled noisily, feeling as if it were folding in on itself, he found himself nodding—casting aside his inner doubts.

It was sometime later Makami sat upon the colorful and richly decorative rug, shielded from the hot sun outside a large tent, rubbing his sated belly in contentment. It had taken all his self-control not to ravenously devour all the food placed before him. Manners had forced him to eat gingerly. Still, he had turned away nothing offered and left the earthen plates piled and empty where he sat. He had nodded along, listening to his host talk—and the old man certainly talked a lot.

Master Dawan, as he had rightly guessed, was a trader. He bartered everything from fine fabrics to oils, making at least two trips each long season across the desert. Nearby his tents were at least four *baushanga*—great shaggy beasts larger than oxen with down-turned curving blue horns. They were slow and lumbering, but their hardiness made them the preferred pack animals of desert traders.

Now an elder man, Master Dawan claimed he had not spent his entire life in the desert. And that when he was as young as Makami, he had traversed far and wide, seeing and hearing of many wondrous things—from giant water serpents that lived beneath the seas, to creatures that were part men and part hyena, who roamed the scorched grasslands. Some things made Makami's eyebrows rise, like the people who worshipped the many-handed god who it was said stood upon a great stool that rotated even as he spun, forever laughing at some great joke, which kept the world turning with him. Other stories however—like the one related to Master Dawan by a fellow trader of lands beyond the known world, where white sand cold to the touch covered everything, and men with skin like a pig's belly and hair of spun gold draped themselves in furs, riding into battle covered in metal and armed with broad steel blades—were simply too much to believe.

"And this is a feather from the great bird I spoke of," Master Dawan said, "that lives high in the mountains of the East—so large it could snatch away a man." He passed the giant grey feather speckled with bits of red to Makami. The thing was easily as long as he was tall. He ran a hand across the long soft fibers, feeling the hollow quill beneath.

"Ah, more tea?" Master Dawan offered. One of his daughters had come to pour more of the warm liquid into small rounded cups of polished stone at their feet.

Master Dawan had several daughters, six so far Makami had counted, and there was a seventh out at market. All were fairly young, ranging in ages close to nearing the cusp of womanhood. At least four wore two long braids that fell forward at the right sides their heads, red and black beads adorning them, while tinges of indigo stained their lips—signs among the desert people that each would soon be ready for marriage.

As the girl knelt in front of them, mixing goat milk into his tea, Makami smiled and nodded thanks. She only regarded him coolly behind dark eyes surrounded by lines of black ink. That was the usual response he received from each of Master Dawan's daughters, who frowned or glared at him with open displeasure. It seemed they did not share their father's charity to seeming beggars—but they held their tongues as well as their noses.

Like most desert people, Master Dawan's daughters displayed a range of skin—varying from their father in either direction. The blessings of three wives, the old man had called them, all now gone—two lost to childbirth and one to the desert. Like her sisters this daughter was dressed in long robes of deep indigo that flowed down to her sandaled feet. Jewelry of crafted copper, silver and colorful stone adorned her everywhere, even tying into her lengthy braided hair. Most noticeable however were the markings. On her hands, arms, even her feet, were intricate designs and patterns etched in dark ink. The artistry was superb. But unlike his, these did not move. In all the fantastic tales Master Dawan had related, none came close to describing his curse.

"Beautiful yes?" the old man said, catching his gaze. "The work of my eldest daughter. She is quite gifted." He paused. "So then, friend Anseh," Master Dawan continued. "I have spoken at such length I have not heard your tales."

Makami took a deep sip from his tea. Anseh was his real name, from his people, the one he had been given. Whoever hunted him here, only knew Makami, the name he had taken for himself in these lands. After the past night, he had decided it was best he was Anseh once more.

"I am afraid my tales are not as grand, Master Dawan." Makami did not flinch at his own lie. The horrors he had seen could compete with the best stories.

"Where do you come from then?" Master Dawan pressed. "You speak the trader's tongue well, but your speech marks you as a man of the south."

Makami nodded, impressed with the old man's perceptiveness. "Far south, yes. But I have lived much of my life in the great cities of the west."

"Ah!" the old man said with a knowing wink. "That explains your love of music! Some of the sweetest sounds to grace my ears have flowed from those lands."

Makami nodded. "In the city of Jenna, I stood in attendance to the funeral of the late king. A hundred bards who played three-necked *koras*, a hundred drummers and a hundred more musicians and singers marched in procession as the king journeyed through the city, laid upon a bed of gold so heavy, that it was pulled by twenty stout war-bulls of purest white, their great horns too wrapped in sheets of gold. As he passed, the drummers struck their instruments in unison, while jombari players strummed gracefully, and the bards cried out so haunting a song, that the very sky opened and wept in mourning."

Master Dawan listened, rapt by the tale. Sitting back, he released a breath of awe, looking Makami over with a wistful expression. "I say these words not as insult friend Anseh, but for one who has seen such wonders, you now seem overcome by misfortune."

If it would not sound so bitter, Makami would have laughed aloud. Instead, he merely nodded.

"Well misfortune can be met with fortune," Master Dawan said. "Soon, before the rains begin, my daughters and I will journey across the sands to the east lands. If it pleases you, join us."

Makami looked at the man in surprise, taken aback.

"I can offer food and drink once more, but for so long a journey I shall expect you to work," he said sternly, "—and listen to my tales." At this he gave a smile and wink.

Makami smiled back. Perhaps his misfortune was easing, if only slightly. He opened his mouth to speak but was cut off as a sudden blur of feathers streaked past his vision. It was a bird—a large hawk. As Master Dawan held up a hand, it landed on a stretch of leather that covered the old man's forearm, extending its bright blue wings wide before folding them against its golden breast.

"Ah Izri!" Master Dawan greeted the bird brightly. "I trust you have brought my eldest daughter safely back from market."

The way the old man spoke to the hawk, Makami half-expected it to answer. Instead it turned its gold crested head before again stretching its massive wings, taking off in a flapping blur and soaring straight towards an approaching figure.

Master Dawan clapped in delight. "Praise you Kahya! You have trained him well!"

The approaching figure didn't answer immediately, dark piercing eyes passing over Master Dawan, and then Makami. A free hand moved to the veil which covered the figure's face, pulling it down to reveal a surprising sight—a woman. Dressed as she was in dust-ridden flowing trousers and a billowing shirt, she was easily mistaken for a man.

"He is your bird Father," she said, thick black hair spilling down to her shoulders as she pushed back a hooded shawl. "I do not see why I must take him with me each morning." With a series of clicks and whistles she lifted her arm and the hawk flew away, this time landing atop a wooden stand that stood beneath their covering. It perched there, gazing down at them.

"To watch over you dear Kahya. I trust Izri's eyes as well as my own."

The woman grunted and made a face, dropping down to sit cross-legged with them. "I handle myself well enough." She poured herself some tea, sipping it slowly before glancing to Makami. "Another stray?" Her nose wrinkled with a grimace. "Can you at least choose one who wears more than rags and smells better than a wet baushanga?"

"Ah this is friend Anseh," Master Dawan said, wincing slightly at his daughter's sharp remarks, "a traveler who has fallen on ill fortune.

I have offered him food and drink for work, from now through the crossing of the sands." Makami started to make his own introductions, but the woman abruptly turned away.

"That dog Zaba tried to trade me moth-eaten cloths for near twice their worth," she said, changing the subject. "But I bested him in the end. He parted with them for far less, and I received several jars of sweet oil as well—for nothing more than a few cones of salt. A worthy trade I think."

Master Dawan nodded in appreciation, turning to Makami with a grin. "My daughter's skills at haggling surpassed my own long ago." He rose to his feet. "I will make the arrangements for Zaba's goods. If you will, see to friend Anseh."

Makami watched the old man walk away, leaving him with his eldest daughter. The woman continued to sip her tea slowly, as if he were not there. After a long awkward bout of silence, he opened his mouth to speak, but once again she beat him to it.

"Father is fond of strays," she said, never looking to him. "Most do not last three days. Some less than two. It is the gift of free food and drink they are after, not true work. Stay on more than three days, and I will be impressed. Attempt to steal from us or take advantage of my father's generosity, and I will send you back to the streets with less fingers than you arrived. Touch any of my sisters, and you will lose more than that." Finishing her drink, she set the cup down and rose to her feet. "Now come, let us see if there is a way to rid you of that unbearable stench."

As she walked away, Makami hurried to follow. He did not doubt the sincerity of the woman's insults, or her threats. But fortune to him was rare in these times, and he was grateful for whatever form it took.

Three days passed. Then six. Then more than thrice that number. And Makami remained. The work was tiresome. He hauled heavy goods, combed the tangled mats from the baushanga's thick fur, and toiled at varied tasks from morning until the sun set. It was the kind of work he had shunned in favor of a life as a skilled thief. But after all his recent troubles, there was something about the simplicity of it all that brought a brief moment of ease.

Master Dawan was true to his word, providing food and drink—and endless stories—for his labor. And he provided clothing as well as shelter. Makami now dressed in loose trousers and a long white shirt. He covered himself in the blue robes familiar to the desert people, and even took to donning the *afiyah* veil, especially concealing himself when they went into town. He did not allow this small reprieve to lull him into complacency. Somewhere out there were men, who hunted him for dark purposes. And as long as he had to remain here, he hoped to put them off his trail.

In fact, he did a great deal to change his look. He shaved his bushy hair, leaving his scalp bare—opting instead for a beard which he wished would hurry and grow thicker. Reliable meals and hard work filled him out some, bringing back his sleek frame. Cleaned up, he looked a world apart from the vagrant first brought to Master Dawan's tents. And the old man's daughters took notice. Now and then he caught them stealing looks as he worked, whispering to each other before breaking into laughter. At first he thought himself the object of one of their jokes, until one of the young women blushingly slipped a bracelet of threaded blue stones onto his wrist—a signal of courtship. None of them actually thought him worthy of marriage of course; the daughters of even a poor trader could do much better. But he had proven attractive enough in their eyes to play in the game of mock courtship young Amazi indulged in.

He took care to hide away the blue stones quickly, lest Master Dawan believe he had improper intent upon his daughters. And Kahya's threats still lingered in his ears. If the eldest daughter was impressed at his having lasted so long, she never showed it. The most she spoke to him were orders and tasks, ignoring his attempts at conversation. Still, the days among the trader and his daughters were the most peaceful he had known for some time. The nights, however, were another matter.

The markings on his chest never ceased their dance. And at night they only grew worse, a burning weight that lay upon him. They moved about so furiously at times, he could not drift to sleep. And when slumber did finally claim him, only terrible visions came. Some were from the past—like the angry drunk who had followed him after a night of gambling, intent on fighting or doing worse, torn apart by the winged monstrosity that had flown from within the strange markings. Or the cutthroats that attempted to rob him, slashed to pieces by the claws of a beast he had unwittingly unleashed. And of course, Kesse was always there, sweet Kesse who he could not save from the evil that lived inside him. Other visions were of his fears, where vile things with dozens of legs and endless mouths crawled out of him like an army of insects, devouring Master Dawan and his daughters as they slept. Those dreams more than any sent him awake, and he would lie there, eyes wide open, waiting for the dawn.

It was some twenty-eight days later that they finally picked up and began their trek into the vast, hot sands. With the baushanga laden with goods they set upon a path Master Dawan claimed had been used by the Amazi for generations beyond measure. Makami had never seen so much sand, like an endless ocean that Master Dawan aptly called the Desert Sea. He himself could discern no path. Each way looked much like the next. But the old man seemed to know his way, putting names to sand dunes, and tracking their movements by the sun in the day and the stars by night.

For Makami, his first few days had been spent suffering from what the old man called "sun sickness." The relentless heat of the desert was unlike anything Makami had ever endured, and he had been forced to ride upon the back of a baushanga to keep from passing out. After a few days however, his endurance improved. And soon he was laboring under the scorching sun with surprising ease.

His days followed a familiar routine. He awoke to feed the baushanga, see to their needs, sat down to a meal with Master Dawan and his daughters and then helped pick up the tent to continue their trek. Most of his time he spent listening to Master Dawan recount endless tales. The old man seemed to always have something new, and never repeated himself. For a long while all seemed tranquil, until the storm.

Master Dawan claimed to sense it coming, and ordered them to pitch their tents in a circle, placing the baushanga on the outside. Even as they tied down their dwellings the normally inert desert filled with a brisk wind that only grew fiercer with each passing moment. By the time night fell they were in the midst of a raging sandstorm that blotted out even the moon, turning the already dark night into an impenetrable blackness.

Outside, his veil wrapped about him to ward off the stinging sand, Makami checked upon the slumbering baushanga. Stripped of their packs they curled their great shaggy bodies into balls, hiding their heads from the winds and acting as a buffer against the storm. Still, Makami had to go out and check upon them several times, to make sure the beasts were still properly tied down. Master Dawan claimed baushanga had been known to wander off in the middle of sandstorms. Disoriented they could travel so far it would take days to find them again. Making certain their harnesses remained fastened about them he fed each a bit of pinkish fruit Master Dawan claimed would keep them peacefully at rest. Barely lifting their heads against the sharp elements, they managed to down the fleshy fruit in noisy wet crunches between their block-like teeth.

Finishing his task, Makami picked up the oil lamp he had set beside him—the only light available in the thick sand-filled gloom. The winds were so strong he had to push hard against them, lest they knock him over. Stopping at his tent he lifted the lamp to look at the large symbol painted on the canvas. Smeared in goat's blood, it was a ward against evil Master Dawan insisted be placed on all their tents. He claimed that storms often brought out demons that dwelled in the deep desert, things that crept up while you slept and drained all your blood or enticed men to wander from their dwellings to their deaths with haunting songs. Whether the old man was merely superstitious, Makami did not know. But he had accepted the ward all the same. He knew that monsters and demons were all too real.

Rubbing at his chest he walked into his tent, pushing closed the flap behind him. Since the storm began, the markings on his chest had started to move about—much more than usual. It troubled him. He had long ago decided, were he to lose control again, he would abandon Master Dawan and his family and flee headlong into the desert, hoping to spare them from any danger. If it came to that, he would do so now, even in this storm. Better that than bring these good people harm.

Unveiling, he shook out sand from his afiyah before laying it flat upon the blankets he usually slept upon. He pulled off his shirt, dusting it off and throwing it to the ground. Standing there, with only the flickering lamp for light, he looked down to the arcs and lines which continued their odd movement across his skin. Putting a finger to them he traced their movements, as if touching them would somehow bring him insight. So engrossed he soon became, that he did not notice the figure entering his tent until too late.

"I wanted to remind you to wake up early, before the dawn, to push away the sand from the baushangas—"

Makami turned in surprise as Kahya strode through the flap he had left partially open. She carried a lamp and was wrapped in dark cloth. At sight of him she stopped speaking, her eyes going wide. With a silent curse beneath his breath he realized that he was still facing her, bare-chested and wearing only his flowing trousers. It took a moment—too long a moment—for his mind to tell his body to turn his back. And he knew immediately, she had seen. The lamp he had was small, but so was his tent, and it illuminated the space all too well.

"What is that?" he heard her ask breathlessly. Makami closed his eyes, cursing to himself deeply now, praying the woman would go away. Those thoughts were dashed as her hand touched upon his bare back.

"Stop jumping!" she admonished at his reaction. "Those markings on your skin—let me see!" When he did not respond, she released an indignant breath and pulled his shoulder hard, with more strength than he thought her capable. He turned to face her and she lifted her lamp to his chest, bending down to gaze at the markings in wonder.

"They move!" she breathed. Looking up to him, her dark eyes were wide. "How did you come by this? Did you make them yourself?"

"No," Makami managed to answer. "This wasn't my doing." He released a sigh. "It would be too hard to explain."

She gazed at him oddly, with a look that was different than her usual dismissive demeanor—as if only noticing him for the first time.

"And you can make them move," she said.

"What?" he asked confused. "No, not me. They move on their own."

Kahya wrinkled her brow. "Nonsense, the markings never move on their own."

Setting her lamp upon the floor she turned her back to him. And then, to his surprise, began to disrobe. The dark cloth that covered her slipped past her shoulders, falling about her arms and her waist, revealing her bare back. Pushing her hair to the front, she tilted her head to him slightly.

"Watch," she said.

Makami looked down to her back. A series of lengthy twisting marks covered its length like vines upon her dark skin. They looked much like the inked designs her sisters wore on their hands, with one remarkable difference. These markings moved.

He almost took a step back in shock, blinking to make certain he wasn't seeing things. But no, the markings were moving. They didn't circle and dance like the ones on his chest, but they slithered about, seeming to grow and vanish only to reappear again, like thin serpents upon her skin. And then just like that, they went suddenly still. Finishing her display, the woman turned to him, holding her robes to her chest.

"You've never met anyone else with the gift?" she asked curiously. Makami stared at her perplexed. Gift?

She moved towards him, reaching a hand for his chest. He flinched slightly but did not pull back when her fingers touched the markings on his skin, slowly tracing their movements.

"I had thought I was the only one as well," she said, "until I met another. She was a woman, older than me by perhaps a few seasons. She too had the gift. The markings she wore covered her whole body, even her face. And she too could make them move."

"What is it?" Makami found himself asking. He looked down to his chest where her hand still lingered. "What are they?"

"Skin magic," Kahya said. "That's what the woman called it. She said only few were born to it, a magic woven into our very skin. Patterns like the ones we wear, marked into our skin, can bring that magic alive. I first learned of the gift when I was young. I thought my ability was to only make the art I worked into my skin move. She showed me however, that it could do more."

"More?" Makami asked. His heart pounded. Could the answers he had sought have been right here all this time? Did the gods delight in teasing him so?

"It allows us to work magic." The woman smiled slightly. "Sometimes I am able to create patterns that allow me to not feel the heat of the sun. Or heal a slight sickness. Or speak with my thoughts. Once I even managed to make water spring out of the sand. The woman said that with time I could learn to do even more—fantastic things. But I have no need for such power. I am kept satisfied by my small magics." She looked up to him, those dark eyes probing. "What do yours do?"

Makami stiffened at the question. That answer was more than he was willing to give. Besides, he had another question.

"You made yours stop. How?"

"It is the skin that is magic," she replied matter-of-factly. "Whatever patterns we place upon it are ours to control." Seeing his blank expression she frowned slightly and squinted with curiosity. "You truly don't know?" He shook his head. Magic of the skin? He had never heard of anything like this.

"Fine then, I'll show you." Placing her palm flat against his chest she closed her eyes and exhaled deeply. "Breathe," she told him. "Breathe like I do. Clear your thoughts of nothing but the markings, see them stilled, and breathe."

Makami watched her for a while, attempting to emulate her actions. It took a few tries, but finally he matched her breathing, taking breath and releasing as she did so. Closing his eyes he saw the markings in their normal dance, swirling about beneath his skin. He tried to see them stilled, imagining what they would feel like, finally at peace. It was a pleasant thought.

"Good," Kahya said. "You learn quickly."

Makami opened his eyes. He was readied to ask her what she meant, until his eyes fell to his chest. The markings had gone still. They sat there, unmoving, as if trapped in time. He gaped at them in wonder, a surge of happiness threatening to escape his mouth in a mad laughter. Looking to Kahya he saw a slight smile on her lips, as if amused by his own joy. He opened his mouth to thank her when a familiar feeling suddenly came. Gazing back down to his chest he found the markings moving again. They did so slowly at first, but soon built up speed, returning to their normal pace. His own smile vanished, at the loss of this minor triumph.

"Worry not," Kahya told him soothingly. "You only need practice. Your magic is strong. It will be harder to control. If you like, I can teach you."

He pulled his eyes from his chest, looking up to her. Teach him?

"Yes," he nodded, unable to hide his eagerness. "I would like that. Please."

Kahya lifted her shirt back to her shoulders, pulling it more firmly about her.

"Wait a while," she said picking up her lamp as if preparing to go. "Then come to my tent." Covering her face, she walked out into the howling storm, leaving him alone.

Makami did not waste time, hurriedly dressing. He had never wanted to learn a thing so much in his life. It was some time later that he found himself outside Kahya's tent, a large one she reserved for herself. He stood hesitantly, uncertain if he should announce his entrance. In the midst of his thoughts her voice suddenly came, amazingly in his thoughts, telling him to enter. Doing as instructed, he pushed back the flaps and walked inside.

Master Dawan's eldest daughter's dwellings were at least twice the size of his own and more. They were filled with soft cloth and other strewn items. An iron brazier with red-hot coals kept the space warm, and provided the only illumination. A bowl of water was suspended above it, sending out steam to fill the tent in mist. Beyond the thick vapors there was a sweet scent in the air that tickled his nose. Of course, there was also Kahya.

The woman sat in a corner of her room, reclined upon several thick reams of red cloth. She had retired her usual billowy shirt and trousers, and now lay wrapped in light blue cloth that left her shoulders and most of her legs bare. Beads of water rolled down her bare skin, as the mist of the room clung to her. Leaning back, she held a long and ornately carved thin pipe in her hand, pulling from it and exhaling the sweet scent that filled his nostrils into the air. She lifted a hand, motioning for him to come closer. As he did so she looked up to him, her dark eyes tinged with red—an effect of the intoxicating herbal concoction he well recognized.

"You will need to be in your skin," she told him.

Makami's eyebrows rose as he caught her meaning.

"Do not take all night," she chided.

Following her commands, he pulled off his shirt and then his trousers.

"Come," she said, patting the space before her. "You will have to learn it the way I did."

As he knelt down she discarded the cloth that hugged her, urging him forward. In moments the two sat touching, their sweat-slick skin pressed against each other. It was a soothing warmth, one that Makami had come to forget. Meeting his gaze she parted her lips, blowing thick smoke upon his face, directly into his nostrils. He coughed but inhaled, feeling the sweet vapors enter his mind.

"Now breathe," she told him, her heaving chest pressed against his own, arms now clasped around his back. "Breathe in time to me." He took a deep breath, following her lead. On his chest, he knew the markings were still moving but slower. He could feel them.

"That's it," she whispered, her breath warm in his ear. "Breathe. Just breathe."

Makami found himself matching her rhythm now, drawing and releasing breath. And he did so as long as she urged him. It was well into the late hours of the morning that he drifted off. But when he did, the markings on his chest had ceased moving. And for the first time in what seemed a lifetime, his dreams were not nightmares and he slept in peace.

"THREE MEN. AND they come swiftly."

Makami took the looking glass from Master Dawan, peering through. It made the objects that appeared as mere dots against the sand in the distance seem close enough to touch. They were three men, their faces veiled. Each rode upon their own *mjaasi*—a giant sand lizard that could travel the desert at vast speed, and required little water.

"Blue men?" he asked.

Master Dawan shook his head. "Blue men would not so easily announce their coming."

Blue men, or the Taraga, were strange desert people—some say a lost branch of the Amazi. None knew much of them, except that they dressed in robes of deepest blue, and even covered their skin in the rich dye. They often raided caravans, carrying off goods and people—mostly women, children and young men. Those who had survived their attacks claimed the Blue men merely appeared, as if out of nothingness, and then vanished just as quickly.

"Whoever they are, they've spotted us, and are riding hard in our direction." Kahya had taken the looking glass and now peered through it as she spoke. "We can't outrun them. Stop the baushanga. I'd rather we met these strange men with our faces than our backs."

Makami nodded. The woman did not even look back at him before she turned to converse with her sisters. It had been some eleven days now since their encounter during the storm. Since then he had shared her tent each night, and they had held each other, as she taught him this skin magic—and how to control the markings upon him. On those nights she was a different person, adventurous, daring—even playful. But in the open day she was just the serious-minded daughter of a trader, and treated him as she always had. He did not think Master Dawan or her sisters knew of their secret meetings. Both had been quite discreet about that.

Moving off to the baushanga, he pulled on their reins, making the clicking noises of reassurance to stop them. Looking into the distance he could make out the three approaching figures much better now, without the need of the looking glass. They would be upon them in moments.

"Friend Anseh." He turned to find Master Dawan standing nearby. "I do not know these men, and every precaution is necessary. I will speak to them in peace, but if that does not work..." The old man reached into his robes and drew out a knife. "Can you use this?"

Makami took hold of the weapon, noting the intricate golden hilt. He unsheathed the curving blade and with ease twirled it across his hands, causing Master Dawan's eyes to widen slightly.

"I see then that you can," the old man said, a bit of excitement in his voice. Makami had a feeling he would one day be asking to hear the tale of how he had learned that ability.

"Here they come," Kahya declared, coming to stand beside them.

Makami looked up to see the three men riding down a dune directly in front of them. The brown and white-striped mjaasi they rode kicked up billowing puffs of sand as they more scampered than ran, their clawed feet barely touching the ground. They brought their riders just up to the caravan, stopping short when the leather reins tied to their necks were pulled. The baushanga shifted slightly at sight of the creatures, eyeing them warily, their normally blue horns changing to a dull orange—a clear warning. Despite their size, mjaasi had small teeth. Exceedingly sharp and numerous, they were better suited for devouring rodents and would not fare well against the tough hide of a baushanga. But the pack beasts didn't take chances, and would charge with their great horns if these strangers came too close.

"Manhada," Master Dawan said, palming his forehead in greeting. "The goddess smile on you with good fortune."

The three men did not respond right away, shifting their gaze down to the old man and his caravans. Each was wrapped in dark fabrics that enveloped them completely. With their veiled faces all that could be discerned were their eyes which were unreadable. But there was something odd about the way they sat, so casually upon their steeds, showing none of the caution anyone would at meeting strangers out in the deep desert.

Finally one of them, the one whose steed stood closest, began to unwrap his veil. In moments his face was visible, that of a man—the flints of gray in his beard showing he was older certainly than Makami, but younger still than Master Dawan. His broad frame was visible beneath his clothing, matching his large hands. He stared at them all a while longer, his dark eyes piercing. Then quite unexpectedly a bright grin of white teeth crossed his ebon skin.

"Manhada," he replied back in greeting, his voice a deep baritone. Palming his own head, where only a strip of hair grew in the middle, he nodded slightly. Makami took note of the man's accent. He knew the customs of the desert people well enough, but he did not share their dialect. He spoke trader's tongue impeccably, like someone who was well-traveled. "May the goddess smile upon us all. May she smile on you even more, if you so happen to have water."

Master Dawan motioned to one of his daughters who stepped forward. Gingerly, she offered up a leather pouch filled with water. The man looked down from his mount, his smile unwavering. Reaching down he took hold of the pouch and paused. Makami's hands tensed on his knife, anticipating trouble. But the man only took the pouch with a solemn nod. In moments he was downing its contents, much of it running down his beard and soaking his clothing. His thirst quenched, he tossed what was left to one of his companions, who caught it and began to drink just as heartily.

"Many thanks," the man said, wiping his mouth with the back of his hand. "I thought we would die with sand in our throats this day."

"The sands do not show mercy," Master Dawan remarked. "What finds you so deep in the desert friend?"

"My men and I were guarding a caravan. But we lost them in a storm."

"A fierce thing," Master Dawan noted. "It passed over us some nights past."

"Most likely one and the same," the man grunted. "We have not been able to find them since. I fear them perished—as were we until we spied you in the distance. My men and I are hungry, thirsty. Our mounts need feeding as well. If you could spare a bit more to drink, to eat, before we set out—"

"What can you offer in trade?" It was Kahya who spoke. She had donned her veil once more, her muffled voice and clothing making it hard to discern if she were man or woman. Makami knew she had spoken quickly, lest her father in his generosity offer away the little supplies they held for nothing.

The man smiled knowingly. Reaching into his robes he took a small pouch and tossed it over. Kahya caught it nimbly, snatching it from the air and opening it, peering inside. Gold dust, Makami could see.

"A week's earnings," the man said. "More than enough I hope."

Kahya nodded curtly. The gold dust would resupply them and more at the next trading village.

"I am Master Dawan," the old man said warmly, now that such matters were finalized. "And I offer you food and drink friend…?"

"Abrafo," the man answered.

"So it is then, friend Abrafo," Master Dawan said. "Night draws near, you may camp with us and we will share food, drink and tales."

The man Abrafo gazed down, smiling wide, as if that was what he had been waiting to hear.

It was well into dusk, as the sun lowered in the horizon, taking with it the last shafts of light in the desert that the caravan and their new guests sat in a circle about a fire eating, drinking and talking. Master Dawan's daughters had slain a goat, preparing enough food for them all, and they sated their bellies. A few of the young women even danced, showing skills at balancing knives and swords atop their heads as they twirled to a rhythm beat upon a flat drum by their father who chanted some unknown song in the Amazi tongue.

The big man, Abrafo, seemed to delight at this, clapping heartily as he ate, and listening riveted to the tales Master Dawan eagerly spun. Makami sat back, eating his own food slowly, but saying little. The other two strangers—muscular men with rough faces named Cha and Kadori—said even less. Their stone demeanor betrayed nothing but seemed to take in everything at once.

Something about them did not set right with Makami. More than once he thought they glanced in his direction. But they had looked away so quickly, he began to wonder if it wasn't his own mind playing tricks. Still despite this seeming calm, he kept his eyes open, the knife Master Dawan had given him tucked away safely beneath his shirt. He hoped he would have no need of it. Kahya did not eat with them, taking her food inside her tent where she claimed to be handling business. In all this time Makami had only seen her a few moments, still veiled and not even looking his way. He wondered to himself if tonight, they would still be able to have one of their lessons.

"You are blessed with beautiful daughters and fabulous tales Master Dawan," Abrafo was saying, his rumbling voice filled with mirth as he drank from a wooden cup. The skin on his powerfully built arms glistened in the fire's glow. Since settling down the three men had discarded their lengthy cloaks, revealing long loose-fitting trousers and dark shirts. All had weapons strapped to them. Nothing alarming for caravan sentries, but still—it made them seem like leopards.

"Friend Abrafo, you are too kind," the old man said, graciously accepting the compliment. "But surely, in your work, you have tales to share as well?"

The big man laughed, sipping again from his cup. He cast a glance to his men, who glanced back. It was such a swift thing that most would not have noticed. But Makami was keeping his eyes on them. In his homeland he had seen leopards hunt often as a child. And they too had a silent way of speaking.

"Tales I have in great number," Abrafo said finally. He settled back lazily on one elbow, the cup held before him while a wistful expression stole his face. "Here is one you may find of interest—it is about a thief and a sorcerer."

Makami stopped the cup that he was lifting to his own lips, his ears perking to life. Staring at Abrafo the big man did not seem to be looking in his direction, but his words had set Makami's heart fluttering.

"There was once a thief," the big man said, "who lived in a city to the far west, in one of the great kingdoms, between oceans of water and oceans of sand. He was a good thief, whose fame was celebrated on the streets of the city for his daring thefts. One night he decided to increase his fame. He would steal a prized jewel from one of the richest men in the city. What the thief didn't know was that this man was a sorcerer, and not a man of simple magics or one who you go to for healing. No, this man practiced dark magics, forbidden in the kingdom. He belonged to a secret brotherhood, and they had become quite wealthy dabbling in their terrible practice."

Makami's heart beat so fast now that he thought it might jump from his chest. And for the first time in some eleven days, the markings on his chest began to move. Since his first lesson with Kahya he had been able to control them, keeping them still while he slept and in the days while he worked. But his breathing had become sharp and chaotic listening to the big man's tale, and what control he had slipped away. This tale was becoming too frightening, too real.

"That very night," Abrafo went on, "the sorcerer was working one of his greatest magics—markings etched with blood and ink upon stone. Unknown to him however, a thief had entered his home. The two stumbled upon each other, quite in surprise—the thief thinking that the darkened home was empty, not expecting to find anyone within. Any other day, the sorcerer would have killed an intruder outright. But the magic he dealt in was powerful, and required all his concentration. In that moment of distraction, the sorcerer was seized by the very forces he sought to control and pitched forward—dead."

"And what of the thief?" Master Dawan asked, his eyes alive with intrigue.

"Well that is where the story gets interesting," Abrafo said with a wink. "The sorcerer died, but his magic did not. You see the thief himself could wield magic—a deep and old magic that rested within his skin. And magic, good or ill, is attracted to magic—it seeks it out, is drawn to it. The dark magics of the sorcerer came alive at sensing him. They left the stone they had been etched upon, latching onto this thief, burying into him, marking his skin."

Makami glared openly. So this man knew his story, knew it in detail that no one else could, and now gave answers that he himself could only have guessed upon. He still remembered that terrible night, standing with the dead sorcerer at his feet, watching as the strange markings etched onto the ground had slithered across stone, seeping into his skin, crawling up his body and embedding into his chest. The pain had been so great, he had almost passed out. Only fear had kept him awake long enough, to flee into the night and back home…

"But the unlucky thief didn't know what had happened to him," Abrafo continued. "You see the sorcerer had been creating doors with those markings, symbols that opened pathways to other worlds where unknown things dwell—demons and dark spirits. The unsuspecting thief returned home, this wicked magic buried into his skin. And there he fell into a deep sleep. But the magic worked upon him yet stirred. That very night as he slept, the markings upon his chest opened a door, releasing a monstrous demon that killed his wife, who herself was with child. When he awakened the room he slept in was covered in her blood. Some say the thief went mad that night, and fled the city, forever running from the monster he had become."

Makami released a sob, the tears he had tried to hold back choking him. Images of sweet Kesse flashed through his mind, and the events of that terrible night. The man knew much, more than Makami ever did—but not everything. He had not awakened to find Kesse dead; he had awakened to see it happen. He had watched as the terrible thing with endless arms, bristling with black hair, had emerged from his chest. He had watched it grab onto Kesse, and seen her wide terrified eyes as the monster ripped her to pieces. And he had been too weak to stop any of it. He had indeed gone a bit mad that night. But if these men still sought him, knowing all they did, they were madder than he.

"What do you want?" he asked, his voice matching the resignation on his face.

The big man Abrafo slowly finished draining his cup before turning to Makami, a slow smile creeping across his face. "So the thief finally speaks."

Makami did not reply. Casting eyes to the two other men, he could see they now stared at him openly. No, it had not been his imagination after all. Leopards these men were—and eager to hunt. Turning back to their leader he released a weary sigh.

"Whatever you want, whatever you think you'll get from me—there will only be death in the end. You have come all this way, for nothing. Go now, please."

Abrafo only returned a wider smile. Master Dawan frowned deeply, looking from Makami to their new guests in puzzlement, trying to fit the pieces together in his head. The old man may not have yet understood what was going on, but he could certainly sense the dangerous tension that now filled the night air.

"It is not about what we want friend thief," Abrafo replied calmly. "Your fate is not ours to decide." He paused. "Take him."

At least that's what Makami imagined had been said, because the big man spoke his last words in an unfamiliar tongue. But his leopards pounced at his command. They were upon him so quick there was barely time to react. Strong hands grabbed and wrestled him to his knees. The knife he had held was twisted from him, skittering onto the sand, as a longer sharper blade was placed to his neck. About him Master Dawan's cries of protest mingled with his daughters' screams. Then suddenly, there was a cry of pain.

Makami saw Kahya from the side of his vision, unveiled and wielding her large blade. The commotion had drawn the woman from the tent and she had emerged, weapon at the ready. One of the men that had held him down clutched at his arm, cursing at the blood that seeped through his clothing. Kahya moved at him again, deadly intent her eyes. But the leopard was faster. He slid out of her way, and with his good arm caught her by the wrist, wrenching it cruelly until she cried out and released her grip. A quick blow to the woman's side seemed to take her breath, and she doubled over in agony, the fight momentarily gone from her.

"There's no time for this," Abrafo growled. He grabbed Kahya, tossing her towards her family and drawing a large sword with a jagged end. "As we planned! Hurry!"

Makami watched the unfolding chaos about him, lost in a void of pain. The markings on his chest had begun to move long ago, rising with his own fear, and they burned with an intensity that threatened to overwhelm him. He barely noticed as his shirt was ripped away, or when a hand touched his chest, slathering on something cold and liquid. And then, quite unexpectedly, the pain diminished. It ebbed away, all but vanishing. Soon, he could feel nothing at all.

Makami looked down to his chest in surprise, to where two strange markings in red had been freshly painted, still dripping from him like cold blood. Whatever the symbols were, they numbed his skin, making it feel as if cold needles were prickling him. The markings on his chest slowed their rhythm and then went still.

"Good then," Abrafo said, his toothy smile returning. He looked down to Makami and winked. "You see, we have our magics as well. Weak yes, but enough to keep us all safe."

Makami stared at his chest, dumbfounded. Looking back to his captors he glared. Men who not only hunted him, but who knew how to subdue him. These leopards had been well-prepared.

"Who are you?" he asked behind clenched teeth. "How do you know about me?"

"We are couriers," Abrafo replied plainly. "Sent to retrieve and deliver you."

"Deliver me? To who? Who do you work for?"

Abrafo walked over, crouching low to meet Makami's gaze. "The sorcerer who you came upon that night, belonged to a secret brotherhood." He pulled forth a strip of red cloth tucked into his shirt, opening it for all to see. Upon it in black ink was printed the dismembered hand of a great cat, its claws ready to strike. "They call themselves the The Leopard's Paw. The sorcerer who died was one of the most powerful among them, and his brothers have been unable to recreate the magic he worked that night.

But why recreate, when you can merely steal...eh, thief?" The big man laughed at his own wit.

"They want this." He pointed to the markings on Makami's chest. "And they have sent us to find you. Or rather a courier was sent to hire us—the The Leopard's Paw never shows its true face. The brotherhood could sense you and offer guidance in our hunt...but only when the markings were moving, or when a doorway opened, when the magic was at its strongest.

"It flared greatly in the trading town you spent time in, about the same time I mysteriously lost three men I had ordered to search for you. You would not happen to know of them?" Makami winced slightly and Abrafo's smiled widened. "No matter, greed is often the end of fools. But by the time I arrived you had gone into the desert. We followed, only to have the trail end. The brotherhood was unable to sense you, as if the markings had gone silent." Makami said nothing. Kahya's tutelage had unwittingly spared him for some time. If only he had known all of this earlier, how many more lives could have been saved.

"But I know little of magics," Abrafo shrugged. "My business was to find you, with or without the brotherhood's help. We must have gone through near a score of caravans in this cursed desert, searching for you, killing and taking food and water as we needed, leaving no sign of our passing. But the goddess of the Amazi must have smiled upon us with good fortune today." He turned to Master Dawan and his family, who remained huddled together, fear painted on their faces. All except Kahya, who knelt before her father and sisters protectively, her dark eyes glinting steel. A pang of regret washed over Makami as he thought of the danger he had brought them.

"These sorcerers," he said. "They can remove these markings from me then?"

Abrafo laughed, glancing to his companions who responded in kind. "Remove them? Oh yes. That is their intent. My men and I have a wager on how the brotherhood will claim the markings. They think the sorcerers will cut out your chest and mount it on a wall, from where they can call their dark spirits. But I believe they will peel the skin from you, and perhaps wear it over their own flesh." Makami stared at the man aghast. "As I have said, I know little of magics. But the courier explained to us that the markings and your skin had become one—which is why the brotherhood needs you brought back to them. Whoever controls your skin will hold power over the markings and the dark beings they call forth. You carry with you a weapon thief, which they intend to wield."

"A weapon?" It was Kahya who spoke, her eyes now wide in alarm. "And you would hand it over so willingly? If these markings hold such power as you say, do you not worry to what purpose these sorcerers will put it?"

Abrafo shrugged. "Perhaps they will wield it against their enemies. Or perhaps they will unleash horror upon the lands. It is not my concern or care. So long as I receive payment."

"Friend Abrafo." It was Master Dawan now who spoke, his voice gentle. "Certainly there are greater things in this world than wealth. What these dark men of foul magics would do to this man, what they would do with this power, surely it must weigh upon your heart."

"Wealth?" The big man laughed. "You mistake us Master Dawan. Wealth is not what the sorcerers have promised us for this prize." He moved to kneel and look the old man directly in the eye. "We are to be gifted with magics that will make our skin invulnerable to weapons, our blood immune to poisons, bodies able to heal from any wound or affliction. We will be immortal. Whatever may come, we will survive it—and then we can become as rich as we wish." He came to his feet and released a lengthy breath. "But for now Master Dawan, there will be some unpleasantness to come, for your eyes and ears have witnessed much—and the brotherhood greatly values its secrecy."

As the grim meaning of those words sank in Makami felt his stomach go hollow. A look of horror crossed Master Dawan's face as he reflexively reached for his daughters. Then just as quickly, he returned to his jovial self.

"Come then friend Abrafo," he urged pleasantly. "There is no need for such talk. Surely we can arrive at some understanding. My family and I are but simple traders. We spend much of our lives in the desert. Who can we tell such tales to?"

"Ah, Master Dawan," the big man smiled, wagging a finger playfully. "But you are a lover of tales. And this story may be too great to keep. No, there is no understanding to which we will come."

The pleasantness on the old man's face slowly slid away, and Makami felt his stomach tightening. Abrafo sounded like a man who would regret the slitting of a child's throat, but slit it all the same.

"Please, I beg you. If you must silence any tongues this day, let it be mine."

Master Dawan's daughters screamed as one at his words, clutching and pulling at their father as if he had already gone. Even Kahya looked stunned, her face trembling.

Abrafo stared at the old man, seeming to mull over his words before shaking his head.

"No, I cannot grant that wish Master Dawan," he said finally. "But, you offered me food and drink, and for that I am grateful. So I will promise that at the least, you will not have to watch your daughters die." He gave an order and one of the other men grabbed the old man, pulling him away from his family who wailed and tore at his clothing. Kahya rose up, as if she intended to fight all three of their captors with her bare hands alone. But Abrafo caught and easily wrestled her to the ground, bringing his jagged sword to the throat of a younger daughter in threat. Master Dawan was brought to the forefront, and placed upon his knees. His eyes were closed and his mouth moved rapidly, speaking words in his native tongue. A prayer, Makami knew. It came like a song that rose and fell in a rolling fashion.

"Yes old man," Abrafo said soothingly. "Finish the prayer to your goddess. You will be reunited with your daughters soon enough."

Makami watched the unfolding scene in horror. The knife at his neck had been pressed so firmly into his skin that it now drew blood. Catching a glance of Kahya he met her eyes to find she was staring directly at him, her gaze stabbing into him and her mouth moving. At first he thought the woman was praying as well. But no, she was saying something, directly to him, shouting it in fact, above the screams of her sisters and her father's sorrowful entreaties. *Breathe*, she was saying. *Breathe. Breathe. Breathe.*

Makami listened puzzled as she repeated the words, almost pleadingly. He had heard them before, whispered into his ear during their nightly sessions, as they lay wrapped in each other's skin. It was how she taught him to slow the markings, to control his skin. He was struck suddenly by his own thoughts, mingling with the words Abrafo had spoken earlier. *Control his skin. The markings as a weapon. Whoever wielded it...*

He met Kahya's eyes with sudden understanding, and attempted to do as she asked—breathe.

It took some trying, the chaos about him distracting his thoughts. He had to find a way to concentrate. It came amazingly from Master Dawan. The old man's prayerful chant flowed into his ears, offering him the bit of peace he needed. The markings shifted upon his chest—only slightly, but enough to give him renewed hope. He did not dwell on the irony that the very curse that had robbed him of so much, might now offer salvation. *It is the skin that is magic.* That was what Kahya had taught him. Whatever was placed upon it was his to master. Yet, try as he might, the numbness on his skin robbed him of control. It was like trying to move a boulder. But wait...something else moved.

Yes! It was the other markings, the ones just placed upon him. Abrafo had called them weak magic, and indeed they moved easily. In short moments he made quick work of one, shifting his skin until it broke and peeled away. Sensation returned quickly to his chest, and his own markings began their familiar dance. Concentrating he worked upon the second symbol. It twisted and then gave, untying like a knot undone and dripping away. And then there was pain, flooding his body as the markings on his chest swirled about furiously. The lines and arcs began to fit into each other, falling into place, creating a symbol before going still. He braced for what he knew would come next.

Makami heard his own screams as fire erupted from his chest. He did not seem to burn, but the heat was more intense than anything he had ever felt. The thing that emerged from him was shrouded in flames, and he imagined that whatever place it came from was an endless inferno. Its massive bulk towered into the night, like a flaming beacon in the darkness. Unknown symbols like writing adorned the skin of its pale and reddish muscled body which slightly resembled that of a man. Its head had no face or features of any kind—only a crown of endless horns, curving and pointing like spears to the heavens. Where forearms should have been, the flesh extended into two large blades of bone that glistened like steel.

By now, Master Dawan's prayers had ended, and all had gone silent, bearing witness in awe to the nightmare before them. The first person Makami heard speak was the man who stood over him. It was a whispered prayer as the great being swiveled a horned head to look down at them with its eyeless face. It raised one of its arms and there was a blur as the great blade came down swiftly. Makami felt the knife at his throat fall away, along with the half of his captor that held it. The man had been sliced in two, the heated blade cauterizing the wound so well that no blood splattered.

At sight of his companion's demise, another of the men cried in fear and made as if to run. There was another blur as the creature's arm came down, this time cutting cleanly in one stroke from head to crotch, impacting heavily against the sand which was sent up in a billowing cloud. It shifted its horned head then to Abrafo.

The big man stared up at the behemoth that dwarfed him, his sword hanging limply at his side. He turned to Makami, a look of absolute wonder in his eyes. Then, as a familiar smile crept across his rapt face, he uttered one word.

"Magnificent!"

It was his last, before the great being lifted a thick fiery leg, bringing it down and crushing the man beneath several tons of flesh and flames. It stood there for a moment, seeming to exult in its kills. And then it turned that horned and faceless head to those who remained.

Master Dawan had long ago scrambled towards his family, and now spread his arms protectively against his daughters, as if that could possibly shield them. The great being gazed down at them hungrily, lifting its blade with murderous intent.

"No!" Makami was surprised that the cry came from his weakened lips. He was even more amazed when the great being turned to stare at him, with its odd eyeless gaze. *Whoever wields the magic*...he recalled.

"It is the skin that is magic. And as the markings are drawn onto my skin, I hold power over them—I hold power over you." The great being reared up—the flames that shrouded it flaring and roaring in anger. It stalked forward, in two giant steps coming to tower above him. Makami could feel its terrible heat fierce upon his skin, but yet he spoke. "I hold power over you! And I command, you leave them unharmed!" Makami knew his words would have sounded stronger if he was more certain, and they didn't come in ragged breaths. He was not sure what he expected to happen next. This monster could kill them all.

But instead, the great being did the unexpected, suddenly dropping to one knee and bowing deeply. Makami grimaced as words emanated from that face without a mouth, echoing in the still night and ringing within his ears. The language was unlike anything he had ever heard and it pounded against his skull. But he understood it all the same.

As you wish.

Makami released a breath of relief, his body shuddering. "Go back," he said hoarsely. "Return from where you came. I command you."

The great being's return through the doorway in his chest was painful, as it always was. But when it had gone the markings broke apart again and returned to their usual movements. Eyeing Master Dawan and his family he could see their awestruck faces. Kahya too glared. And he thought that perhaps, for the first time, he had impressed her. Those were his final thoughts before darkness claimed him and he could think nothing more.

MAKAMI FITTED THE straps onto the remaining mjaasi tightly. They had set the other mounts free into the desert, to erase all traces of Abrafo and his men. But he had kept this giant lizard as his own steed. It would serve well in his coming travels.

"Take more water than that." He looked to find Kahya offering him yet another pouch.

"I cannot take it all from you," he said. She wrinkled her unveiled face at him.

"Do not be foolish. I would not have us die of thirst in the desert. I offer it to you because we have enough to last us and know where to find more."

Makami took it, smiling his thanks. Despite all that had occurred, her demeanor towards him had not changed greatly. He was thankful for that. He might have kissed her openly, if he did not think she might cuff him in turn.

After the happenings of three nights past he had expected Master Dawan and his family to have left him in the desert, and to have fled as far as they could from the madness he had unleashed upon them. Instead he had awakened in Kahya's tent, finding she and her sisters caring for him. Master Dawan had greeted him cheerfully, sharing tea and tales while he recovered his strength. They had not abandoned him, even after all they had seen. But now, he was abandoning them.

"Friend Anseh." He turned to find Master Dawan walking towards him, his pet hawk Izri on his protected arm. "Can I still not convince you to see us through our travels?"

"I would like to," Makami replied thankfully. "But it is perhaps best for us all if I went my own way. Besides, it's time I stopped running, and confronted what has happened to me."

"You will hunt down this…Leopard's Paw?"

Makami felt his teeth tighten and he rubbed at his chest. A brotherhood of powerful sorcerers who wielded dark magics was not someone you eagerly sought out.

"Better perhaps than being hunted," he said. "But first I want to learn more about this skin magic."

The old man looked concerned but did not voice his disapproval.

"In the southlands, there are a people who scar their whole skin with intricate patterns," he said. "I have heard they know much of this magic of the skin."

Makami nodded, exchanging a quick glance with Kahya whose eyebrows as well rose with interest. He had not revealed her secret. He supposed she would tell her family of her abilities in her own time. Or perhaps her father knew more than she thought.

"I will find them out if I can," he said. South was home—and he had not been there in a long time. He wondered if he was ready. Looking up at the sky he took note of where the blazing sun stood. "It is time I went." Swinging up onto the mjaasi he sat in his seat, pulling the straps of the giant lizard which rose to its feet, already eager to run.

"Manhada," Master Dawan said, palming his forehead. "The goddess keep you in her thoughts." Makami replied in kind, turning his gaze to Kahya. Uncertain of what to say, she spoke for him.

"Farewell. Keep safe, so my eyes can touch upon you again in this life."

He nodded deeply, deciding he would hold onto those words and this parting vision of her in the lonely time to come. Veiling his own face, he gave a series of clicks and spurred the mjaasi to action. In moments he was galloping away, the sound of Master Dawan's daughters Amazi tongue rolling chants of farewell and luck dying in the distance as he rode into the new day.